*Ak,
I hope you ... this!
Best wishes
Frankie Masters
"Maeve Hunter"*

BLOODLINES

BLOODLINES

A Novel

MAEVE HUNTER

Bloodlines

Copyright © 2016 by F. H. Masters

All rights reserved. No part of this book may be used or reproduced by any means, graphic, electronic, or mechanical, including photocopying, recording, taping or by any information storage retrieval system without the written permission of the publisher except in the case of brief quotations embodied in critical articles and reviews.

This is a work of fiction. All of the characters, names, incidents, organizations, and dialogue in this novel are either the products of the author's imagination or are used fictitiously.

For Vicky

Prologue

Prussia, 1823

It was a warm night, but a cool wind blew through the cave. It arose from a clear stream that flowed over pebbles worn smooth from years of chafing by the water, and into the air, keeping it a constant temperature. It was the refreshing breeze that first caught their attention and the Balfours stopped at the opening as if testing it. They had learned caution through the years. It was a caution born out of great trial and more often than not defeat, but as their confidence grew, they stepped through the opening and into the dimly lit cave.

Brother Cavanaugh carefully eyed the five men as they entered. He had been waiting for them, knowing they would come. Sooner or later all such men came to him, and in the Balfour's case, their reputation preceded them. Carefully, he watched as they picked their way across the uneven ground.

They were a handsome group of men — the last of the Balfours. The burning torches that lighted the cave played on their faces and Brother Cavanaugh studied them as they approached.

The monk was seated on the floor of the cave, cracking nuts on a large flat stone. As they drew near, he raised a burly hand and slammed a fist sized stone against the smooth, hard surface. The shell broke into a dozen pieces and he carefully picked the meat out of the rubble. The five men stopped as one.

"So, you have come at last," the monk said, never once looking up from his task. "I have been expecting you."

"Brother Anton sent us."

"No. The Great Almighty has sent you."

No one responded.

"So, you are ready at last, are you?" Brother Cavanaugh mused, more to himself than to them.

"Ready for what, my friend?" Stefan asked. "We were told you could help us. That you could show us how to defeat Demetrius."

The monk looked up for the first time. He was not an old man although he had lived years longer than the expected life span. He was tall and solidly built, but all of this was masked by his position on the ground. He locked eyes with Stefan and neither man wavered.

"Yes," he said after a moment of consideration. "But there is great cost. I wonder if you are ready for such great sacrifice."

"We are ready," a young man standing behind Stefan suddenly spoke. He was different from the others, fair and blonde, and the monk recognized him for who he was. No doubt, he was Marius, the girl's fiancé.

The girl! Lorna had been her name, and she had been a beautiful girl, they said. After seeing her father and brothers, the monk could believe it. In the beginning, the Balfours had been a large, close-knit family. Stefan was the father of seven sons and one daughter, but now, all that remained were the three handsome men standing before him. One was no more than a boy.

The monk knew her story. It was a story that struck pity and sympathy in his heart. It was what made him want to help them although he wondered if they had what it would take — or the courage either. It would take a special kind of courage to do what he was about to suggest — a courage that few men could imagine, much less conjure. The Balfours had to have more than just a desire for revenge. They had to want it so badly they would go through anything to get it.

"You give us the tools and the knowledge to defeat him and we will show you how ready we are," the young man continued with passion. The monk never even changed expression.

Stefan put a hand of caution on the young man's arm. "We have come a great distance in hopes you could help us. We understand sacrifice. We have sacrificed so much already."

The monk came to his feet in one smooth, easy movement. He was tall — taller than any one of the Balfours and strongly built, more like a wrestler than a holy servant of God.

His eyes took in all five of them at once, but they rested only on the youngest son.

"How old are you, boy?" he asked.

"Sixteen," the young man readily answered. He was one inch less than six feet tall, dark of hair and eye just like his father, and lean and slender.

The monk grunted. "So young," he said. He seemed to lament the age — or perhaps the boy's lost youth, but he only shook his head and he shrugged with indifference. "Come, my friends," he said, as his mood changed "You must be thirsty.

Drink with me." He walked away and the five men stared after him. They were weary, but more heartsick than tired. What they wanted was encouragement and knowledge, but it didn't appear they would get it here. Stefan moved after him and the young men slowly followed.

The monk led them to a stone table in the corner and once there, he poured wine into crude cups. They sat down and drank and Brother Cavanaugh leaned his back against the hard wall of the cave, his drink in his hand, and a weariness on his face to match that of the Balfours.

"So, I ask you again," he began. "Are you truly ready? Would you really sacrifice everything for your quest?"

"Sacrifice is not new to me," Stefan said. "I have lost my wife . . . four sons . . . and my daughter is lost to me. What could be greater than that?"

"But you have not lost everything. You still have three sons — and a would-be in-law," he added. "But unfortunately, you will lose all of them, too, on your present course." He spoke with an indifference that belied his concern.

"Then what are you offering?" Stefan frankly asked.

The monk toyed with his cup, turning it in his hands before responding. When at last he spoke, there was no answer in his words.

"Demetrius is one of the elders, you know — one of the first — and he is old, very old." He looked down at his drink and continued to turn his cup. "You have been lucky so far —yes, lucky, I say," he quickly added as they all flashed hard looks his way. "To hunt the vampire, Demetrius, when you have only the strength and the power of mortal men is nothing less than suicide. Yes, you have been more than lucky. The Lord Himself is protecting you."

A palatable silence met him. No one said a word or even changed positions.

"You have not destroyed him, because you cannot destroy him — not in your present state," the monk continued.

"We have killed vampires," Marius proudly boasted. "Two to be exact. If they can be destroyed so can Demetrius."

"Minions," the monk calmly said. "They were nothing compared to Demetrius and still, it has cost you three years and four brothers." The monk shook his head. "Not good odds, I would say."

Stefan set his cup down and looked more closely at Brother Cavanaugh. He didn't understand, but he knew the monk was leading up to something more — something great, in its own terrible way.

"What do you suggest?" he asked.

"Have you heard of the Peregrinias?"

Stefan looked far away as he thought. "No," he finally answered. "I cannot say that I have."

"I have," the oldest son, Artemus, said, speaking up for the first time. "A mythical coven of vampires who have supposedly been converted, and they hunt their own."

"Not exactly," the monk said but his eyes arose with approval. "To begin with," he continued, leaning forward so that his eyes shined in the dim light, "they are not mythical. They exist. And they do not hunt their own — only they can.

They are able if the need arises. You see, they are not vampires — not anymore, that is."

"And we are to recruit them? Is that your suggestion?"

"No, you should become one of them."

Five blank stares met his proposal; then very slowly, Artemus, Marius, and Joseph arose to their feet. Victor remained seated, keenly looking at his father. Stefan, however, did not seem at all shocked.

"Become a vampire? You must be crazy," Marius said, his fair face now red with fury.

"No, become one of the Peregrinias," the monk corrected him. "If you want to destroy Demetrius, then you must have the same power he has — and more."

"This is blasphemy! Come, father, let us leave this place now!" Joseph declared.

"No," Stefan said with a slight shake of his head. He was calm and his eyes held great interest. "How do you know they exist?" he asked. "Or that they have the power to destroy one of the elders?"

Brother Cavanaugh laughed aloud. "*I* am one of the Peregrinias," he said. "The first, in fact. I can be a teacher and a guide for you just as I have for those that have been carefully chosen before you. And if you are willing to give up everything so that you can gain everything, I can take you to a plane of existence you never could imagine. And then, my friend, not only will you have the power to destroy Demetrius, but more than enough power. You will surely have your revenge."

Chapter One

Present Day

All of man's great achievements first began as a whimsical thought in the mind of a dreamer.

Or that was what Emry thought. She was a devout and well-practiced dreamer, although she had never aspired to greatness nor imagined wonderful things that would change history the way Edison and Einstein had.

She had, however, traveled through time and space, flown to the stars, and created worlds that would astound even the gods. And she had done it all without erudition, special powers, or even effort. Sometimes all that was required was a boring classroom, a quiet corner — or a long ride — the kind she was taking today.

Interstates can be very conducive to daydreaming as Emry soon realized. The long trip from Charlotte, North Carolina to Florida had kept her quiet and occupied. She shared the middle seat of the mid-size SUV with her sister, Crystal. Her parents, Stanley and Maggie, occupied the front seats. They had been traveling since early morning and by afternoon, Emry had traveled a lifetime distance farther than anyone else in the car.

Her mother was driving. Since Stanley's accident, she'd done a lot of driving. In fact, she had done a lot of things she'd never had to do before. It was taking its toll. Emry could see gray in her nut brown hair and a deepening darkness under her soft brown eyes. She had always been a quiet woman — almost stoic, but lately she had receded further and further within herself, much the same as Emry had done.

Stanley, on the other hand, had handled things quite admirably, even retaining his sense of humor. But maybe that wasn't true either. His hair had receded to the back of his head and he had put on thirty pounds — nervous eating, perhaps.

Crystal was the only one who seemed totally and completely unaffected by the change. She sat in her seat, leaned back, a pair of tiny white earbuds crammed tightly in her ears as she listened to her Mp3 player. Occasionally, she would sing an abstract line that hinted as to which song she was hearing at the moment, but otherwise, she was happily just riding along, undisturbed by the move.

In fact, she was rather excited. She had the idea it would be all swimming pools and beaches, but then she was only fourteen years old. Maybe Emry would have felt the same at fourteen, but she didn't think so.

They were going to Bostwick, a tiny community south of Jacksonville, where Stanley's mother, Ellen, lived. Emry was really Emerald Ellen Winters, named after her grandmother, but she had spent very little time with the source of her namesake, just holidays and special occasions. What time they had had together was mostly by Ellen's efforts. She had driven to Charlotte in the Chevy Caprice she had bought new the year Emry had been born and she would stay for short periods of time. Over the years Emry had watched the car age — just like its owner.

Ellen's farm was on the outskirts of town. It was just a small parcel of land but the property would be Stanley's inheritance one day. When they lost their home in Charlotte, Ellen graciously pointed that out to him. She had always wanted the family to move to Florida. Emry guessed she could read her grandmother's mind concerning this — and her father's too, but Stanley had very few options at this point. Emry supposed she should be thankful. Stanley had not worked in two years, so where else could they go?

She slumped deeper in her seat and they kept moving steadily south on I-95. Emry stared out the window as the scenery whipped by, dreaming of a world where she was not the new girl in her senior class, and where all her friends were not hundreds of miles away in another city. It occupied her mind and her time so that the afternoon sped by. She was surprised when Maggie flipped on the blinker, leaving the interstate for highways with unfamiliar names and numbers. It didn't seem possible to be arriving so soon, but forty-five minutes later, Maggie was again making a significant flip of the blinker, announcing as she did that they were practically there.

"Next stop grandma's house," she said.

Crystal pulled the earbuds from her ears and leaned forward, showing interest in her surroundings for the first time in hours. She couldn't remember Bostwick. She had been only four years old the last time they were here, so the rural community was a curious attraction to her.

It held a fascination for Emry as well, and maybe their reasons were not as different as one might imagine. They both curiously noted the single caution light that marked the entrance to the community and that the narrow paved road was lined with more trees than houses.

They bumped across a railroad track and immediately took a left onto a smoothly paved road. It stretched on in a straight line as far as the eye could see, the railroad track running parallel to it. Emry seemed to remember this road even though she had been only seven years old on their last visit. She definitely remembered the long driveway they turned into and the house that lay at the end of it.

The old house had been built in the 1930's, but it was well kept and picturesque in the shadow of the gathering darkness. It was a white two story frame farmhouse with a porch that ran all the way across the front of it. On each end were red chimneys and on top was a green metal roof. Large oak trees shaded the yard and the house was surrounded by hedges of azalea bushes. On the porch were hanging baskets of geraniums, making a line of red on each side of a bright green door. Behind the house and completely out of sight was a garden, and beyond that was a strip of woods that separated the Winters' property from the actual town of Bostwick.

From an altruistic point of view, Emry had to concede that this was a move that was not only necessary, but unavoidable. That fact didn't ease the pain of the move, but it did give her reason to go quietly. Her parents had problems of their own and Emry knew her little senior high crisis was nothing compared to their trouble. She reminded herself of this as she stepped out of the car and stretched.

Ellen Winters was on the porch, snapping beans. She sat in an old ladder back rocking chair that gently moved as she nudged the floor with her toe, but as the car came to a halt at the end of the driveway, so did the chair. Ellen laid the bowl aside and came to her feet. She was a petite woman in her mid-sixties, dressed in jeans and a plaid camp shirt. Her gray hair was short and straight, framing a face that was still pretty and her eyes were a bright blue, just like Stanleys.

"At last!" she exclaimed as she hurried down the steps. "I was beginnin' to wonder what'd happened to y'all. Welcome home!"

She reached Emry first and crushed her in a tight hug; then one by one she repeated the greeting with all the others.

They were still passing hugs around when a friendly shout from the neighbor's yard made them all look in that direction. A man was standing there, waving a burly arm at them. The house behind him was a long ranch-style block house and in the driveway was a police cruiser.

Jim was Stanley's cousin, and he was a clean-cut guy, thickly built, but not fat. His eyes were friendly, but squinted as if he was perpetually looking into a bright light and his brow was always creased even when he smiled. It didn't take him but a minute to cross the yard and when he arrived, he vigorously shook Stanley's hand while at the same time; he patted him on the back. He hugged Maggie and kissed her on the cheek, and was just turning to the girls when a large yellow dog interrupted the greeting — much to Emry's relief. He was a friendly mutt of a dog and he happily pranced around, wagging a shaggy tail, and grinning from ear to ear while barking out his own welcome. His name was Tripper. Emry was told that when Tripper was a puppy, he stayed under foot, tripping the unsuspecting, and thus, the name.

Close on his heels was a teenage boy who ran up to them and took the dog by the scruff of the neck. If Emry hadn't noticed the dog before, she certainly would have once he had a grip on him. Casey was his name and he was an eye-catcher, cute rather than handsome. His blue eyes stood out against a suntanned face and his blonde hair was stylishly unkempt. He was slender and firmly built and he had a smile that was almost bashful. Emry did a double take, looking once and then looking again. She cleared her throat and mentally reprimanded herself. "He's your cousin," she reminded herself, and then she calmly smiled as he greeted her.

They were unloading when Betty arrived. She was Jim's wife and Casey's mother, and neither her looks nor her personality came as a surprise. In fact, in Emry's opinion, she was the stereotypical country homemaker. She was short and overweight and she appeared to tiptoe across the lawn as she made her way to them, her arms held up like someone wading through water, and her high-pitched voice calling out a welcome. She smiled and bumped cheeks with Maggie while continuing to talk the entire time. Between her incessant talking, the dog's joyful barking, and the constant reprimands being given out every time someone almost fell over Tripper, there was a chaotic atmosphere that was all but comical.

Dusk turned into night but Emry's eyes had so accurately

adjusted that the change was imperceptible. Only when she walked into the artificial lights of the house and back out again did she notice that it had grown quite dark.

Betty took Tripper and went home, but when Emry walked outside again Jim was still there, standing in the yard, talking to Stanley.

She walked to the car and began looking for anything that might have gotten overlooked. There was an mp3 player somewhere, she told herself, and was just beginning her search when she heard a step behind her.

It was Casey. He had come out of the house so quietly that she hadn't heard him until he was right beside her. He placed a hand on the open door and looked down at her.

"So . . . are you lookin' forward to school? Dad tells me you're going to be a senior."

"That's right."

"Me too."

"Hey, that's great," Emry answered. She looked over her shoulder at him. His profile was etched against the light behind him and he was cuter than ever.

"Maybe we'll have some classes together," he said, giving her his timid smile.

"I certainly hope so. It's hard not knowing anyone."

"I could show you around — help you get oriented on your first day," he suggested. "The school's a real maze if you don't know your way around."

"That would be cool."

"I could give you a ride too — if you want it."

She had thrust her hand into the sleeve on the back of the seat and was digging around. It was crammed with travel trash — an empty water bottle and paper wrappers from snacks, but she found her Mp3 player and pulled it out before answering. "Dad says he's getting me a car, but I'll take you up on that if it falls through."

She cringed at the thought of riding the school bus.

"Sure," he said just as Jim called out to him.

"Let's go home," Jim said and Casey waved a careless hand at Emry.

"See ya'," he said as he walked away.

Emry slowly wagged her head as she watched him follow Jim across the yard. He was much too cute to be a cousin.

Emry's room was upstairs. It was small, but large enough for a double bed, a dresser with a mirror behind it, and a corner desk. Most of their belongings had arrived a couple of days before by way of a moving van and Ellen had arranged things, setting Emry's three year old computer on the desk. A regular, straight-backed chair was pulled up to it.

She walked to the side of the bed and laid the things down she was carrying. This was the room her parents had occupied when they had come for their last visit. The only thing Emry remembered, though, was the wallpaper. It was white with the print of a tiny rosebud spray that ran in every direction like a climbing vine. A lace curtain framed one tall window that looked toward the north and a pair of old-fashioned mini-blinds filled the opening.

Crystal knocked at the door and then stepped inside

without waiting for an invitation.

"I can't believe it!" she said. "I have my own room."

Both she and Emry had imagined they would be sharing a room, so they were relieved when that scenario hadn't played out.

She walked to Emry's bed and fell over backwards on it. She was a gangly girl of fourteen, tall and thinly built. Her hair was blonde and her eyes blue and Emry looked at her with a bit of envy. Her own hair was blonde as well, but her eyes were brown, like Maggie's. She thought that blue eyes were the perfect complement to blonde hair and she was disappointed the lucky gene had gone to Crystal and not to her.

Crystal pushed herself up to her elbows and smiled, swinging her legs as she looked around.

"This is going to be great," she went on to say. "Hey, what'd ya' think of Casey? He's lit, isn't he?"

"He's your cousin," Emry said.

"No, he isn't. He's Jim's stepson. Grandma just told me."

It was true. Casey was Betty's son from a former marriage so he was really no kin at all.

"Still, that's a little awkward, don't you think?"

Crystal sat up and shrugged. "No, not really. Hey!" she quickly exclaimed, changing the subject, "Did you know we live next door to a haunted house?"

"Really?"

"Yeah, the guy that once lived there was an axe murderer — or something," she added, her voice tapering off as she considered that.

Emry gave her a curious look. She did seem to remember there was an old house next door.

"This is so-o-o-o cool!" Crystal went on to say.

"Don't you have some unpacking to do?" Emry pointed out.

She did, but she didn't want to do it. It got her out of Emry's room, though. She got up and walked away, and Emry just stood there, one hand on the door and the other propped on her hip as she stared at nothing.

After a minute, she closed the door behind Crystal and then she looked into her new room. It was neat and clean, but still, it had the odor of a room long closed. The smell prompted a memory of her mother reading bedtime stories to her while they lay side by side on this very bed. Her favorite had been the fairytale of a young girl whose brothers had been turned into swans by an evil witch and in the end, because she gathered briars at night to make garments that would restore them to their human form, she had also been accused of being a witch. Emry smiled at the odd feeling of enchantment the thought prompted.

She took a shower and then she dressed for bed. As she left the bathroom, she called out a good night in the general direction of the downstairs. One by one, an answering reply came to her from all over the house, reminding Emry of the Waltons. She had an irresistible urge to say, "Good night, John Boy," but she didn't. Instead, she returned to her room, smiling all the way. When she entered it, however, the same feeling of enchantment came over her again. She turned off the light and walked to the bed. Moonlight was streaming through the blinds, making a pattern on the floor as she crawled into the bed. She pulled the pillow under her head and with a sigh; she rolled onto her back, and stared up at the ceiling.

So, this is it. In the darkness, the glad feeling of a moment before left her. The home she loved in Charlotte was now nothing more than a memory. She felt her eyes tear up even though she fought against it. She hated to cry.

The unbidden emotion made her angry. She huffed and turned to her side, beating the pillow with her fist as she stuffed it under her head. With another sigh she settled down and gradually she relaxed.

She was lying there, looking at the vertical lines of shadow the blinds made on the floor when a distant sound brought her head up. She listened and then she laid her head down again. They were now living in the country so she could imagine that some animal had howled into the night. A minute later, the train rumbled by, blowing its whistle as it neared the crossing at Palmetto Bluff Road. Maybe that was all she had heard before — the distant sound of the train whistle.

The sound, though, gave her a strange feeling, a curious feeling, one that made her want to look outside even though it was dark and she knew she couldn't see anything. She climbed out of the bed and walked to the window. She pulled the blinds up so that she stood fully exposed in the tall opening and then, she simply stared outside.

The moon was full and everything was bathed in a dim light. It was bright enough that the trees made shadows on the grassy lawn. She looked down on the scene in fascination and felt bewitched by the strange beauty. The sylvan landscape was magical in the moonlight and her fairytale thought came to mind again. She could almost imagine seven swans wearing golden crowns, alighting on the grass, and changing into young men as the light of the moon gave them the power to do so. The sun was their enemy. By day they were swans, but as the day turned into night, only then could they be men.

She heard the sound again and her eyes immediately moved to the dark outline of forest at the edge of Ellen's yard. A distant star winked in and out of the trees and against the vague outline of the woods she saw a fence that stood tall and formidable.

And then she remembered the old house. It was behind that fence and all but hidden amid years of runaway growth.

It's the Balfour's house, she thought and then she tried to remember what she knew about the old place.

Nothing much came to mind except that Stanley had never let her get near it — not even near the fence that separated the two yards.

She stood there for a few minutes, just looking out the window, but then for no apparent reason, she began to feel uneasy. It was a curious feeling, as if someone was watching her from the deepest part of the shadows. Her eyes ran across the moonlit yard and even though she saw nothing, she stepped back and closed the blinds. An uncontrollable shiver suddenly ran down her spine.

Like someone has stepped over my grave, as the old saying goes. It brought another slight tremor to her body.

She walked back to the bed and crawled in, but now she was consumed by a curiosity that took precedent over her previous melancholy. Tomorrow she wanted to have a look at the old house. She didn't feel restrained by Stanley's restrictions of ten years ago. Besides, she was old enough that surely they no longer applied.

Well, she thought, *it's better than just moping around.* And it gave her something to look forward to.

Tomorrow she'd check out the haunted house.

Chapter Two

The Balfour's house sat far off the road, even farther back than Ellen's house, and it was almost hidden behind moss-laden oak trees and a tangle of Florida vegetation. It was a huge house with large vacant windows that seemed to stare toward the road. The roof was long and slanted and on both ends of the house were rounded balconies. Surrounding the property was a high wrought iron fence with points like spears that shot up every few feet at alternating heights. At the entrance an enormous gate of intricate design was set on two cement columns that stood one on each side of a leaf strewn driveway. A path wound onto the property where it quickly disappeared into a dark overgrown yard.

Emry stopped by the fence in the shade of a giant oak tree and placed a hand on the smooth iron bar. It was sturdy and cool to the touch, and she leaned into it, looking, but not seeing anything significant. She walked down the fence line, noting how high and strong was the fence. Everything inside was pressed against it, pushing so hard that it seemed as if the fence was there only to hold everything inside rather than the other way around. Emry imagined that should there be a breach in the wall, something evil would be released like a genie from a bottle.

When she came near the back corner, Emry stopped in

surprise. There was another gate there almost hidden behind tall golden grasses. She stood there and stared, the unexpectedness of it making her look in wonder.

This gate wasn't tall and overpowering like the one at the front of the property. It was a friendly gate, a neighborly gate, but a locked gate nevertheless. Emry waded through the tall grass and stood by it, looking over it into the overgrown path that wound into oblivion beyond.

No one had used it in years, but Emry could see where it had once been a well-used and maintained access to their property. The back of the Balfour's house could be seen from here through a tiny window of opening in the trees, and Emry could see a seedy garden that must have once been a beautiful display of landscaping marvel but was now only dry fountains and low stone walls, overgrown flower beds and an old greenhouse that was in disrepair.

It looked as if a permanent gloom had settled over the place. The trees kept the sun from reaching into the interior, giving the yard the tenebrous look of a witch's garden. It was enchanting in its own way, although the enchantment was more like the quiet still of a cemetery rather than the charming delight of a fairytale dream.

Still, it had its own charm. Occasionally the sun managed to get through, and when it did, it made lacy patterns in the depths of the gloom that when the trees moved; it made tiny spots of light that seemed to sparkle as if the sun laughed at the thought of penetrating into the forbidden area. A single shaft of light struck the path and Emry was surprised when she heard the incongruous sound of birds singing in the heart of what appeared to be a cursed garden.

As she stood there, a cloud passed before the face of the sun. The sunlight disappeared in the wink of an eye and a gray mantle again settled over the path and the yard into which it ran. The sudden change affected Emry strangely and her eyes immediately arose to the second story of the house. The windows were dark — almost black. It wasn't the kind of darkness that comes from lights being turned off, but rather the absence of light all together. It was as if there was nothing inside except the darkness itself.

Baby, Ellen's calico cat, came around the corner of the barn and tentatively meowed in Emry's direction. Emry stooped down with a beckoning hand and the cat came to her, winding around her legs and rubbing against her. She was the barn cat. She lived outside, never coming inside the house, but when Emry began walking home, Baby ran ahead of her, guiding the way. She ran onto the porch, jumped up to the swing and settled down on the flower-print pillows lying there. Emry walked inside and went straight to the kitchen just as Betty arrived at the back door.

There was to be a dance at the community center that night. Betty brought the news, telling Emry about it over a cup of coffee. With nothing better to do, Emry decided to go. She made arrangements with Casey and that evening, he picked up Emry and Crystal in his little silver Kia, and they all went to the dance together.

They arrived just before dark and already, there were a

dozen vehicles in the parking lot, most of them pick-up trucks.

Standing beside a two year old green Ford was a small group of boys. They waved as Casey stepped out of his car and then they began to move in his direction.

They were all remarkably alike — all of them except one, that is. They wore jeans and button up shirts that were open at the collar. Some of them had on cowboy hats and pointed leather boots, but the rest were in t-shirts and they wore caps with a brim. All of them, it seemed, wore fancy belts with buckles as big as their fists — except one.

The exception was a free spirit. His clothes were more Abercrombie than Western World, and his hair was an unusual color of florescent red that stuck out from his head in every direction, framing a long, rectangular face. Among the coterie of solemn, frank faced boys who sauntered with predictable and determined steps, he was a light breeze, buoyant, bouncing along with an energy that made him engage in random acts of physical activity. He almost skipped as he moved around the other boys, the energy bursting forth from him, making him run to a parked car and slide harmlessly across the hood. He landed on steady feet beyond it and then he ran back to the others. They completely ignored him, but Emry watched in amazement. He was quite entertaining.

His name was Lawrence, but everyone lovingly called him Beaker because of his uncanny resemblance to the Muppet character. The other boys were Brad, Cody, Joe, and Robert. They were alike as peas in a pod.

The community center had once been in the cafeteria of an

old school, but it had burned down. The Volunteer Fire Department now occupied that property, but next door, a new building had gone up for community activities and that was where the dance was being held.

Casey led them to the double doors that opened into a room with nondescript tables and chairs. A table had been set up at the entrance and two women were taking tickets. The admission was a dollar. They paid their money and entered the room.

A group of girls were already seated at a table to the right and that was where Casey went.

Introductions were passed around — Ann and Natalie, Jessie, Courtney, and Cindy. Emry knew she'd never remember the names and she didn't. They helped her out all evening — every time she called someone by the wrong name.

They had been there for about fifteen minutes when two more girls arrived. The first of the two was a short girl with dark hair and eyes, full figured with rounded hips and large breasts, but the girl with her was a perfect ten. She had a long slender body that was curved in all the right places and red hair that was dark and smooth. It was straight and hung to her shoulders in silky strands, not a split end in sight, and her eyes were a soft brown, large and framed by long dark lashes. Her ivory skin was without blemish and her lips were full, the color deep and rich.

"The Millers," Brad spoke, just loud enough for those closest to him to hear. All the boys looked up. It was a primordial reaction prompted by natural selection. In other words, the hot girl got the attention, and the tall slim redhead gracefully crossing the room was more than just hot — she was blazing.

"Who are they?" Emry whispered to Casey and he smiled in his deceptively timid way. Emry had the feeling there was nothing shy about him, but his smile didn't give that away.

"The Millers, Abby and Kaylee."

"Sisters?" Emry asked. No two sisters had ever been more different.

"Yeah," he answered, chuckling softly at her astonishment.

Abby, the red-head, went straight to the back and sat down, but Kaylee looked around as if trying to locate someone. Her eyes fell on Emry and she smiled. Immediately, she approached the table and when she arrived, the smile was a happy grin.

"Emry?" she asked as she leaned across the table. "Hey, I'm Kaylee. Your grandmother has been tellin' my mom for weeks about your arrival. I've been lookin' forward to meetin' you."

Emry stood up. It seemed more polite.

"Hi," she said. That sounded kind of lame, so she quickly added an invitation. "You wanna sit here with us?"

Everyone pushed chairs around and made room for her.

There was a stereo system in the corner and a boy standing near it patted the end of a microphone just then causing a loud popping noise and a squeal of a speaker that got everyone's attention. He cleared his throat and laughed nervously.

To begin with, he made a few announcements — where the refreshments were for tonight and then upcoming events for the community center. He ended with an encouragement for everyone to dance — after all, it was a dance. A hum of united laughter arose from the tables.

Someone dimmed the lights, and he put on a slow song to play. Several couples arose from their chairs and walked to the center of the room where all the tables and chairs had been pushed back, leaving room for dancing.

"You wanna dance?" Beaker asked Emry and after the shock of the invitation wore off, she apprehensively accepted. He was like bottled energy and she was afraid what would happen once she was out on the dance floor with him, but remarkably, he was an excellent dancer — much better than Emry who knew little more than how to sway to the music.

There were several adults chaperoning the event, but just as it grew dark outside, another man arrived. The bright light at the door shined like a spotlight on his face, highlighting the white telltale collar under the chin of a Catholic priest.

He greeted the ladies at the ticket table and they shook hands. He was a young man and very good looking, and even though he was a proclaimed celibate, they appeared to be girlishly giddy at his presence. He smiled with friendly ease and stood near them, talking while his eyes roamed around the room. After a minute or two, he casually strolled away from them, making a turn around the room before walking back again.

He stayed the rest of the evening, taking a greater interest in the teenagers than the other chaperones. He occasionally walked outside, but he always returned, constantly walking and looking, his eyes always moving.

When Emry got ready to leave, he was standing near the parking lot, watching as everyone left. He was very friendly, and even though he had appeared to be monitoring them more closely than all the other adults, he never came across as stuffy or suspicious. In fact, everyone seemed to like him, and spoke kindly to him on their way out.

"Who is he?" Emry asked once they were in the car and she knew he couldn't hear her.

"Who? Father Joe?" Casey said.

"Yeah," Emry answered.

"He's the Catholic priest. He usually shows up to help chaperone these events. He'll stand right there until we're all safely in our cars and gone. That's what he always does."

He was standing under the covered walkway and like Casey said, he was quietly watching as every car loaded up and backed out.

They were one of the last to leave and Emry was looking right at Father Joe when his calm exterior suddenly changed, becoming rigid while at the same time, the expression on his face changed to shocked disbelief.

Emry turned and looked. A large SUV was just then turning in, moving slowly as it approached the parking lot.

It was a black Escalade with dark tinted windows that reflected everything just like a mirror, causing the lights from the community center to roll off it in shimmering waves. Father Joe stepped out to meet it just as Casey backed out.

Casey quickly dropped the gear shift into drive, taking off

with more speed than Emry thought was necessary in a parking lot. They passed the dark SUV just as the window on the driver's side silently slid down. The lights that had reflected on it seemed to roll up into darkness and disappear. Before Emry could see who was inside, Casey had accelerated and the little silver sedan zipped quickly past them toward the exit.

"Well, that was interesting," Crystal said, but Emry barely heard her. She was looking back, trying to see what was happening with the dark SUV. They turned a corner and she lost sight of them. "When we got here I thought — this really sucks! But it turned out to be a lot of fun."

She was sitting in the back seat and Casey's eyes flashed at her in the rear view mirror. He smiled his shy little smile. "I'm glad you enjoyed it," he said and then his eyes turned to Emry. "How 'bout you?"

She hesitated but only because she was distracted.

"It was fun," she said, and like Crystal, she was surprised that it had been.

It didn't take but a few minutes to get home. Casey dropped them off and waited until they were in the house, then he backed out and drove next door.

Ellen, Stanley and Maggie were all three in the kitchen. There was a formal dining room in the house, but the long wooden kitchen table was the place everyone chose when eating, visiting, or just simply resting for a while. Besides, there was usually a jigsaw puzzle spread out on the dining table so there was no room for anything else.

"We're home," Emry announced as she walked through the

door. She was expecting a mild interrogation, but their questions were succinct and without interest.

"Have a good time?" Maggie asked.

"How was it?" Ellen said.

"Everything okay?" Stanley quickly threw in.

"Yes . . . good . . . everything's okay," Emry answered.

Emry waited, expecting more, but when nothing else was forthcoming, she shrugged and turned away.

"Well, I'm going upstairs," she announced, expecting the questions to come flying at any minute, but they didn't.

"Okay."

"That's fine."

"Glad you're home."

Emry eased out, thinking they were a strange trio tonight, but she laughed it off and ran up the stairs.

She flipped the light on in her room and walked to her bed where she fell across it with a sigh.

Tonight had been fun, but curiously, that wasn't what was on her mind as she lay there. It was the house next door.

She folded her arms under her head and stared up at the ceiling. It was very quiet in her room. She could hear the crickets singing in the night and the frogs peeping down at the cypress pond, and far in the distance she heard the train whistle.

It drew her to the window and she opened the blinds, looking out just like she had done the night before. The yard was bright in the moonlight and the sky was full of stars, bright stars. She picked out one in particular and marveled at how large and close it seemed until it occurred to her that it wasn't a star at all. It was shining through the trees in the Balfour's yard, a light that emanated from an upstairs window.

Her mouth fell open in surprise. Someone was there in that creepy old house!

And they were moving about. The light disappeared from one room only to reappear in another. Was the place really haunted? Was the ghost of the axe murderer roaming the halls of the old house?

She popped the blinds closed with a quick twist of her wrist and then she stepped back, moving away from the window.

It isn't a ghost, she thought. *It's the Balfours.*

She thought about the black SUV that had arrived at the community center as they were leaving. She didn't know why she thought it, but without a doubt Emry knew it had to have been the Balfours.

"O'ma'gosh!" she said. "They're back!"

Chapter Three

Emry's first week in Bostwick passed by slowly. She got up early every morning and jogged, taking advantage of a small clay track in the park that was on the corner of Palmetto Bluff and West Tocoi Road. There was a short cut just past Jim's driveway that took her in the back way. It was just a path worn down over the years by people cutting through the woods, but it was clear and well-marked.

That helped to occupy her time, but she also rearranged her room and began communicating with her old friends. Already, they seemed so far away and so long ago. It was a little disheartening.

The light she had seen in the Balfour's old mansion, as she suspected, was really the Balfours. They had returned the night of the community center dance and their arrival was all the talk of the small town. Her parent's preoccupation that night was no longer a mystery.

The tales of the Balfour's last visit were many and varying, but none of them were comforting. True, the participants in the old stories were obviously dead and gone, but as anyone in Bostwick was quick to point out, grief follows grief, which was their way of saying, "axe murderers begat axe murderers".

Every night Emry stood at her window and looked across the yard toward the tiny light that gleamed dimly from the old mansion. It was curious since the Balfour's black Escalade left every evening just after twilight and hardly ever returned before morning. The light stayed on, though, burning like a star through the woods.

Emry wondered where they went and what they did all night. No one knew but there was plenty of speculation. The most popular theory was that they were vampires out feasting all night on human blood. Emry chuckled. Jim was the only one who had actually seen them and he assured everyone they were just normal people — well, maybe normal wasn't the right word. But they were just people.

They had driven up to Jim's house a couple of nights after arriving in Bostwick, and had knocked boldly on the door even though it was eleven o'clock and everyone had gone to bed.

Jim was expecting the worst. No one knocked at his door late at night unless it was an emergency. Unfortunately, he'd had a few of those in his years as a deputy — an accident, an unexpected death or a missing child. He was mentally prepared for a disaster but instead, there was just Stefan Balfour standing at his door, making a neighborly call.

"What did he want?" Stanley had asked when Jim told him the story the next day.

"He just wanted someone to know they were here so there'd be no problem with curious visitors. He said he and his sons were making repairs on the family home and would be staying in Bostwick for a few weeks. He looked too young to have grown sons," he dryly added, a new wrinkle finding its way across his already wrinkled forehead.

It was interesting that no one had heard the sound of a hammer or a saw. In fact, during the day, nothing stirred on the property. It was as still and undisturbed as if no one was there at all.

On Saturday night, the whole family went to a barbecue at the community center. Unlike the night of the dance, tonight the wide open space was packed. The noise of voices rose as high as the ceiling and was a confusion of sound that filled every corner of the room. But just the same as at the dance, a ticket table was set up at the entrance.

Miss Tilly was manning the table. She was an elderly lady who had never married, the typical small town old maid, and she took their money with businesslike efficiency.

Emry followed her parents inside and uncomfortably looked around. She saw Courtney and Cindy first and then Natalie and Ann. They joined each other at the serving table where they turned their tickets in for plates of food. Afterwards, they found a table where Jessie, Robert and Cody were already seated. They had just begun to eat when Brad and Beaker came in. Brad sauntered through the door and paused inside, but Beaker — true to his vibrant personality — bounced inside with a tap of the overhead lintel, making an entrance that brought a scowl to Miss Tilly's face. Emry chuckled and everyone looked up.

"Hey, Brad!" Courtney called out, raising a hand and waving at him. He waved back and after buying his ticket, he walked toward her.

Courtney was the organizer of the group. She had a

personality that made her always fixing things whether it was simply making room for two more people at a full table or putting relationships back together.

The table seated eight comfortably, but she pushed chairs together and pulled more chairs from surrounding tables until she had made a place for Brad and Beaker. Casey came in shortly behind them and then the Miller sisters. Soon Courtney had two tables pulled together and everyone seated.

It was just getting dark outside when Father Joe arrived. No one seemed unusually interested when he came in. He was greeted with the normal familiarity, and he and Miss Tilly shook hands. His arrival seemed to arouse no more attention than Emry's had — maybe even less. He walked to the back corner of the room where all the adults had congregated. A few minutes later, the door opened again and two men stepped in from the darkness. Their eyes scanned the room with practiced ease while Miss Tilly primly cleared her throat with a sound that was not unlike a small hiccough.

The older of the two declined the dinner ticket she pushed his way, but he made a generous tip in the donation box on the corner of the table and that seemed to satisfy her. The other man stood quietly solemn, just staring into the room.

"Wow!" Jessie said as she saw them. Emry looked up, not surprised that a man was the focus of her exclamation. Jessie liked the boys — all the boys. "Who are *they*?" she asked.

It was the Balfours. Emry didn't know how she knew that — she just did.

It was hard to tell their ages. They both looked young, but

somehow one of them seemed older than the other — more mature, perhaps. They could have been in their late twenties or maybe their early thirties. Both of them had dark hair and eyes, and they were dressed similarly in dark pants and long sleeved, high collar shirts even though the weather was hot and muggy. The younger of the two wore a thin mustache and a beard that was trimmed to a tiny line that followed his jaw and across his chin, but the older man was clean shaven.

"Too old," Ann said, shrugging as she continued to look at them. "They're old enough to be your father," she then said to Jessie.

"Not unless I was ten years old," Jessie said as she gave Ann a look of disbelief. "You gotta admit — that one's gorgeous!"

He was attractive. Both men were handsome even though Emry, like Ann, thought they were too old for Jessie.

"But who is he?" she asked again.

"It's the Balfours," Emry stated without thinking. Everyone within the sound of her voice looked up. Suddenly, even the boys were interested.

"It can't be," Robert said, but no one paid him any mind.

"I thought they were supposed to be vampires or something," Brad said, wrinkling his nose as if he smelled something that stank. He sounded disappointed.

"Axe murderers," Robert corrected him.

"They look perfectly normal to me," Jessie said. Of course, she would think that. "How did such a stupid story get started anyway?"

Ann looked at Jessie with disdain, and then she turned to Casey and dramatically raised her eyes to the ceiling. He simply shrugged and looked down at his half eaten plate of barbecue. Everyone assumed Jessie's question was spoken rhetorically so no one answered her.

"So, how d' you know it's them?" Brad asked Emry. "You seen 'em this week?"

"No," she answered. She squirmed uncomfortably. Everyone at her table was staring at her. She didn't like being the center of attention. "But it's them. I'd bet on it."

Casey nodded. "It's them," he said and no one questioned it after that.

"Could we *please* talk about something else?" Ann asked and Natalie quickly backed her up. Natalie was a follower, always testing the proverbial winds to see which way they were blowing. Tonight she and Ann were together so anything Ann said, was the direction she followed. "Who cares about the stupid Balfours?"

"Well, I reckon I do," Brad admitted.

Just then a cup hit the center of the table and seemed to explode with cola, splashing and running in every direction.

Everyone at the table jumped up and a couple of the girls squealed.

"Beaker!" Ann screamed at him. He had been playing with his drink — nervous energy, no doubt, and he had somehow lost control. The cup flew out of his hand and landed on the table, splashing and running to the edges and pouring off onto the floor.

"Sorry — I'm sorry," he apologized. He grabbed up the now empty cup and threw a handful of napkins on the escaping liquid. Courtney helped him, being one of the first to recover.

Emry had stepped back. The coke had run off the table and down to her knee, dampening her jeans before she had had a chance to get out of the way, but she was laughing. As soon as the initial shock dissipated, everyone was laughing — except Ann and Natalie. They scolded Beaker and then they walked away, mumbling all the way while occasionally throwing dirty looks over their shoulders as they retreated.

"Don't pay 'em any mind," Courtney said. "They didn't even get wet."

Beaker shrugged indifferently, but it was obvious that it bothered him. It didn't take Emry but a few seconds to understand why — he was interested in Natalie. His eyes sorrowfully followed her as she stomped across the room and disappeared out the door.

They cleared the table, removing the heavy white paper that covered it. Someone arrived with a mop so Emry stepped back even further. Casey was standing right beside her.

They were standing there waiting for the clean-up when the door opened again and this time, an anxious, disheveled young man stepped inside. His eyes were wide and he was staring around. When he saw Jim at the back of the room, he called out and then he hurried in that direction.

The room seemed to go quiet and then it immediately hummed again with the usual sounds. It was Matt and obviously, he was in-character, which meant no one paid any mind to him.

But he was excited and his eyes wild, and Emry couldn't help but watch him with concern.

Jim stood up when Matt stopped beside him. Matt said something and Jim's eyes flashed toward the door, the creases in his forehead deepening as he gave a start.

Several of the adults at the table with Jim suddenly stood up and it was odd that at that moment, the Balfours started for the door with great urgency. They hurried outside but no one except Emry seemed to notice them.

"Hey," Casey said with concern, "looks like Matt's got a problem. I'll be right back."

Jim was leaving, following Matt out of the room, but Casey caught them before they got to the door. They briefly spoke and then Jim pushed past Casey and left. Casey quickly made his way back to where Emry was waiting.

"What on earth's goin' on?" she asked.

"Matt says there's a problem at St. Peter's church. He said somethin' attacked the priest."

Father Joe? He had been there at the community center just minutes before. Emry looked around, wondering when he had gone.

And what about the Balfours? They seemed overly interested in Matt's announcement. Suddenly, she was very much afraid for Father Joe.

Casey left Emry to go to the back table where his mother was sitting. Betty was with Stanley, Maggie and Ellen, but Emry didn't want to join them. She was curiously drawn to the front of the room. She walked there and looked outside through the narrow rectangular glass panels inside the door.

"It looks like trouble," Miss Tilly said from beside Emry. She was still manning the ticket table but Emry had forgotten she was there.

Miss Tilly had a prim way of talking and her voice articulated words with a rise in her rather high voice. Old maids had always fascinated Emry. She wondered if their single lives were due to a simple choice or if they had some tragic story behind them. The romantic in Emry always imagined it was the latter.

"Yes," Emry said. "Matt said Father Joe had been hurt."

"Oh, dear," she sighed and a grave look came into her eyes. Everyone liked Father Joe. Miss Tilly was no exception.

The table where Emry had been sitting had been put back together. Jessie and Courtney were the only girls there now, but Emry decided to join Casey at the back of the room. She located her parents first and made her way in that direction.

"Hey, honey," Stanley said as she took a seat near him.

"Hey, dad. What did Jim say before he left?"

"Not much. The boy—"

"Matt," Casey said, helping him out with the name he wasn't sure of.

"Yeah, Matt, said something had happened up at the church and the priest was hurt. That's all I know."

"I hope he's okay. He's a really nice man."

"Yeah," Stanley agreed, but he didn't comment further.

They went home shortly after that, giving Casey and Betty a

ride because Jim hadn't returned. At about eleven thirty he showed up at their door, apologizing for coming by so late.

"I saw your light was still on," Jim explained.

"Come in. Yeah, we're still up," Stanley assured him. "How's Father Joe?"

"Fine. He wasn't hurt."

"Then what happened?"

"Something — that's for sure," Jim said. Ellen offered him a cup of coffee and he waved it away before continuing. "Thanks, but no. I wouldn't sleep a wink tonight," he explained and then he went on. "A section of the cemetery fence is down. Matt swears he saw a big animal attack Father Joe, but after hearing the priest's side of the story, I decided it was just Jay on a rampage again."

"Jay?"

"He's the town drunk," Jim explained. "He gets drunk and blunders onto people's property, sometimes tearing things up in his stupor. I've arrested him more times than I care to count."

"Why would Matt think it was an animal if it was just Jay?"

"Well, he's been known to smoke the wild wood weed occasionally, if you get my drift. Bein' Saturday night, I figured he'd been at it again."

"Then what's bothering you?" Stanley wanted to know.

He turned his hat in his hand before answering. "I don't know," he said, giving a slight shrug of his shoulder. "You get the feel for people and the way they act when you deal with them. I've dealt with Jay time and time again and this just doesn't feel right anymore. There's something off on this one."

He put his hat on and turned toward the door, but he stopped. "That's why I stopped by, I guess." He hesitated and then continued. "Stefan Balfour was there tonight."

"I know. I saw him."

"No," Jim said. "I mean, he was at the church when I got there."

Stanley's brow wrinkled with concentration. It took him a couple of seconds to sort out what Jim was saying.

"He was there and if I didn't miss my guess, the priest was real nervous — maybe like he felt intimidated by him. But that's not what I came by to say," Jim said, his tone changing. "You got a gun, Stanley?"

Stanley looked up with genuine surprise. He moved restlessly, rearranging the position of his shiny silver cane. It was a thing he did when something bothered him, one of those little nuances done without conscious thought. "My old .22 is here somewhere, and dad's guns are around — why?"

"It was dark and I could be wrong, but I saw the prints of a large animal in the sand near the torn down fence. It looked a lot like a dog, only big, real big."

"If there was an animal there, why would the priest lie?" Stanley asked.

"He didn't exactly," Jim said. "Stefan Balfour told me what happened there. The priest never said a word." He paused and then looked back at Stanley. "Keep a close eye on the girls, Stanley — until I get this sorted out. An', Stanley?"

"Yeah?"

"Find that gun and make sure it works. I've got a bad feelin' about this."

Chapter Four

The sky had just taken on the first glow of morning when Father Joseph arrived at the old house. He walked quietly down the overgrown path, around old fountains, and past the broken greenhouse, giving the surroundings only a casual glance as he hurried by. A morning fog had settled into the low areas and the trees dripped with a heavy dew causing him to pull at his collar as one drop after another unerringly found its way down the back of his neck.

The morning was overcast. The sun would be late in coming out, but to his dismay, it would come out. The thought pushed him. He wanted to be back at the rectory and safe inside before it found its way high in the sky.

He didn't like the sun and he supposed he never would. Some people would find that odd — him being a priest. They would think he should love the light and shun the darkness, but Father Joseph was not the average priest. The only light he cared for was his Lord, the Light of the world, for he was a good priest in spite of his curious oddity.

He glanced around as he entered the yard. The old place was really run down. On a morning like this he could understand why half the people in this town thought the property was haunted. It was eerie in the early light, a gloom making it darker than the surrounding area and the moving fog giving the illusion of a ghostly presence. Toward the back fence the white mist curled and eased along the ground, moving among tombstones whose tops barely rose above the cloud. Few people knew of the old cemetery. It was the private family plot of the Petersons who had originally built the house and established the property back in the 1840's. The tombstones were crooked, many of them leaning over, and some of them broken and lying on the ground.

It should be better cared for, he thought, but there was no one left to take care of that job. The last caretaker had gone away in the 1970's and no one had been on the place since then — until now.

Father Joseph was the reason for the Balfour's return. It was he who had sent for them. He was at the back of the house by then, and he looked up at the old wooden door at the top of the worn and polished stone steps and he considered this, thinking that fate — or Providence — had surely been at work. Not one of the Balfours would have guessed that when Joseph had called them to return to Bostwick, they would find Hugo here. Joseph had not guessed it either although after finding Hugo, he was not surprised.

He didn't call himself Hugo anymore. He had long ago forsaken that name, but to the Balfours, it was the name by which they would always call him. They had pursued him through time and place, seeking his demise, but never achieving the objective. He was wise and careful, and he surrounded himself with no less than a small army — an army that the Balfours had picked off time and time again only to have Hugo make his escape when their victory was all but assured.

Father Joseph sighed with that thought. It had been a long and wearying chase and he had tired of it all. From the beginning he had lacked the same stamina for the pursuit as the others. He could see where it had probably been a mistake for him to join them. He was a man with a quiet soul and a forgiving heart, two things not compatible with the life of The Strangers, but quite adequate for that of a priest. What else was left for a man such as himself? If he could be called a man, that is. He had often wondered about that — wondered what he'd actually become, but then he realized that sometimes new, but strange and different things, are necessary when nature has been manipulated and twisted as it had with Demetrius and now with Hugo. There had to be a balance. Nature always balanced itself and although it took its time in doing so, The Strangers had become that very important weight that balanced the scales.

The door opened quietly under his hand, and his brother, Artemus, met him in the middle of the room. Only a moment was spent in greeting, a quick handshake that immediately turned into a gripping hug, and then they turned into a dark hallway, swiftly walking to the end of it.

A light shone faintly under a door, marking their way, and when the door was opened, only a single candle burned inside, giving the library a shadowy dim glow.

All the Balfours were there and they all greeted the priest with the same enthusiasm that Artemus had. It was a welcome that warmed his heart for it had been a long time since he had been with them.

"You were right, Joseph," Stefan quickly said as everyone settled down. "Your instincts are still sharp even after all this time."

"Yes, but I lament the fact that they need to be," he said, frowning as he spoke. "I understand there is an added bonus — Hugo is here."

"We think so," Stefan said. He leaned back in his chair, touching his fingers together in a steeple that he laid gently against his chin in thoughtfulness. "We have been fools. He knew we would avoid Bostwick for a time. He used the unfortunate incident of our last visit to his advantage. We should have known."

He was referring to the incident that had taken place back in the forties. A man had dropped into town from the boxcar of a freight train. It was wartime and there were young men who often caught a ride in such a manner, but no one suspected that this man was not a man at all — not even when a young girl turned up dead, her blood drained from her body. Stefan had killed the hobo, but not without a witness. From his point of view, it appeared to this witness to be a vicious and heinous murder, and it didn't take long for the Balfours to realize that their effectiveness in the community was gone and departure from the area was their only choice. They had left and only Joseph's call to them now had brought them here again.

"It does not matter," Artemus said. He had a quiet voice and an even temperament and his words consoled them. "We have realized it now. It is enough."

"So, what are your plans?" Joseph asked.

"We are looking for him. We want to find where he is staying, but he guards that secret with great care." Stefan pushed forward again and laid his hands on the desk. "Times have changed and I find people are more the fool than ever. The days of acceptance and understanding for what we do are gone. We must keep our secrets as carefully as Hugo keeps his own. It puts us at a greater disadvantage than it does him."

"He usually works a city and then moves on. It is curious that he has not followed that pattern here," Artemus said.

"I have a theory," Father Joseph said, drawing everyone's undivided attention. "I think Hugo is staying here because he has found another girl."

A slap across their individual faces would have given him the same result.

"What makes you think so?" Marius quickly asked. His fair complexion turned ruddy and his blue eyes darkened with anger.

"It is just a feeling," he said, but no one doubted him. It was his gift and over the years they had all learned to trust his intuition.

"Who is she?" Victor asked. He was the youngest of the clan and this morning he had been quietly sitting aside, just listening.

"I don't know. Like I said, it is only a theory."

Curiously, Victor's thoughts went across the yard to the house next door. Ellen Winters had two granddaughters and one of them was enough to excite the interest of any man. He had curiously watched her when more than once, she had stood before her window, looking out into the darkness, and he had wondered what was on her mind. Surely she couldn't see into the night, but still, she had stood there as if looking for something — or someone. Now Victor wondered if it could be Hugo or more likely, one of his minions. Hugo was too careful to come himself — not this close to the Balfours, but he wouldn't hesitate to send someone.

If she was the girl, then she would have to be taken care of, and who better than he to do that little chore?

"What about the girl next door?" he asked and Joseph's eyes darted in his direction. "I have noticed she is interested in something in the night — and she has the looks."

"Ellen's granddaughter?" Stefan asked. "Yes, it would suit him to choose her. He would consider it retribution for what Thomas Winters did for me so long ago." A distant look came into his eyes as he remembered. "You are best suited for that job, Victor. I lay it on you."

He nodded, knowing it would come, but not liking it. "Very well," he simply said.

The conversation moved on and a few minutes later, Father Joseph came to his feet and made preparations for leaving.

"Get some sleep," he told them. "You all look as if you could use it. And I have a feeling we are going to need all the strength we can muster for this job."

"Then you are with us," Marius said. "I wondered if you would actively involve yourself or if you would take only a passive role in this battle."

Joseph didn't immediately respond. He looked at Marius and gave the statement serious thought.

"There is no getting away from it. I have tried to remove myself from the order, but God has had other plans. It isn't luck that has brought us together for what may be our last battle with Hugo, it is Providence, and who am I to question the motives of God Almighty?"

"You put too much trust in your faith," Marius said.

"It is not possible," he assured him. He then turned to Stefan and his demeanor was more serious than anyone had ever seen. "I have a bad feeling," he said, his voice unusually sharp. "Perhaps my thoughts are taking me back to Lorna, and it clouds my judgment, but I am afraid this is going to end badly — just like it did with her."

Stefan jerked with the portent of that statement and his eyes glazed over with agonizing thought. He had killed her — his only daughter — killed her after she had sucked the life out of her own mother. It was a moment they had all shared, a memory that drove them, making hard men of them all.

A gloom settled over the room and a quiet resolve. If Joseph said it, then it must be true, and unfortunately, they all felt it as well.

Chapter Five

July came to an end and August was suddenly upon them. Only three weeks were left now before school would begin.

Emry felt as turbulent as the thunderstorms that seemed to arrive every afternoon. She anxiously considered those three weeks and sighed with dismay. She was really not looking forward to going to school.

The rain came that afternoon just like she knew it would and she sat in her room with her feet propped up, reading a book while the lightning popped and the thunder shook the house. The lights went off and on so many times that she finally closed the book and laid it aside.

She actually liked the stormy weather, especially when the lightning moved away and the thunder only growled in the distance. The rain on the metal roof was soothing and peaceful, having the same effect as the sound of waves breaking on the shore. Her thoughts turned to more relaxing subjects and gradually the tension left her.

A knock on her door startled Emry and she lifted her head and looked around. She had fallen asleep and the rain had moved on.

"Emry!" the impatient voice of her sister called through the door. "For cryin' out loud! Are you alive in there?"

"What do you want?" she asked, touchy after just being

awakened.

"Daddy wants to talk to you. He's in the kitchen."

"Great!" Emry mumbled as she pulled herself up and dragged herself out of her room. The hallway was dark, but she didn't need any light to find her way to the stairs. Slowly she stomped down them and into the kitchen.

Ellen was cooking and the smell was so delicious that Emry's stomach growled. She put a hand against it and grimaced. Music was playing softly in the background, some oldies tune that Emry wasn't familiar with.

"Have a seat," Stanley offered and she fell into the chair directly across from him. "You look tired."

"I just woke up," she explained.

"Oh," he said and then he cleared his throat in order to continue. "I wanted to talk to you about a car."

Emry was suddenly wide awake. She pulled herself up from the slump she had fallen into and sat up straight in her chair. "A car?" she asked.

"Yes, well . . ." He looked apologetic and Emry figured she knew where this conversation was going. The school bus would be the *coup de grace* after all. Well, what did she expect with the way her luck had been running? "I wanted to get you a new car, some little coupe that would be easy for you to drive."

"I know, daddy. I understand."

"I couldn't swing that, but I've made a deal with the guy who sells used cars here. I hope you won't be too disappointed, Emry. I really wanted to do more, but . . ." His voice trailed off.

Disappointed? Not on your life! She mentally waved

goodbye to the school bus and a smile spread across her face.

"Are you kiddin'?" she said. "Believe me, this is great."

It arrived the next day. Emry, Maggie and Crystal had gone to Palatka and when they returned, a ten year old white Buick was sitting in the driveway.

"Ohmagosh!" Crystal exclaimed as she saw it. "Ohmagosh, Emry! It's your car!"

It wasn't what she had imagined for herself, but she wasn't going to dwell on that. Besides, when she sat down in it for the first time, a feeling of excitement came over her. This was her car! It didn't matter that it wasn't new or even nearly new. It was hers and that was all that mattered. She turned the key and the starter whined but the engine didn't start. She tried again, holding the key a little longer in the on position, and finally the engine roared to life. It sounded good and she gave a thumbs-up to Crystal before dropping the gear shift into reverse and backing out.

The next day when she was sitting at the convenience store in a dead car, Emry wasn't quite as happy anymore.

She walked into Hall's looking for a phone to borrow. She wished she had a cell phone, but she didn't. It was just one of those things that her parents couldn't afford right now. Everyone else, though, seemed to have one. At her request, a half dozen of them appeared as if by magic and she could take her pick. She accepted the phone of a little old woman whose thin gray hair was pulled back in a ponytail. She seemed the least zealous, lacking the overly anxious desire to help that prompted the swift gesture of reply from each of the men in the room, some of them whipping their phones from cradles at their sides as quickly as gunfighters making a fast draw. Emry made the call and then she went outside to wait.

Stanley arrived a few minutes later full of apology. He lifted the hood and looked at the battery, carefully removing the cables and cleaning them.

"Try it now," he said and when Emry turned the key in the ignition, the car fired up on the first try. He was all smiles when he dropped the hood back in place.

And everything seemed to be fine.

The days rolled by and each day seemed to be pretty much the same as the day before. Emry jogged and cleaned house and e-mailed friends. Their replies were coming farther and farther apart and shorter in content until one day, there was nothing from any of them, not even from Stacy whom Emry imagined to be closer to her than a sister.

The next day, there was still nothing. It put Emry in a mood of self-pity combined with disappointment, and also a little anger.

Stanley was reading a paper when she went downstairs. He seemed to have changed since coming to Bostwick — heavier yet, she was thinking. He wasn't as cheerful anymore either.

"Would you look at this," he said as she walked into the room. "Billy Grayson plays mandolin in a bluegrass band. They'll be at the Price Martin Center in Palatka tomorrow night. I went to school with him."

"Yeah? You ought to go see him," Emry suggested.

Ellen walked in from the back yard just then. She was

getting her garden ready for the fall crops and she had been outside talking to the man who would do the plowing for her.

"Whew! It's hot today," she exclaimed as she entered the room. "I bet we have a doozey of a storm this afternoon."

"Don't get overheated," Stanley said, then he added, "Mama, do you remember Billy Grayson? I went to school with him. He plays in a bluegrass band now."

She picked up a broom and began sweeping before answering.

"Was he that short fat kid who married that tall pretty girl?"

Stanley chuckled. "Now that you mention it, he is."

"Move your feet outta the way," she told Emry as she reached under the table with the broom. "If I sweep under your feet, you'll never get married."

Emry raised her eyebrows and looked at Stanley who smugly smiled at Ellen's quaint superstition.

"I heard his band," Ellen said without a pause from her chore. "They're pretty good. And, by the way," she added. "His wife must've put 'im on a diet. He ain't fat no more."

"I think I'll go see 'im tomorrow night. You wanna go?"

"I would," Ellen said, "but me, Lois and Eunice have plans."

They were her closest friends — all of them widows. When she had been living alone, Friday night had been their regular night out. Now that everything was getting back to normal, Ellen was resuming her old habits.

"I'll go with you, daddy," Emry said. She was thinking she

had nothing better to do.

Come Friday night, though, she wasn't as eager to go. Maggie had decided to go, so it wasn't like Stanley would need her or anything so Emry graciously backed out.

The depressing thing was, it seemed everyone had plans except her. Crystal was going to a friend's house and would be sleeping over and, of course, Ellen had her Friday night outing scheduled. Stanley and Maggie were going to hear the Bluegrass band, so that left Emry on her own. She decided to take the opportunity and simply wallow in her misery alone in an empty house. Besides, it would be nice to have the house all to herself even if she didn't indulge in self-pity.

As it turned out, Kaylee called and invited Emry to come over for the evening. With nothing else to do, she accepted. Besides, she actually liked Kaylee. The two of them would be seniors this year and they could compare schedules. Maybe Kaylee could give her some pertinent advice.

Kaylee lived on West River Road which was just a small paved road that followed the curve of the river. It began at US 17 and ended at Palmetto Bluff Road and mostly it was very rural with pastures and small farms, but along the river itself, there were large beautiful houses, some of them magnificent in both size and looks. Along the way and tucked in between these two extremes, were just average houses and it was in one of these where Kaylee lived.

Mrs. Miller was a divorcee who worked at a bank in Palatka. Kaylee looked a lot like her and Emry wondered if Mr. Miller then was who Abby had taken after. If so, he must have been one heck of a good looking guy.

Emry only stayed an hour even though she enjoyed being there. A week before, she would have felt guilty and even disloyal for feeling this way, but after the silence from her friends in Charlotte, she had no such compunction. In fact, she felt motivated to cultivate friendships instead of pushing them away, and reluctantly she admitted that maybe it was for the best. This was probably a good time to simply cut those old ties.

When she got into her car, she flipped on the CD player and turned it up loud.

It was dark but the night was pleasantly lighted by a million stars. The moon hadn't yet arisen, but the sky was a dark bowl generously peppered with tiny dots of light. The old Buick whipped along, and within a few minutes, Emry had left West River Road and was coming into Bostwick. The railroad track was just ahead and the park was coming up on her right when she slowed down at the demand of the speed limit sign.

She had given very little thought to the fact that she'd had problems with the old car. It had been fine ever since Stanley had cleaned the battery cables. That's why she was so surprised when it suddenly and without warning cut off. One minute she was going down the road at thirty-five miles an hour and the next, she was sitting on the side of the road futilely turning the key in the ignition. The car wouldn't make a sound.

She sat there for several minutes, contemplating different solutions to the problem, but in the end, she opened the door and got out. The park was nearby and a lone street light burned at one corner of it. It was the shortest route home so Emry left

Palmetto Bluff Road and walked through the park, taking the short cut that would come out near Jim's driveway.

The quiet little path that was so inviting during the day, however, was darkly forbidding in the night. The trees blocked the street light making it a shadowy place, and so when a voice came out of nowhere, speaking to Emry, her whole body jerked with surprise while at the same time, a startled yelp escaped her lips.

"Car trouble?" the voice asked.

"Ohmagosh, you scared me!" Emry exclaimed, putting a hand to her chest as if to still her racing heart. She peered into the darkness, trying to see who had spoken, but all she could see was the vague outline and a face that towered above the ground as if the man was unusually tall.

She probably should have just run away. She told herself to go ahead and do it — just run, but her feet didn't want to obey. She felt like a bug stuck to flypaper, unable to move, even though in the shadows, a spider was approaching. But then at the same time, she thought that it was probably useless to run. She wished she had a weapon — which she didn't. She had mace, but it was in the glove compartment of the Buick. A lot of good that was doing her.

"My car died and I can't get it to start," she finally answered, wondering why her voice worked when her feet didn't.

He moved and the face that had hovered above the ground, suddenly dropped to an average height. He had been standing on the low-growing limb of an oak tree and as he jumped down, he did it with such grace that it was almost as if he had flown. His feet made almost no sound as they hit the ground or when he walked across the dried leaves to stand within a few feet of her. Emry stood very still and waited, her feet still rooted to the ground.

He was a young man, not much older than she and he was dressed all in black, giving his face the illusion that it floated in the darkness. As he drew near, however, he seemed to magically materialize, the effect giving him a ghostly appearance. Suddenly Emry could see him quite clearly and she was astonished at his fine appearance. His hair was dark and cut short but several strands of bangs fell down to large, beautifully shaped eyes. His face was wide of brow, smooth and angular and his cheekbones were high, his jaw square, and his mouth was a perfect line under a straight nose. He was disarmingly handsome even though he was strangely unnerving, and Emry was struck by his compelling features, unable to look away.

He looked so serious, however, and his eyes were so very intense, staring at her as if they could see right through her, that her heart began to pound — her breath to come quickly like she had run a long way.

"Walking home alone — in the dark — without even a flashlight." It was an observation, not a question, but Emry felt an answer was in order.

She opened her mouth to speak, but no sound came out. She wasn't sure if it was fear or his good looks that unmanned her, but it took her two tries before she was able to respond.

"I didn't know I'd need one," she finally managed to say, then as an afterthought she added, "I just live around the corner. My dad'll be lookin' for me." It was a lie and she knew it, but it made her feel better to say it.

"No, he will not. He is not home. Neither is Jim. In fact, you are all alone, Emry. It is just you and I."

That was chilling. For the first time, she looked at him — really looked at him. Who was he? And how did he know all that? And her name — he knew her name.

"Who are you?" she demanded, the fear giving her boldness.

"I am your neighbor," he answered. "Victor Balfour."

Chapter Six

Emry's mouth went as dry as if she had swallowed a desert. She couldn't have screamed if her life had depended upon it — and, she thought, it might very well. She stared at Victor with eyes that had grown large with apprehension — and maybe even wisdom.

He saw the change and quickly responded.

"You do not have to be afraid of me," he said. "If I had been going to hurt you, I would already have done it."

He talked with a preciseness that was a little strange almost as if he had a slight accent or like he had learned English from a dictionary.

"Then what're you doin' hanging around out here in the dark?" she asked, and immediately she regretted it.

He was a Balfour and that should have been explanation enough. He probably wasn't quite sane and so she was thinking she shouldn't say anything to antagonize him. She was afraid the whole bunch of them were mental cases and maybe the old stories about them were not so far off the mark. It was a pity, though. He was such a fine looking man. It seemed an awful waste.

"I was looking for something," he calmly answered and Emry mentally nodded.

In the dark? Well, good luck with that, she thought, but

she didn't say it.

"Where have you been?" he suddenly asked — no, demanded. It was more of a demand than a question.

He seemed to test the wind as if catching a scent on it that caused him to look suspiciously at her. His whole demeanor changed and she realized that if he was mentally unstable, then he had just turned a corner that might lead to her demise. It was time to get out of there — if only she could move.

"I was at a friend's house," she carefully answered, wishing she felt comfortable in just telling him to bug off and mind his own business. "I've got to go home now. My dad's waiting for my call."

Another lie, but she felt that all was fair . . .

"Whose house?" he demanded.

Crazy or not, she was very close to telling him to get lost. "Kaylee," she said instead.

"Kaylee?" He appeared to be confused. It was as if he thought he already knew the answer and was incredulous at her response.

"Yes, Kaylee," she firmly said. Why was he so interested anyway? "Well, I'll be going now. It's late and daddy'll be home any minute. I'd better be there when he gets home or he'll come lookin' for me." She was saying anything she could think of to distract him and also to plant the idea that a search party would be out in force if she wasn't home soon. "I don't want to get in trouble by missing my curfew. Did I mention Jim's a policeman? He carries a gun, you know."

"No," he stated as if he hadn't heard a word of her

rambling. "I know who you have been with. His scent is all over you."

Well, that was just weird. And, yes, he *was* crazy. She was afraid of that.

"Look, Vince, Vick — whoever you are," she said, stumbling over her words as she slowly backed away from him. "You seem to be a very nice man, but I can't stand out here and talk to you just now." She was talking like she would to a child who needed placating. "Maybe some other time, okay? I've really got to be gettin' home now. Well, I'll be seeing you — goodbye."

She turned to run, but just as she lifted her foot in preparation, another man stepped out of the darkness. She set her foot down in exactly the same spot from which she had just lifted it.

Oh, my God, she thought. *I never thought it would happen like this, but I'm about to die.*

Chapter Seven

The man looked nothing like Victor. He was fair and blonde and his face was long with a high brow and chiseled cheekbones. His lips were full with a bit of a pout to them and his eyes were turned down ever so slightly. He looked like a model for a Calvin Klein commercial, but as he walked toward them Emry felt hope die inside her. She didn't know if she even had the strength to attempt an escape.

"Get her out of here *now*," he said in a commanding voice. "Someone is coming."

Oh, good! Emry thought. Maybe there was reason for hope, after all. Perhaps a good strong scream was in order, too, but when she opened her mouth and took a deep breath, Victor slapped a hand over her mouth with such speed and precision that she had no time to do anything. He dragged her aside, but strangely, he did not appear to want to hurt her. He was speaking softly in her ear and the sound was oddly reassuring. She began to relax even though she was so frightened she could hardly stand on her own two feet.

"Quiet," he said, "and do not move. Just calm down and be very still. That is good . . . very still . . . very calm . . . I am not going to hurt you."

Her back was against him. He had one arm around her waist and the other held a hand over her mouth. The sound of his voice was hypnotic, lulling her into a state of apathy. Gradually, she stopped fighting and he relaxed his embrace.

"Good," he said. "Now, listen closely. I need to get you out of here and I have no time to explain."

She felt an anxious moment and as she restlessly moved, he tightened his grip.

"Sh-h-h," he softly whispered to reassure her again. "Do not struggle . . . be calm . . . trust me . . ."

She did not understand why, but suddenly she felt calm and safe in his arms.

"I am going to get you to safety. Trust me . . ." His voice trailed off in a euphony of words that led her, guided her until she was practically putty in his hands.

She nodded an agreement not caring about anything except the pleasing and agreeable sound of his voice.

He released her, dropping his hand from her mouth and at the same time, turning her to face him. A part of her wanted only to hear him speak to her, to talk in his reassuring voice, but deep inside her was a tiny voice crying out for her to run. She couldn't have run at this point if she had wanted to, and, strangely, she didn't want to.

"Close your eyes," he said and she obeyed even though that little something in the back of her mind told her she should not.

It felt like someone pulled a cloak around her and she wondered if he had been wearing one and she just hadn't noticed. She forced her eyes open, but she couldn't see anything. She was cradled against him, and it was like being inside a cocoon that hid the night from her and her from it. He picked her up. She felt her feet leave the ground and then it was like she was flying!

Or was it just a dream.

Emry awoke and it was morning. Ellen was in the kitchen, cooking breakfast. Emry could smell bacon frying and coffee brewing and she could hear a rooster crowing in the barnyard.

She was home — that much she was certain of, but how she had gotten here was a mystery.

She tried to get up but she was a bit disoriented and she literally rolled out of the bed. She hit the floor and put a hand on the side of the bed to pull herself up again. She looked down at herself. She was wearing the same clothes she had worn to Kaylee's the night before.

"Hey! You alright in there?" Crystal asked as she opened the door and looked inside.

"What're you doin' home?" Emry asked, thinking Crystal was at Vicky's house.

"What're you doin' on the floor?" she countered.

"Huh?" Well, what *was* she doing on the floor? "I . . . well, I'm lookin' for somethin'," Emry said and as quickly as it was out of her mouth, she remembered Victor Balfour saying the same thing to her the night before. "Ohmagosh!" she exclaimed and then she scrambled to her feet.

"What's wrong with you?" Crystal demanded as Emry pushed past her and ran, stumbling and tripping to the front door. She threw it back and looked outside in astonishment. Her car was sitting in the driveway just where she always parked it.

"No way!" she said.

Crystal had followed behind her, but at a safe distance. She watched as Emry stumbled out the door and ran to her car. The keys were in the ignition and the door was unlocked. She opened it and sat down under the steering wheel. As soon as she turned the key, the engine fired and the old Buick ran like a top.

"No way!" she said again.

When she came back inside, Crystal was looking at her like she thought she had lost her mind and Emry was beginning to wonder if she had.

She tripped back up the stairs and opened the blinds at her window. She looked across the yard to the Balfour's property and what she expected to see, she wasn't sure. All she knew was something extraordinary had happened the night before, and it was Victor Balfour that had made it happen. For certain, she would never again think about a Balfour in quite the same way.

"How did you do it, Victor Balfour?" She spoke to the empty air, voicing one of many thoughts that was running through her mind like a herd of wild horses. "And what are you — really?"

That was a sobering question especially with all the nonsense she had heard about them. Crazy axe murderer? Vampire?

"You aren't crazy," she told herself and she was surprised at how much that relieved her. "And something tells me you aren't an axe murderer either."

Vampire? Well, he hadn't bitten her the night before so

that ruled that out — or had he?

She quickly turned to the mirror and jerked her blouse aside so she could examine her neck. Smooth unblemished skin stared back at her and she laughed aloud.

"I knew it," she said, feeling a little silly in spite of the fact that no one had seen her. She placed her hands on the dresser and leaned forward, looking out the window. "But you are something special, aren't you?"

Emry pushed herself upright and waited as she regained her equilibrium. It was coming back quickly and she was beginning to feel normal again — as normal as she could under the circumstances. It was a peculiar thing that had happened the night before and even though she was mildly concerned, she was even more curious.

She went downstairs for breakfast and when she came back to her room, she threw herself down on the bed and looked up at the ceiling. There was a mystery here and it frustrated her that she had no idea how to solve it. But it excited her, too.

She continued to stare at the ceiling, thinking about all the things she knew that concerned the Balfours and in her aimless wanderings, she began to consider where they went every evening. Their shiny black SUV always went out around sundown. It took them someplace and although she had heard all the ridiculous speculations, she hadn't really given it more than a passing thought. She did now.

"It would be fun to find out," she said aloud and then she laughed at the very idea. But strangely, the idea persisted until she grew excited with the thought of tailing them to see where they went every evening.

She lay there thinking about this until she began to feel guilty, then she made herself get up and do something productive. The morning passed and soon the afternoon was waning too, but curiously, the thought of following the Balfours wouldn't leave her. It was as if she had two minds. One kept working out scenarios for a clandestine tailing operation while the other kept tearing the thought apart, reasoning with her other half, and demanding caution and sense.

As it usually is with this kind of war, the adventurous mind won and the sensible one quietly retreated. Emry worked out a suitable plan and with an impatience that can only come after a completed scheme, she scheduled her first operation for that very evening, but like so many schemes, it failed in execution. Casey came over and he didn't leave until Emry saw the Balfour's SUV pull out of their driveway and speed away.

She wasn't to be deterred, however. The next evening, she drove her car to the end of the road and parked it cat-a-cornered to the park. She had a perfect view of the West Tocoi Road, and she could sit there in relative safety, waiting until they came out for the evening. When they did, all she had to do was start the car and pull out behind them — at a safe distance, of course.

The trouble was, her surveillance point turned out to be the most crossed intersection leading into Bostwick. Almost every car that turned off US 17 crossed the railroad tracks and then went through this intersection. It wasn't long before Brad and Beaker came along, and thinking that her car had broken down, they pulled up beside her and offered help. Before she could get rid of them, the Balfours came down the road, made a rolling stop at the traffic sign, turned onto the main road, and disappeared into the distance.

The next evening, she tried a new tactic. Beginning with a new surveillance point, she set out to wait, not alone on the side of the road, but in the busy parking lot of Hall's convenience store. It was located on the corner of Palmetto Bluff road and US 17 and she parked to the side, her car backed in for easy take off and the front of it pointed toward the north where she had seen the Balfours go before.

It grew dark and still she waited. The lights of the convenience store came on and the parking lot grew bright with the artificial light. People came and went, but there was no sign of the Balfours. Finally Emry gave up and decided to go home. Just as she reached down to turn the key in the ignition, the big black Escalade pulled up and stopped at the flashing traffic light on US 17.

Emry was so excited that her first attempt to crank the car was a failure. She fumbled with the key and only half turned it in the ignition, succeeding in turning on all the lights in the dash, but nothing else. Besides that, the Balfours turned south which meant if she wanted to follow them, she had to make a u-turn to do so. By the time she got pointed in the right direction, the Balfours were nowhere to be seen. This detective work was harder than she imagined and she went home, disappointed one more time.

The Balfours had become an obsession. The idea of

following them was something Emry thought about all the time. No matter how many times she went out to follow them, though, she was never successful. It had become a challenge and one that she was determined to overcome. The trouble was, she had a problem getting out of the house every evening. She had used every reason she could think of until now, she was running out of excuses. Besides that, lying had become second nature. It was scary how easy it was to lie and how adept she had become at it.

To distract herself, she tried hanging out with some of her new friends, but she spun scenarios in her head the whole time she was with them until she wasn't much company. She knew she was obsessing, but she simply couldn't make herself stop. She just had to know where the Balfours were going and what they were doing! It was a matter of pride now as well as curiosity.

The thought that they might be FBI or CIA or some other organization that used an acronym for a name crossed her mind repeatedly. It was just one of the many theories she considered. Without a doubt, she knew there was something unique about them and although she liked to fantasize about time travelers and aliens or super heroes and vampires, she laughed at the very idea. It's just that Victor Balfour had done something unusual the night she had met him and she could not get past it. Everything had been just what she might have expected that night, right up to the point when he had grabbed her. It was his voice that had changed things. He had spoken to her so earnestly — no, that did not explain it. She couldn't explain it, but something in his voice had changed everything. All she knew was, after a while, it had all become like a dream — a fantasy, something she couldn't quite remember or explain, just as if he had some special power. It bothered her and it excited her, but mostly it just intrigued her. She had to know.

Casey walked across the yard and sat on the porch with Emry that evening. She liked being with him. He was easy going and fun to be around. Of all the boys she had met in Bostwick, he was the most desirable, but one she couldn't quite make herself romanticize about. He still felt like close kin even though he wasn't. They sat together on the porch swing, swaying slowly as he talked softly, occasionally smiling his shy smile. Emry could almost have been distracted, but she wasn't.

He wanted to go to the beach the next day and he asked Emry if she and Crystal would go with him. Jim never let him go alone — safety reasons, and Casey wanted one more trip there before school began. They made plans and he came by early the next morning and picked them up.

They drove to St. Augustine in Casey's car and were there by ten o'clock, but Crescent Beach was already filling up. They found a spot that wasn't too crowded, parked, and set their things out.

It was a beautiful day, blue skies and a gentle sea breeze. The clouds began to stack on the western horizon just after noon and soon they turned black. The sun continued to shine on the beach, but you could see a storm was raging somewhere inland.

It was hot. Emry applied the sun block generously and

repeatedly, but still she felt the burn of the sun.

"Here, let me get your back," Casey offered as he reached for the plastic bottle. Crystal was in the water so they were alone.

"Thanks," she said, moving her hair aside for him. She had wanted to talk to him about the Balfours and this seemed the perfect opportunity. "Casey, did Jim find out anything about the incident at the church? I've been wondering what became of it."

He shrugged. "I don't think so." He was silent for a few seconds and then he added. "But something's goin' on. Daddy doesn't say much, but I've overheard him talkin' and he's worried. I believe it's something to do with the Balfours. Their name keeps comin' up."

She had the urge to tell him about her meeting with Victor, but she didn't. She thought it was best to keep that a secret for the present. If word got back to Stanley, she knew she'd never get out of the house again to follow the Balfours.

"What does he say about them?" she asked.

Casey leaned back and closed the bottle of sun block with a snap. Emry let her hair fall across her bare shoulders and then she leaned back, too.

"He called 'em a bunch of liars. He was on the phone and I don't know who he was talkin' to, but that's what he said. He also said he'd believe Matt's story over theirs any day and Matt's nothin' but a dope head."

"What story?"

"You know, what happened at the church that night." Casey

drew his legs up and relaxed his elbows on his knees before continuing. "Did you know, the next morning when dad went by to check on the damage, the fence was already mended?"

"What? The fence that was knocked down at the cemetery?"

Casey nodded. "The fence was back up and the ground around it had been swept clean. There wasn't a mark left within a thirty foot diameter around it."

"But how?"

Casey shrugged again. "Father Joe said he imagined it was concerned parishioners that had taken care of it. Daddy thinks it was the Balfours."

"But why? What could possibly be their reason for lying and then fixin' the fence in the middle of the night?"

"Who knows? They're kinda crazy, you know."

"Yeah, I know," she said, thinking about her own meeting with them. Victor Balfour was a peculiar man, if not downright crazy, but she couldn't feel an aversion to him even though she knew he was not quite right. The funny thing was, Casey's story only made her want to find out more about him rather than the other way around. And the more she thought about it, the more excited she became about following them.

She stretched out on her towel and turned onto her stomach so she could rest her chin on her folded hands. She stared at the breaking waves and watched Crystal as she rode a boogey board to the shore. When the water became shallow enough to ground her, she picked up the purple board and ran back into the water. Emry watched her, but her thoughts were on the Balfours — Victor, in particular.

She was obsessing again. This time, though, she relived her meeting in the park with Victor, letting herself think about how he had looked standing in the shadows and how it had felt when he embraced her — the smell of his body as her head rested against his shoulder.

She literally jerked as she mentally slapped herself. Was it so easy to forget how frightened she had been? Or how strange he had acted? Or about the other man that had come out of nowhere, scaring her half to death?

She reminded herself that it was just creepy for them to be hanging out in the park at night, in the first place.

He had been looking for something, he had said, and for the first time, Emry wondered about that.

"What do you think about them?" she suddenly asked Casey.

"The Balfours?" He paused as if thinking. "I don't know. Rich and eccentric, maybe."

"Not axe murderers?"

They both chuckled. "Too messy. But it's funny that there've been some peculiar deaths in the area since they arrived."

"What'd ya' mean?"

He looked around as if fearful of being overheard, and then he spoke in almost a whisper. "Don't say anything, okay? But I heard there've been some bodies found that were all slashed up and their blood gone."

"Vampires?" Emry jokingly asked.

"No. But you know what daddy thinks? He says, he knows there's no such thing as vampires, but if someone wanted to be a vampire bad enough, he might roleplay that he is one and then go out and kill people — take their blood."

"And he suspects the Balfours."

"Yeah. You have to admit, they do things that make you wonder about them — never coming out in the daytime, for instance."

"I know," Emry admitted.

"And you know what else? A person that thinks he's a vampire can be as deadly as if he really is a vampire — just as dangerous."

Crystal picked up her boogey board and ran across the beach, arriving just as Casey finished his statement. She threw the board down and grabbed up a towel.

"Do you see that cloud?" she asked, looking across the dunes as she spoke.

Emry looked over her shoulder. A purple cloud was making a backdrop behind the swaying sea oats. It was rising ominously into the sky and stretching forward, moving toward them.

"Dang," Casey said. "We're in for it."

"Somebody's gettin' a soakin'," Crystal agreed, just as lightning brightened the dark cloud.

It was a long way off and no present danger, but the lightning unnerved Emry. She didn't want to be on an open beach in a thunderstorm so she put in for them to go home. It wasn't a hard sell. Both Casey and Crystal readily agreed. They packed up and left the beach, driving right into the storm. It was raining just west of St. Augustine and rained all the way home.

The sky was gray in Bostwick, but it stopped raining as soon as they arrived. Emry was exhausted. The sun and the water together had sapped her strength and she dragged herself upstairs. She took a short shower to get the sticky salt feeling off her, and then she took a nap. When she got up, she was refreshed, so she went to the kitchen and helped Ellen and Maggie prepare dinner.

Maggie had been looking for a job and she talked about the possibilities. Kaylee's mother had mentioned a position that might be coming available at the bank where she worked and Maggie was going the next week to put in her application. She had been an elementary school teacher before Emry had been born, but she hadn't worked outside of the home since then. It was just another one of the things that was changing.

Emry had decided to lay low for a couple of evenings and not go out on her surveillance, but an unexpected opportunity arose while they were eating dinner and she grabbed it.

Kaylee called and asked if she could come over. It was the perfect excuse to go out.

The sun was still up when she left home. She had plenty of time to visit Kaylee and still make it back to Bostwick before the Balfours made their usual evening trip. She had it all planned out. When she left Kaylee's house, she went straight to Halls.

The parking lot was almost empty. There were several places on the south side of the building where she could park, so Emry backed into the one that gave her the most concealment.

A half hour later, she was still waiting and when fifteen more minutes crawled by, she decided that either she had missed the Balfours or they had taken another route. She reached for the key in the ignition and gave it a turn. The Buick fired up like a brand new car and Emry dropped the gear shift into drive.

Just as her foot touched the gas pedal, the Balfour's black SUV pulled up to the intersection and stopped at the flashing light. She was no more than thirty feet away from them, sitting in a car that was running, and pointed in the right direction. When they pulled out onto US 17, she spun out behind them.

They accelerated with great speed just as they always did and Emry's Buick was no match for their power. She fell behind, but not too far. It was actually a good distance.

She followed them, moving past miles of pastures as she kept pace with them, but as they approached the curve at Seminole Electric, Emry was afraid she would lose them, so she sped up. They made the turn and went out of sight, but she was close enough that when she came around the curve, they were still within view.

Oddly, she found herself gaining on them so she slowly eased off the gas. Soon she had to slow down again. US 17 was a four lane highway and she knew she couldn't keep falling back or they would know she was tailing them. She would have to go around and that meant she would lose them one more time.

She looked into her rear view mirror. A semi-truck pulling

a long trailer was approaching in the left lane. She couldn't get over until he passed so for the moment, she was stuck behind the Balfours.

Without warning, though, the black SUV ahead of her braked. Emry slammed on her own brakes to keep from rear-ending them but they quickly pulled over although they never completely succeeded in getting entirely onto the narrow skirt. The semi whizzed by and Emry waited as two more cars followed.

She was looking in the outside rear view mirror and that was why she didn't see the dark figure that stepped into the glare of her headlights.

It was Victor Balfour, but Emry did not see him until the passenger side door opened. She looked up in surprise and then she gasped with fright. Her first impulse was to hit the gas, but there was nowhere to go. The Escalade was ahead of her and cars were speeding by in the other lane. She watched in horror as Victor got into her car and slammed the door shut.

She looked at him with eyes wide and mouth agape. She was frozen behind the steering wheel and stunned into immobility.

"Go!" he demanded, as the Escalade pulled entirely off the road, but she hesitated in stunned silence. "Go," he repeated. "Before someone runs over us."

"Okay," she meekly said and her foot touched the gas. "Where to?" She was so nervous her hands trembled on the steering wheel.

"Just drive," he said.

They went through the intersection at West River Road and as they did, Victor pulled the seat belt around and clipped it into place. He looked over his shoulder, out the back window, and Emry glanced into the rear view mirror to see where he was looking. The black Escalade had pulled back onto the road and was just then turning down West River Road.

The armrest was between them but Victor moved it. Emry wondered what his purpose was for doing that. It intimidated her and she supposed that was his reason for moving it. Having it between them had given her a barrier that, mentally, at least, protected her. Now that it was gone, she felt more vulnerable. He laid his arm on the back of the seat and Emry watched him out of the corner of her eye.

He leaned forward and quizzically looked at her.

"You really should lock your doors. You never know who might drop in."

"Like you, you mean?"

He leaned back and smiled. "Yes, like me. I want to talk to you."

Talk? Emry hoped that was all he wanted to do. She anxiously looked at him.

He was calm — relaxed — innocuous enough, she supposed. Nothing about him seemed to be threatening, but then she had heard that even serial killers were normal appearing people, sometimes even fooling their own families. She gave him another glance across the car and then she stared straight ahead, wishing she knew what to do.

"About what?" she ventured to ask.

"Well, a couple of things, actually," he said. He paused as if considering which subject to open with. "Shall we get the unpleasantries out of the way first?"

Unpleasantries? What did he mean by that, she wondered. He raised a questioning eyebrow as he waited for her answer.

"The unpleasantries then," he said when she didn't say anything. "No more following us, understand?"

"I wasn't—" she started to lie, but it stuck in her throat. "Uh . . . how did you know?"

"It was rather obvious," he said. "You have been giving it a try for about a week, I think."

"A week and a half," she admitted.

"Well, no more. Do you understand?"

She didn't immediately answer so he leaned toward her to get a better look at her face.

Her hair was a little longer than shoulder length and straight with bangs that fell down to her eyes. She usually pulled it back in a loose knot or a ponytail, but after her shower she had just brushed it out and let it fall naturally. He caught a wisp of it and brushed it out of the way. It was just a simple touch, but oddly, she felt it all the way to her toes.

"I am giving you the opportunity to stop all on your own," he said. "However, if you insist on following us after this, I will have to stop you. I do not think you will like that very much," he added with meaning.

Well, that was enough to kick in the adrenaline. Her pulse took off like a race horse and her respirations rose to match it.

"I'll stop," she simply said.

He leaned back again. "Good, then we can move on." His arm went to the back of the seat again, but this time, the tips of his fingers rested carelessly on her shoulder. It made her acutely aware of his presence — for more than one reason. "How would you like to help me with something?" he asked.

"Like what?"

"Just some information."

Well, that was peculiar, and the last thing she had expected. She wondered if he was really serious or if he was playing some deep game with her. After all, he didn't know her any better than she knew him.

"What is it?" she cautiously asked.

"Not one to blindly commit, is that it?" he said with a smile.

"Well, I don't want to get in over my head," she said. That seemed to amuse him.

"If you do, we will both go down together," he promised. "So, you want details before you agree to anything."

"Well, no . . . it's just that I don't want to agree to anything illegal or immoral or something. You know," she lamely ended.

"Fair enough," he said. "You have a friend. I believe her name is Kaylee."

He was quick to begin, no hesitation, no delays. He launched right into the proposition in an almost businesslike manner.

"Yes," Emry said with a nod. She glanced his way, wondering where he was going with this.

"She has a sister, I believe."

Well, she should have known. He wanted to know about Abby — all of this just so he could hit on Abby! But then, why not? Every other man in the area was interested, so why not him? In fact, he was the male counterpart to Abby, in Emry's opinion — handsome, sexy, the eye catcher in any crowd. Emry could imagine all the girls turning to look at him when he crossed a room just like all the boys did Abby. It had to be destiny that brought two such people together.

"Abby," she flatly answered, but this time she didn't take her eyes off the road.

"Tell me about her."

"I don't know anything about her. When I visit Kaylee she's hardly ever there."

"Does she live there — at home, I mean?"

"Yes, but she goes to school at St. Johns in Palatka." That was St. Johns River State College, but everyone shortened the name.

"Does she have a boyfriend?"

"Yes," Emry answered, mentally scolding herself for feeling unexplainably happy about that.

"Who is he?"

"I don't know. Van something or other. I've only met him once."

"The night your car broke down."

"Yes," she said. *Now, how did he know that?* "Why do you want to know?"

"Just curious."

Emry thought about that for a brief moment before saying

anything else. The fact that he was a Balfour caused her to imagine sinister reasons for his interest — imaginings that included murder of the rival so that the playing field was wide open.

"Where does he live?" Victor asked, interrupting the thought that had momentarily sidetracked her.

"I have no idea. Palatka, maybe."

"Can you find out?"

Emry looked at him. What on earth did he want to know that for? She stared at him so long that she crossed the line and a car blew its horn at them.

"Why?" she asked after jerking the car back into her own lane.

"I think I might know him."

"Why not just ask Abby? She'll put you in touch with him."

"That would not be a good idea. You see, I do not want him to know about me."

"Why not?"

"It is a long story," he said. "In fact, it is important that he does not learn I am even asking questions about him. It is a serious matter."

"Oh," Emry said, suddenly realizing that the gossip in Bostwick didn't even begin to grasp the enormity of the Balfour's true identity. There was indeed something going on here.

"Look, I have to go. So tell me. Do you want to help or not?" He suddenly sounded impatient.

"What do I have to do?"

She carefully asked the question, but in all reality, she was excited. This could prove to be an interesting adventure — even if she was getting in league with one of the Balfours.

"I need to find out where Van is staying. Can you find out — I mean, without raising suspicions?"

"I can try."

"Very well," he said with a cautious nod of his head. "But you have to be careful. Do not ask too many questions and do not dig too deeply. It could get dangerous if he thought you were checking up on him."

Emry thought about that and her brow creased with worry. If Abby was involved with a man that was dangerous, then someone should warn her. Victor saw the change in expression and tilted his head, getting a better look. At the same time, he leaned toward her and the hand that was on the back of the seat, reached up and moved that same strand of hair again.

"It's alright," he said, seeing that she was upset. He tucked the loose hair behind her ear and she cast a glance at him. "Do not do this if it makes you uncomfortable. It is just that I have come to an impasse and the others —" he meant his family. "Thought it would be a good idea to involve you. I reluctantly agreed."

"No, I'm comfortable with it. That's not what's bothering me. I was thinking about Abby," she said. "If he's dangerous, I should tell her."

"And then what?" he asked. "She will want to know how you know. You will have to tell her, but even if you do not, it will not matter. She will go straight to him. The first thing he will do when she does, is find you."

His face suddenly went blank and then he leaned back, the look of shock on his face.

"Oh, my God!" he said, "This is a bad idea." He slowly shook his head from side to side. "We are going to forget this," he went on. "And you are going to go home." He was upset, but not at anyone. It was his deductive reasoning that had brought it on, a flash of insight as if he had had an epiphany. He unfastened his seat belt and indicated a gas station up ahead by the dip of his head. "Put me out at that convenience store."

He was suddenly in a hurry to be gone.

But Emry was momentarily stunned. The atmosphere in the car had changed with surprising swiftness. She drove right past the store without even slowing down and Victor calmly watched as it fell behind them.

"Or the next one," he said. "If that one did not suit you."

"If you can find Van, does that mean he'll be going away and Abby won't get hurt?" she asked without even acknowledging the fact he had suggested letting him out of the car.

His body had tensed to razor sharpness, but he seemed to relax and he eased back against the seat. As he did, he gave Emry a prolonged look.

"I cannot promise that, but she has a better chance than she does now. I am afraid she is already in too deep."

"What are you, a policeman of some kind?"

"No," he readily answered.

The sharpness of his voice made her look at him.

"What did Van do?"

He suddenly smiled but there was no humor in it. "Just let me out, Emry. Anywhere will be fine."

"I want to help," she said, afraid her chance was slipping away. "I can do it. And if it'll help Abby, then I *want* to do it."

He was still for so long Emry wasn't sure he had even heard her. She looked across the car again, but a pickup truck suddenly pulled out from a side street and she had to slam on brakes. She lamented the fact that the road needed her undivided attention. Driving was too much of a distraction for a conversation like this.

"I was a fool to ask you," he finally said. "I suddenly realize how dangerous it can be for you." He paused. "But maybe not any more dangerous than your driving," he added with a wry smile and she shot him a dirty look. His mood had changed again. He seemed more relaxed, but still pensive. "Besides, you are not going to leave it alone, are you?"

"I can be discreet," she said to encourage him. "I'm really good at cloak and dagger."

That made him laugh. "Like you were at following us, you mean? That is not very reassuring."

They both laughed, but then his face went still again, and that serious look came back into his eyes.

"I was wrong to ask you, Emry," he said. His voice sounded far away — and sad. "It is a little more complicated than just telling you to let it go and expecting you to do it. I have a feeling I can expect you to do the very opposite. It is a mistake I do not know how to correct — except in one way." He eased back against the seat again and from all appearances, he was now just talking to himself. That was scary — considering who he was. "There is just the obstacle of you driving home afterwards. But then, I suppose, I could take you home if you are not able to drive. It could still work and you would be safe."

"Like you took me home from the park that night?" she said, giving him an askance look across the car. "How did you do that?"

He didn't answer right away, but gave it some thought before casually replying. "Who said I took you home?"

"No one — but you did. It's just that I don't remember anything and when I woke up — it was like I was drunk or something. You didn't — I mean, you didn't drug me or anything — did you?"

She flashed a nervous look his way. He was a dangerous man and the way he looked at her was more than just deep. He had something on his mind and even if half the things said about him were true, then nothing he could be thinking could possibly be healthy for her.

"No," he answered. "But I do not want you to think about that right now," he went on. "Just let it go. We will talk about it some other time." He touched her shoulder as he spoke but Emry wasn't really aware of it. The sound of his voice mesmerized her and she felt oddly relieved at the idea of just letting go of that subject.

Her mind automatically reached out for another and when his fingers reached up and brushed aside a loose strand of hair, she found it without any trouble.

It wasn't what she had planned to think or even what she had imagined she would be thinking. It was a sensual thought that caused her to take a deep breath and then to roundly scold herself. The trouble was, Victor Balfour was an extremely sexy guy and she could not deny that about him no matter what else she thought of him. She felt his presence like heat radiating from a stove, filling her with something more than just warmth. It was actually frightening how easily she was affected by him, but then, she was no more immune to the attentions of a good looking man than any other girl — less than some, she imagined. It didn't even help to remind herself that he was Victor Balfour, the community axe murderer's grandson or possibly the town vampire. She could take her pick. Either way, she was in for trouble.

"Pull over," he said and she snapped out of her reverie.

"What?"

"Pull over," he repeated. "Before you have an accident."

She pulled over at the first empty lot she came to and then she stopped, but she kept her foot on the brake as the car idled in drive. It was a rather dismal place, dark and empty. She could see the river, but everywhere around her there were just closed up buildings and quiet lots. She should have picked a better place to stop.

He was severely looking at her. She thought she could read his mind, though. He was trying to decide what to do with her. She looked out of the car window and the vacant windows of dark buildings looked back at her. This was no place to have stopped with a strange man in the car. Why had she let him get in, anyway? She should have just run over him when she had the chance. She looked at him again, and she knew why. He stirred something inside her every time she looked at him. He did it without even trying and Emry rebuked herself to no avail.

"Put the car in park," he said. "So you can take your foot off the brake."

Emry looked down at her foot, but she did not move. It seemed a strange request since he was getting out, anyway. He was getting out, wasn't he? She cast an anxious look his way.

He didn't seem to be in any hurry now that they had stopped. Emry could see his mind working and she could only imagine what he was thinking — or plotting.

Did he really want her to help him? Emry supposed he did, but he was torn between the idea of allowing her to help versus just simply making her forget they had even met. She didn't know how he did it, but somehow he had the power to make her forget what he didn't want her to remember.

"Aren't you gettin' out?" she asked.

"In a few minutes," he said. "Are you in a hurry for me to leave?"

"I guess not. I thought you were in a hurry to go."

"I am, but not until we do one more thing," he said. "Put the car in park."

What was he suggesting? Emry decided she needed a good slap in the face to bring her back from the place she had unwittingly gone to with her thoughts. But then, she wondered how many women had heard the sound of his voice and had thought the same things she was thinking right then. There was that quality about him, that something special that made you want to do whatever he suggested. She had to ask herself, though, why he wanted the car in park in the first place. What difference did it make?

She was considering this when out of the corner of her eye, Emry saw Victor move toward her. She turned with a start, but when he slid across the seat, he only took the gear shift in his hand and carefully moved it over until it came to rest in park. Emry had gasped, but it wasn't until her breath left her that she realized she had been holding it.

He paused for a few seconds, one hand on the gear shift and the other on the back of the seat behind Emry's shoulders. The green glow from the dash lights settled in his eyes, and at that moment, he looked for all the world like the vampire he had been accused of being. Emry looked away. She couldn't look at him when his eyes were so eerie.

"You can take your foot off the brake," he said as he eased back into his seat. "The car is not going anywhere." He took the same posture as before except that his left arm stayed on the back of the seat.

"I know what you're doing," she said, still not looking at him.

"Do you?" he asked.

She nodded. "You're going to hypnotize me or something just like you did that night in the park."

"Is that what you think?"

"Yeah, it is."

"I think you give me too much credit."

She ventured a look at him.

"No," she insisted, "but you can prove me wrong, if you like."

He smiled and then he looked away from her, chuckling wryly as he did so.

"You have been listening to the town gossip," he sardonically said. His head slowly turned until he was looking at her again. "What do you think happened that night?"

"I don't know. You made me forget."

"You seem to remember just fine. What do you think you have forgotten?"

Well, what did she think she had forgotten? She suddenly felt silly.

But then, she remembered the exhilaration, the feeling of flight and nothing more until she awoke the next morning, disoriented and confused. Her car was in the front yard, too. She didn't remember driving it home or getting it to work. It had been dead on the side of the road, the last she remembered.

She didn't want to tell him that. She didn't even want to answer his question. She wished he had not asked it, in fact.

"Emry?"

"What?"

"Take your foot off the brake."

She looked down. Her foot was still on the brake. She carefully moved it and the old Buick rocked as it settled in place.

"That is better," he said. "You were making me nervous."

Victor Balfour nervous? He was the epitome of sang-froid.

Emry had never met a man with such equanimity.

"Relax, Emry," he then said. "Forget about the park and let us talk business so I can go."

Emry looked up with renewed interest. What business was he meaning? She had to chide herself again when a provocative thought popped into her head.

"I think I have learned a few things about you," he said. Curiously, she had forgotten about the park. "You like to be in control and you do not take orders very well." He paused to give her time to consider this. "And once your mind is made-up, no one is going to talk you out of anything. That is why I know you will go right ahead and ask questions that will get you into trouble. I also have a feeling you have not learned your lesson about following us. You will do it again."

"No," she insisted with an adamant shake of the head. "There's no way I'll follow you again. I promise."

"Very well. I hear a believable promise — but only on one subject. What do you say, Emry. I do not want to scare you, but if you say the wrong thing to the wrong person, your life could be in danger."

She looked sharply at him. "Who is this guy? And who are you — I mean, really, who are you?"

"It does not matter," Victor said. "I want you to forget it. And for your own sake, you have to forget it."

He reached for her, but Emry pulled away before he could touch her. She had realized something. He always touched her when he made a suggestion she could not resist, and she had the idea that he needed the contact to make it work. She knew that sounded crazy, but what he did was crazy. It was one reason she had the feeling he was more than just a human being. Maybe alien didn't sound too farfetched, anymore.

"I will not hurt you," he said. "I promise."

Why did everything he said have to sound so sensual?

"Please, let me help you," she said. "I'll do whatever you say."

"Anything?" he asked and Emry's face flushed.

Whew! The heat that question generated consumed Emry. She took a couple of quick breaths before she got herself under control.

"I promise I won't be foolish," she quickly said, hoping he couldn't read her mind. "I don't understand why, but I understand there's a danger involved. I'll be careful. I won't ask a bunch of questions or try to follow him or anything."

"Follow him?" he said. He wilted against the seat as if her statement had taken the strength out of him. He shook his head and then he turned and looked at her. "No, you will not follow him." He flatly stated.

"I said I *wouldn't* follow him," she pointed out.

"I know, but it is the very idea you even thought about it that troubles me." He tilted his head as he glanced across the car at her. He was silent for a moment, pensively looking at her. "Very well," he finally said. "I guess we will give this a try. You can do what I say?"

"I can," she assured him.

"You seem a little nervous."

"I am," she admitted, "but I'm excited, too."

"Well, don't get too excited," he said. He smiled as if she amused him. But then, his expression changed and his look took on a seriousness that caused Emry to take a deep breath. He leaned toward her, his posture menacing. "If I hear you go out and do anything stupid, I am coming after you, understand?"

She drew back. "Okay," she meekly said and he eased back, settling down in his seat just as he had been before.

"I mean it," he said and there was nothing pleasant about the sound of his voice just then.

She nodded with great gravity, and then without warning or a goodbye, he opened the door.

"Victor," she said as he leaned into the opening. In another second he would be gone. She should have been glad, but she wasn't. "How will I get word to you when I find out?"

"I will be in touch," he simply said.

Emry nodded. She was at a loss to think of anything else to say although she hated to see him go. That was as great a surprise to her as it would have been to him had he known.

"When I get out of the car, lock the doors," he said.

And then he was gone.

Emry sat very still and watched him walk away. He was wearing dark jeans and a long sleeved, button down shirt that was rolled up to his elbows. His arms were smooth and muscular and his hands were shapely and strong. He was the most striking figure of a man she had ever seen. Too bad he was a Balfour!

When he was about twenty feet away, he pulled a cell

phone from his pocket and began making a call. He kept walking and not once did he turn and look back at Emry, but she sat there until she couldn't see him anymore and then she put the car in gear and eased forward. Before leaving the parking lot, she pressed the button that locked all the doors and then she sighed. A ride in this car would never be the same.

Chapter Eight

When Emry arrived at home, Maggie and Crystal were sitting on the couch in the living room watching television. Ellen was in the kitchen and Stanley was somewhere. Emry didn't know where. She raised a hand and gave a weary wave in everyone's direction.

"How's Kaylee?" Maggie asked, but she really wasn't wanting an answer. She was watching a rerun about FBI agents who used mathematics to solve crimes and she was in the height of the story.

"Fine," Emry mumbled anyway and then she went straight up the stairs.

Once she was in her room, she walked to the bed and just fell face forward onto it. She couldn't believe how the evening had turned out. She was mentally exhausted.

And then, there was Victor. She rolled over and looked up at the ceiling. She knew she shouldn't be thinking about him, but there he was — on her mind.

She reminded herself of his reputation and his lineage. It didn't matter. There was something besides his good looks that made her think about him, and she couldn't decide what it was. It was something alluring, something almost magical.

She huffed and came to her feet, the fairytale of the seven swans coming to mind again. She didn't want to think of that either, but her thoughts were not cooperating with her this evening.

"Maybe I should've let him hypnotize me — or whatever it is he does," she said. But then that took her thoughts in another direction — an unexpected direction.

It began with the thought of what he really was.

Maybe there really are aliens among us and he's one, she thought.

It wasn't the thought of aliens, though, that made her lie down on the bed again and wearily roll over. It was vampires. That was the unexpected change of direction her imaginings were taking.

Was Jim right? Could people imagine they were vampires and actually roleplay until in all actuality they were vampires? Could the Balfours be those people?

They certainly gave every indication that they were.

She felt a chill of fear that quickly passed. Victor had not tried to hurt her and he had had the opportunity twice. In fact, the way he looked at her made her feel anything but threatened — not threatened that way, anyhow. Unfortunately, the threat was an unbidden desire that came easily and did not leave.

"Oh, Emry," she sighed, talking to herself in the quiet of the room. "Put him out of your mind and do it now. It can't be healthy."

She got out of the bed and stood beside it curiously thinking about the fairytale of the seven swans again. She walked to the window and opened the blinds, but there was no moon tonight. She couldn't see anything except the solitary light at the Balfour's house and the magic it held did not conjure up the images of princes or golden crowned swans. It was a lonely sight like a tiny star lost in the woods.

She walked back to the bed and stacked the pillows against the headboard. She climbed into the bed and positioned herself among them and then she just sat there, looking out the window, watching the Balfour's light as it winked in and out.

She told herself she was not sleepy, so hours later when she awoke, cramped from falling asleep in an awkward position, she was surprised. The house was quiet. The television was off and no more footsteps tramped through the rooms and hallways. Everyone had gone to bed. She pushed herself up and then she slid under the sheet and was asleep again almost before she got the pillow straight under her head, but her sleep was restless and she dreamed dreams that involved a lot of running — which of course she couldn't do. Her legs were heavy and everything moved in slow motion.

Suddenly she was wide awake and she was breathing hard. The room was still dark, but there was a hint of dawn light coming in through the open blinds.

She sat up and threw her legs off the bed, sitting there until she became oriented and then she stood up and walked across the room to the window. She reached up to twist the wand and close the blinds, but lights moving across the Balfour's property stopped her. The black SUV was coming home.

Emry stood very still and watched the lights weave up the winding path and stop, going dark almost immediately. Instead of closing the blinds, she pulled them up and opened the window, feeling the heavy, hot air like a wet blanket, cover her.

They were a long way off, but in the still night air, sound carried easily. Emry distinctly heard three car doors slam as she leaned her ear into the receding night. *Victor was home.*

But where had he been all night? More importantly, what had he been doing all night? Emry peered into the gloom surrounding the Balfour's house, her eyes trying to penetrate the dense jungle but without success. As she watched, the flickering yellow light inside the house went dark and off in the distance, a rooster crowed. It was morning.

Chapter Nine

Emry was up and wide awake, so she decided she might as well go jogging. She pulled on some running shoes, shorts and a halter top and walked outside. After some warmup exercises, she ran to the park and then jogged around it.

She jogged and then she jogged around again, and then again. After a while she lost count of how many times she went around, but she continued to push herself until she could go no further. She began to walk and as she came around the back side of the park for the last lap, a man wearing sunglasses was standing near the track, waiting for her.

It was Father Joe from the Catholic Church.

"Good morning," he said as she neared him.

She was almost out of breath and she stopped, resting her hands on her knees as she answered him.

"Good morning."

"You are out early," he said.

"So are you."

"Yes. I like the early morning when the sun is just warming the sky and everything is coming alive. It is a magical time of day."

That was poetic and totally unexpected coming from him. The sunglasses seemed unusually strange after that statement, though.

"Do you always jog this early?" he asked.

She pushed herself up and took a deep breath. "No, not this early. But since I was awake anyway . . ." She didn't finish the sentence. She didn't want to explain why she was awake so early.

"I like a brisk jog myself," he said. "But it appears to me you have something on your mind besides running. Something that requires punishing yourself? I wonder, did it help?"

He was a wise man, it seemed.

"No," she admitted. "It didn't."

"I am curious why you run here when you have a wonderful layout on your own property," he said, sagely letting the other subject go. "I think that if I lived on a farm like yours, I believe I would find it the perfect course for my jogging. A few times around it would be a very nice workout."

He was right, Emry thought. It hadn't occurred to her before, but it would make a very good track and one that wasn't quite so monotonous.

"I hadn't thought of it," she admitted. "But you're right."

"It would be safer too, I'm thinking."

She gave him a curious look.

"I only mean, it is so isolated here, but there — well, there you would have so many eyes to look after you."

Yes, she would. Stanley, Ellen, Maggie, Jim, Betty, and Casey. All of them could see her at least at some point around the property. The only blind spot was the back corner where the gate led into the Balfour's back yard.

"Well, I must be going," he said, casting a glance toward

the eastern sky. He pulled on his collar, straightening it as if it had gotten too tight. "It was nice talking to you. Oh, and let me know how the track works out. I am curious to hear how you like it."

"I will," she said as he walked away.

Father Joe walked to the edge of the park and then he stopped and looked back. Emry was leaving, going home by way of the short cut that came out near Jim's driveway.

"At last," he said to himself. "I see what all the fuss is about." He chuckled softly, but then, his expression changed and his eyes took on a sad and worried look. "Victor, my dear brother, no wonder you are so irritable. But I can tell you, you can fight it, but you are not going to win this one."

Chapter Ten

The week went by so quickly that Emry wondered where it had gone. Suddenly it was Sunday night and everyone was preparing for school the next day. To her dismay, Emry had not found out a thing about Van.

She had gone out one evening with Kaylee and Abby, and he had met them. Emry had been tempted to point blank ask him where he lived, but something about Victor's reaction to him made her wisely use caution.

He was an interesting man and so remarkably alluring that Emry felt small and shy around him. He was young, maybe as young as Victor — funny how she had begun to compare every man to Victor. Van was not a particularly handsome man although there was something about him that was both attractive and appealing. He had long, brown hair, pulled back in a ponytail, and a narrow face with a rather pointed nose. His complexion was fair and his eyes were dark and he moved with a gracefulness that was as fluid as a dance.

She had seen Victor only once since their clandestine meeting, and that had been one evening at Hall's. She was at the gas pump filling the Buick's tank when a vehicle pulled up to the pump behind her. She heard the swipe of a plastic card and then the release of the nozzle as it was removed from the cradle and crammed into the car. She ventured a glance and it was the car that made her turn all the way around.

It was an Indigo blue Jaguar and her eyes ran from one end of it to the other before she ever once looked at the driver. He was leaning against the car, and he smiled when her astonished eyes met his.

"Hello, Emry," he said only loud enough for her to hear.

"Hello," she replied, self-conscious to the point of timidness. "Nice car."

"Want a ride?" he asked, his eyes full of something Emry couldn't quite interpret. He was teasing her, but was he flirting? Her heart pounded at the very idea.

"Maybe," she said.

His eyebrows rose ever so slightly. Other than that, there was no significant change in his expression.

"You are not afraid?" he asked, his voice so soft she hardly heard him.

She wanted to say no, but for some reason she couldn't say anything. "I will arrange it, then," he said as if her silence was a confirmation. Her eyes anxiously flashed and he smiled derisively. His expression suddenly changed and he glanced around as if double checking to make sure no one could hear them. "Find out anything?" he then asked. The smile was suddenly gone from his face.

"No," she answered, shaking her head.

He had immediately popped the nozzle out of the Jaguar's gas tank and hung it on the pump. He must not have needed gas at all, so she guessed he was there only to talk to her.

"Be careful," he said before he walked away. She watched

as he stepped into the car and drove out of the parking lot, turning right on US 17 and disappearing into the distance.

"Did he speak to you?" Crystal anxiously asked when Emry got back inside the Buick. She had been sitting there waiting while Emry filled up the car.

"I said hello, he said hello."

"You know who that was? It was one of the Balfours!"

"Yes, I know," Emry calmly replied. She knew only too well.

"Wow," Crystal sighed, easing back in her seat. "I didn't know he was so good lookin'. I gotta tell Vicky! She'll never believe it!"

That had been several days before and still she had not found out anything for him.

Well, Van would have to wait. She had school to contend with now. It was a thing that gave her more butterflies in the stomach than he did, and that was saying a lot.

She and Casey worked out a schedule for carpooling. He would drive one week and she would drive the next. The first week was his turn, so come Monday morning he arrived in his little silver Kia to get her and Crystal.

They rushed out of the house in a flurry of chaotic commotion, and all the way to school, Emry obsessed over the day.

Her concerns were not without merit. When she walked into the school, the halls were crowded and everyone was milling aimlessly around, it seemed. Emry had to weave her way through a host of students, all of them appearing as clueless as she. She stayed lost half the time and was late for almost every class. The rest of the time, she was just overwhelmed. Fortunately, she had two classes with Casey and one with Kaylee. They helped her out, and she ran across familiar faces along the way — Brad and Beaker, Ann, Jessie, and Courtney.

At the end of the day, though, she was just mentally exhausted. Unfortunately, she could not say it had been the result of a stimulating curriculum. It had not. She hated the school and was sure she would never get used to it.

The next day was no better. Schedules were still being worked out, and to her surprise, Beaker turned up in her AP Biology class. He walked into the room with a nonchalance that belied his personality but then when he saw Emry, he skipped across a desk, placing his foot in the chair and bounding over it to come to rest in the seat next to her, an action that did nothing to endear him to the teacher, but it pleased Emry. She laughed with genuine pleasure and then she wondered if it had put her on the teacher's blacklist the same as Beaker.

By Wednesday she was ready to quit school all together, but she knew her parents would never go for that. She dragged through the day and when the last bell rang, she was the first one to Casey's parked car.

He arrived a few minutes later and unlocked the doors. The temperature inside the car was sweltering so he cranked the engine, turned the air on full blast, and then rolled down all the windows.

"Was today better?" he hopefully asked. He knew she was having a difficult time.

"When I'm a minor, would they give me probation if I burned the school down or would I be looking at hard time?"

He smiled. "Seriously, is it that bad?"

"No," she grudgingly admitted. "I'm just looking for sympathy, I guess."

"It'll get better. I'm sure of it."

Crystal arrived at that moment and her enthusiasm made Emry roll her eyes and then simply close them so she couldn't see her annoying exuberance.

"Today I met the cutest boy!" she exclaimed. "Hey, Casey, do you know Mark Baskins?" She inched up on the edge of the back seat to rest her arms behind Casey while she talked. "He's a Junior. I think he lives down West River Road."

"I know his brother. He's a senior like me."

"Ohmagosh!" she exclaimed. "Emry, if he's anything like Mark, you have to meet him."

"Let's go home," was her reply to that remark. Casey grinned and put the car in drive.

They followed the steady exodus out of the crowded parking lot and were soon on the road that took them to US 17. Casey turned north and within minutes, they were in Bostwick.

The days were getting shorter. It was getting dark now around seven forty-five and Stanley was becoming a stickler about the girls being home before then. Emry figured it had something to do with the things Jim kept telling him. She had overheard them once and it was enough to make her see his point. This person was dead and that one was, too. There seemed to be a regular epidemic of unexplained deaths. And not surprisingly, the Balfour's name always came up in these conversations even though Emry wasn't sure they were actually connecting them to the rash of murders.

According to Jim, people were dying of exsanguination. It was murder, he said, and it was so strange, that if there had been bite marks on the victims' necks, he would have been the first one to admit that vampires existed. He suspected the Balfours and their roleplaying game. Just like everyone else in Bostwick, he needed no proof. Everyone was sure they already knew everything they needed to know about the Balfours.

The restriction made it difficult to do anything — even jog. Emry liked to jog in the cool of the evening, but Stanley flatly put his foot down on her going to the park alone. So Emry laid out her course around the property line like Father Joe had suggested and began running there. After a few days, she had a well-marked path all the way around.

The perspective of Ellen's property was totally different when viewed from this angle. It was the vantage point few people ever got. Everything was backwards, it seemed, because everything was viewed from the back side. Even the house looked different. Emry saw it through the grape arbor and behind the chicken coop and barnyard, and around the tool shed. The only place on the new track where she couldn't see it was when she made the turn at the northeast corner. The barn and the biggest oak tree Emry had ever seen blocked it from sight. It was just at the point where the Balfour's gate made a break in the fence.

Her mind was always active while she was running, but

mostly she just daydreamed. Today her thoughts were on the subject of what she was going to do about Van. With school going strong, she hadn't had time to go to Kaylee's or to do any investigating, and more than anything, she didn't want to let Victor down.

Victor . . .

She sighed when she thought about him, and unfortunately, she'd been doing a lot of that lately. It actually frightened her how much he had been the motivation behind almost every plan she made. The desire to see him was a constant companion and she looked for him everywhere. The one night at the gas station had been her only relief and it had been so brief that it hardly counted.

This isn't good, Emry, she told herself. *He's a Balfour . . . He's a Balfour . . . He's a Balfour!* She had to keep reminding herself, because when she stopped, her thoughts were decidedly uncooperative.

She passed the gate again and she looked beyond it just like she did every time she passed by. Everything was dark at the old house. Not a sign a life anywhere, and Emry knew that's how it would be until the sun was completely gone. Just like vampires, they never came out in the sunlight.

It made her consider the impossible.

What if — just what if, he really is a vampire? she thought. She waited for the scoffing rebuke in her mind to make her laugh, but it didn't come. *There are no such things as vampires*, she deliberately made herself think, and then she repeated her earlier mantra. *He's a Balfour . . . He's a Balfour .*

. . He's a Balfour . . . It didn't really help. Her mind was too rebellious. It took off in another direction, reasoning why it didn't seem so ridiculous to consider whether he was a seriously handsome mythical creature anymore. But what did she really have to base such a theory on other than the fact that they never came out in the daylight — never!

Well, people were dying all over the place, for one thing — from blood loss too. That hadn't happened until the Balfours showed up. And she couldn't get past the fact that Victor was uniquely competent in matters of making her forget things. She wondered if she really remembered everything that had happened in the car the night they had made their secret pact or if she was remembering only what he wanted her to remember. There did seem to be an incongruity between their last conversation and the actual time he had left the car. Had something happened in that interval that he had made her forget? It rankled that she didn't know for sure.

This thought led to another and then another until she wasn't surprised when she began thinking about vampire characteristics. She had read Braum Stokers *Dracula*, the abridged copy, anyway, and although it was pure fiction, she wondered if it could be the result of legends and stories about bloodsucking creatures that had really existed at the time. Hadn't she heard somewhere that fairytales were local legends of real people and events? What everyone thought about vampires could simply be facts that had turned to fiction as the years watered down the truth.

But what was the truth? She didn't know. Perhaps no one

really knew, but the thought led her off into an analysis of characteristics that, crazy or not, she had heard through the years. She began by asking herself what she'd heard about vampire characteristics.

Blood drinkers who couldn't stand the light of day was a constant, special powers or supernatural tendencies, and alluring and seductive. That put Victor right at the top of the list. He obviously had some kind of power. Even if it was only a parlor trick, he had successfully worked his magic on her, and he was definitely alluring and seductive. Blood drinker? Well, she didn't know, but he certainly didn't like the daylight. She never saw him except at night.

She'd also heard that vampires were obsessive compulsive. She'd have to untie her shoe laces the next time she was with Victor and see if it bothered him — or scatter seeds and see if he had to pick them all up before he could do anything else. She'd love to see if he could enter her house without an invitation. She didn't know how she'd manage that. Suggesting he come over could be construed as an invitation, so would he be able to come in if she didn't actually say, "come in"?

She wanted to test him. It's strange how her ideas and feelings had changed in the past few weeks. Such a thought would never have entered her mind until now.

Well, she told herself, *I'll eliminate possibilities one at a time, beginning with the most unlikely — vampire. That should be easy to disprove.*

Friday came none too soon. When the last bell rang, Emry let out a sigh that caused several heads to turn toward her. She didn't care. She smiled and stood up, waiting for the classroom full of students to crowd out the door before she did.

She saw Jessie in the hallway and they walked to the parking lot together. Casey was already at the car and they stood there, talking until Crystal arrived a short time later.

Casey and Jessie wanted everyone to get together and do something over the weekend and Emry was okay with that, except that she had a job to do for Victor. She had planned to use her free time this weekend to find out what she could about Van. Besides, the sooner she found out something, the sooner she could see Victor.

She told herself she felt this way only because of the excitement of the game she was playing with him, but she had lied so much that it was hard to recognize a lie anymore even when she told it to herself. Well, she'd go to Kaylee's after dinner and see what she could find out.

But Stanley refused to let Emry go to Kaylee's after dinner. He wouldn't budge on his decision no matter what Emry said, so she wondered what new information Jim had fed him.

"I'll be fine," she promised him. "I'll be in the car and then in the house and then back in the car again. No problem."

"Not after dark," he adamantly said. "Go now and be home before dinner."

"Oh, dad," she sighed. "You're being unreasonable."

But she did what he said. She called Kaylee and went straight there. To her surprise, Abby was home. Emry hadn't expected that, but there she was, sitting at the kitchen table, a laptop in front of her, and books piled around. She smiled when

Emry walked in.

Abby was a beautiful girl. She was not overly friendly, but she was nice. Emry gave her a careful study and wondered what would happen when she found out that Van was not what he appeared to be.

The phone rang and Kaylee answered it, so while she was waiting, Emry sat down across from Abby and the two of them talked quietly.

"How's school?" Emry began.

"Fine," Abby answered. "I heard you were having some trouble, though."

"Not really. I just hate it, is all."

"I hated high school, too," Abby said. "but St. Johns is okay. I *am* a little upset that I'm having to go to the college here, though. I wanted to go to UF, but the finances didn't come through."

"I understand," Emry said, thinking that she'd probably be going to St. Johns for the same reason. "How's things with you and Van?" she ventured to ask.

"Great," she said, a smile spreading across her pretty face. She lit up like a Christmas tree and Emry wondered how a bad man could make a girl so very happy.

Maybe he isn't bad, the thought came to her. *Maybe Victor is the bad man and she was playing into his hands.* She shook her head. That couldn't be true — she didn't want it to be true.

"I'll be meeting him later."

"Where?" Emry quickly asked, hoping she didn't sound too prying.

"At the mall in Orange Park. That's where I first met him."

"In Orange Park? Oh," Emry said.

Abby laughed. "I'll never forget that night," she said, the peal of laughter fading into a smile. "I was in the book store, sitting on the floor as I looked at books on the bottom shelf, and he almost fell over me."

She laughed again.

Emry had trouble imagining that. He was so graceful, she didn't see how he could ever be clumsy.

"He was reading a book and turned the corner where I sat. He couldn't see past his book," she explained. "He bought me a cup of coffee as an apology, and — well, the rest is history."

"He's a really cool guy," Emry said.

"He's more than cool," Abby said quite seriously.

This sounded like pertinent information. Maybe Victor couldn't find Van in the area because he wasn't in the area. He was in Orange Park. Suddenly, she was anxious to go. She wanted to get the information to Victor, but she didn't know how she was going to do that. It was still light outside so he would be holed up in that creepy old house and wouldn't be out until after dark.

She thought about him talking on his cell phone and wondered why he hadn't just given her his number. She supposed he simply didn't want her to have it.

Well, that was depressing.

Casey, Brad, and Beaker were at Emry's house when she arrived. They were sitting on the porch, rocking in the chairs while making plans to go to the beach the next day. It was the last thing Emry wanted to do, but she reluctantly agreed. Victor wouldn't be out during that time anyway, so she wouldn't miss an opportunity to see him. Her eyes strayed toward his property and she wished everyone would just go home, but chances were, she wouldn't be able to find him even if they did.

She was right. Her friends left, but there was no sign of Victor. Emry waited on the porch, looking around the dark property until her daddy made her come inside, but she saw nothing of him.

Well, what had she expected? Did she think he was going to walk up to the porch and address her with his usual greeting? No, she didn't, but it was a thought that was more than just appealing.

The next morning, there was a whole caravan of kids that showed up to go to the beach. Even Ann came along, dour attitude and all. Natalie was with her and so was Jessie. Courtney and Cindy arrived with Brad and Beaker, and a new guy, one Emry hadn't met, was with them. His name was Johnny Patton and from the first introduction, he had eyes for only Emry. She, Kaylee, and Crystal rode with Casey, but as soon as they arrived at the beach, Johnny was by her side.

They chose to go to Anastasia Island. No cars were allowed to drive on the beach. It was a state park so it was fixed up really nice. There was a snack bar at the parking lot and bathroom facilities, and the beach was beautiful. They carried their paraphernalia across the white sand, between sand dunes waving with sea oats, and down to the edge of the water. The tide was going out as they arrived and they set things up only to have to move them forward a short time later to keep near the receding waves.

The sun was bright and the wind was blowing with some force — more than just a gentle sea breeze. Emry kept sunglasses on for both reasons, but by noon, she was squinting anyway. She suddenly wondered if Victor would ever come to a place so bright and sunny — if he *could* come to a place so bright and sunny.

Probably not, she decided. *He would probably burn to a crisp.*

Which made her wonder about the ethics of what she was doing, planning to help him find where Van lived. Van seemed so pleasant — so good — and he made Abby happy. It was hard to imagine him as the bad guy. But if he wasn't, then Victor probably was.

She almost huffed at that thought.

Why did he want Van's address anyway? she wondered.

She had drifted into daydream mode and didn't come out until the frisbee Brad and Beaker were tossing back and forth hit her and bounced to the ground.

Beaker skidded to a stop beside her and snatched it up, apologizing on the fly.

"No harm done," she said as he took off again.

The boys were all goofing around, tussling and shoving and pushing — all except Johnny. He was sitting on the ground beside Emry's chair and occasionally he would engage her in conversation, simple things like how she was getting along at school and what she liked to do when she was on her own time.

He was a nice looking boy, cuter than Casey, but not as handsome as Victor.

Now, where did that come from! The thought startled her so that she jerked the sunglasses off her face and stood up.

"Wanna swim?" she asked Johnny and he immediately came to his feet.

He was tall, six feet or more and his body was the typical healthy, teenage boy physique. His hair was wavy and light brown in color and his eyes were very blue. They walked into the water and when waist deep, Emry dove into a wave, coming up on the other side of it as it rolled away from her. Johnny followed her example and soon they were competing at simple games of their own making like how far you could body surf before being grounded. Emry was the lightest so she always went further and was the clear winner. They played for a little while and then ran back to where the chairs and the towels were laid out on the dry beach.

The other boys continued to throw the frisbee and it wasn't long before Jessie joined them. Emry was surprised she hadn't done it sooner. Jessie loved the boys and was always flirting with them. After a couple of minutes, Casey took the frisbee and she tried to get it from him. Emry watched as the two of them playfully wrestled for it, Casey hiding it behind his back so that Jessie had to reach around him to get it. They were laughing, both of them enjoying the contact, until Beaker suddenly slid in and snatched the frisbee from Casey's hand. He came to his feet and spun the disc with precision to Brad and then in triumph, he turned a cart wheel that was followed by a string of gymnastic flips and turns that astounded Emry. She had no idea he had had gymnastic training, but she really wasn't surprised. His parents must have had to do something to give him an outlet for his unbridled energy. What better way?

When he came to a stop at the end of his routine, everyone applauded, even strangers, and Beaker bowed with great animation.

His attention, though, and probably his motivation for showing off, was still Natalie. By the afternoon, she had warmed up to him and by the time everyone began gathering their things to go home, Beaker and Natalie were together. He held her hand all the way back to the parking lot.

Emry considered his choice and wondered what he saw in her. She liked Beaker, but in all honesty, she didn't like Natalie. Next to Ann, she was the most disagreeable person Emry had ever met. Well, what could she say? Everyone's taste is different.

It made her look at Johnny. He was walking beside her as they trudged through the powdery, white sand on their way back to the cars. He was a nice boy and she could tell he liked her. Victor Balfour suddenly came to mind again, and she mentally slapped herself. She immediately told herself that besides being a little crazy, Victor was probably some weird hybrid or something, and she couldn't keep comparing other boys to him.

What is wrong with you! she asked herself and to prove she could overcome the Balfour obstacle, she smiled at Johnny and then boldly took his hand. He smiled back and tightened his fingers around hers in a very agreeable manner.

Wind, water, and sunshine had a way of tapping Emry's strength. When she got home, both she and Crystal dragged themselves inside. All she wanted at that moment was a cool shower and a long nap. She got the shower, but afterwards, she felt refreshed and decided that she didn't want the nap, after all. She dressed in shorts and a tank top and went downstairs. The house seemed deserted. There wasn't a sign of anyone anywhere. In a house of five people this was rare.

But as she listened, she heard the muffled sound of voices in the back of the house, and she realized it was her parents, talking loud enough that she could hear them all the way from their bedroom.

They were arguing. How long had it been since she had heard them argue? Years.

It made her feel funny inside, hurt, but frightened also. She couldn't stand it.

She put her hands over her ears and walked into the kitchen. Where was Ellen? Dinner should be cooking, but nothing was on the stove nor even laid out to cook. The whole house seemed out of kilter, wrong somehow. The feeling was awful — empty and lonely.

She went to the refrigerator and pulled out leftovers. There was enough to make a meal if she warmed everything up, so she set out some pots and got to work. When the smells began to waft through the house, Maggie appeared in the doorway.

"I'll help," she simply said.

She bustled into the room and busied herself with pulling

down plates and laying out flatware, not a word about where Ellen was nor why she and Stanley had been arguing, but the tension was so strong, Emry could feel it radiating from her.

She put three plates out and Emry quizzically looked at them.

"Only three?" she said.

"Your dad isn't feeling well. He'll eat later. I'll call Crystal."

The three of them ate in silence. Crystal hadn't heard the argument, but the charged atmosphere cued her in that something was wrong — and the absence of both Stanley and Ellen.

After dinner, Maggie walked to the sink to begin clean up, but Emry stopped her.

"We'll clean up, mama," she said. "Go check on dad."

"He's okay," she said, but Emry insisted.

"Then go take it easy somewhere. We can do this."

She hesitated, but she didn't refuse.

"I'll check on Stanley," she finally said and walked away.

Crystal carried dishes from the table to the sink and stacked them on the counter.

"What on earth happened while we were gone?" she asked in a low voice.

Emry shook her head. "I don't know."

For a brief second, she was elated at the thought that maybe something had happened that would send them back to Charlotte, but as soon as the high hit her, it drained out again. She was left with a sinking feeling of dread and disappointment.

Charlotte no longer held the draw nor the attraction it had had when she first arrived. Her old friends hardly ever contacted her anymore and her new friends were actually very nice — all except Ann and Natalie, she amended.

And now she had met Johnny. The second she thought about him, her eyes automatically looked out the window toward the Balfour's property. She shrugged and turned back to her chore.

"Dishes done," Crystal announced as she threw down the dish cloth she was using to wipe off the counters and the table. "I'm outta here."

"Where're you goin'? Emry asked.

Crystal shrugged. "To my room, I guess. Maybe I'll call Vicky."

Emry closed the dishwasher and dried her hands. Everything felt so wrong this evening. The house was so empty!

She looked out the window again, but this time her eyes ran across only her own yard. The sun was gone, but it wasn't yet dark. She picked up the cloth Crystal had carelessly thrown down, hung it up, and then she walked out the back door.

A train rumbled by on the nearby track and then there was silence. The evening was calm, and the sound of a lone quail broke the quiet with a sharp, piercing call. Next door, Tripper barked a few times and Emry walked to the fence, passing the grape arbor on the way, frightening a bird that was sitting among the twisted vines. She followed the flight with her eyes and then looked back at Jim's yard, calling the dog as she waited by the fence.

He ran to her and she talked to him, reaching through the fence, petting him and ruffling up his fur. He was a nice dog — always happy, and she needed a happy face to look at just then.

He took off after a few minutes, chasing a squirrel or something, and Emry glanced down the path her jogging had made. It had taken no time to beat down the grass and make a clearly defined path along the fence. The ground was even and in some ways it was better than the clay track at the park. There were no pot holes or cracks from runoff water, just the flatten grass, now turning brown.

She thought about running, but she was too tired for that. She wasn't ready to go back to the house, though, so she began walking, taking her time, just sauntering along, following the path.

Soon Baby joined her and they walked together.

The light from the dying sun turned into velvety soft night, but Emry's eyes were so accustomed to the change that the only indication of the late hour was the fireflies that blinked in and out of the grass as she neared the barn. She wasn't even aware of the subtle change. The soft peeping of the frogs in the nearby pond was pleasant and so was the song of the mockingbird that chose to sing out one last time before roosting in the lemon tree near the backdoor. Everything was clear and undiluted as if all Emry's senses had been magnified. She momentarily forgot the turmoil that had prompted her to leave the house and she strolled along, just enjoying the evening.

When she made the next turn on the path, the Balfour's gate came into view. It was simply a dark line against a darker background and Emry didn't look directly at it. She was watching the fireflies and noting that a couple of rabbits had come into the yard to eat clover. She was surprised that Baby didn't take after them, but then she noticed, Baby's attention was focused elsewhere and she wasn't even aware the bunnies were on the property. She suddenly reacted with hostility, arching her long, sleek back as she hissed, showing all her pointed white teeth, and Emry anxiously looked up, not knowing what to expect.

It was Victor. He was standing at the gate, leaning casually against the post, quietly watching as she approached.

Baby took off, running toward the barn where she quickly disappeared from sight, but Emry only stood there. The cat had startled her but Victor's unexpected appearance had literally stunned her. She looked to the west, an automatic reaction to the thought that Victor wouldn't be here if the hour wasn't so late, and it was then she realized it was actually dark.

She knew she couldn't continue to just stand there. She either had to follow Baby's example and run for it or keep walking. She chose the latter.

He was leaning against the post, his arms folded across his chest and his ankles crossed in a very relaxed manner, but as she drew near, he uncoiled and stepped out to meet her.

Too bad she hadn't untied her shoe laces.

He watched her without a word, but there was a pleasant look on his face that eased some of Emry's anxiousness. He was dressed differently from the last time she had seen him, a simple t-shirt and jeans and his hair was a little mussed. She could see his arms. The muscles were hard and tight under his perfect skin and his biceps were well rounded and smooth. He wasn't heavy with muscle. Like everything else about him, they were just right.

"Hello, Emry," he said. He always started their conversations in this very way and with that same crooked smile he was giving her at that moment. His voice always said more to her than his words did. She couldn't explain it, but the sound of it made her heart race and her breath pull at her lungs as if she had run a mile.

"Hey," she answered. He made her feel self-conscious and timid too, almost the same way Van did. "What're you doin' out here?" she asked.

"Waiting for you."

Wow! Did he mean to sound so sensual? Emry cleared her throat and looked down at her feet, trying to get her emotions under control.

"I saw you coming around," he explained, tilting his head to indicate that he had seen her from his house. She looked up at the second story window and saw that he would have a clear view from there. "You know, you should not be out here this late in the evening," he then said.

Her eyes quickly shifted back to him.

"You sound like my father."

"You should listen to your father. He is right."

She looked toward her house, but she couldn't see it past the barn and the giant oak tree.

"Oh," she sighed and then remembering that she had news,

she quickly turned back to him. "I found out something," she said, her voice reflecting her excitement. "Van may be living in Orange Park."

"Orange Park?" He frowned, but then a faraway look came into his eyes. "That makes sense. That makes a lot of sense."

"Abby told me she met him at the mall in Orange Park — at a book store there."

Victor's eyes flashed at Emry. "Did you ask a lot of questions?"

"No, she was just talkin' and she offered it all — I swear!"

He nodded. "What else did she say?"

"That he made her happy. I could see it too." They both just looked at each other for a few seconds. "What did he do? He doesn't seem like that bad of a guy."

"Take my word for it. He is."

She bunched her shoulders and then let them fall. "I don't know. I like him."

"It is to be expected," Victor said. "Most people do — for a while anyway."

There was something sinister in the way he said that and Emry gave him a curious look.

"Was there anything else?" he asked. He took a step toward her and she instinctively moved back. "I am not going to hurt you," he said, the same exasperation in his voice that was there the last time he had said that to her.

She shook her head. "Sorry, no," she said, answering his question without acknowledging his statement. "I'll keep listening, though."

"Fine," he said. "Now go home. You should not be out here after dark again."

Who did he think he was — her father or something?

"I'm a big girl. I can walk around my yard after dark if I want to."

"What if I told you, you were in serious danger of being hurt this very second?"

"I thought you said you wouldn't hurt me."

"Maybe I lied," he said.

Maybe you did, she thought, and she wasn't surprised at all. His suggestion to go home was sounding better by the second.

"You know," she said as she backed away from him in prelude to turning and going home, "I don't know why I'm doing this — why I *want* to help you. You're actually a very strange man."

He chuckled and it was a pleasant sound despite the fact that he was creeping her out.

"Go home, Emry," he said, "before we both regret it."

"I'm goin'," she said, but as she took another step, her foot came down on a tiny branch that had fallen from the oak tree. It wasn't a large branch, just a small sprig, but it was forked in several places with dead leaves on it and a few tiny acorns. When she stepped onto it, one of the prongs jabbed into her shoe, leaving an acorn behind when it pulled out again. "Ouch," she said, and Victor anxiously tensed. He took a few steps toward her, but he stopped when she added, "There's something in my shoe."

He relaxed again, but not before Emry wondered what had made him react in such a manner. She kicked off her shoe and then she reached down and picked it up. She tipped it and the acorn fell to the ground.

She realized she was holding an opportunity in her hand. She untied the shoe laces and for just a few seconds, she simply held the shoe and looked at it.

"Do you need help?" he asked.

"Yeah — thanks," she said and he came close enough that she could hold onto him for balance while she slipped the shoe back onto her foot. His arm was strong and firm, and pleasing to the touch. She tried not to think of that while she pushed her foot into the shoe.

But when she straightened up, she came face to face with him and the thought of tying her shoe laces left her as if she had planned it. In fact, she was spellbound and almost breathless with a feeling she had never had before.

"Your shoe is untied," he softly pointed out, breaking the spell she was under. She looked down at her shoe, but she made no move to tie the laces. "Do you want me to tie it for you?"

"No," she quickly answered. "I'll do it when I get home."

She considered the perfect opportunity that lay before her, deciding it was better to dwell on it than on the subject her mind kept straying to.

She took a couple of steps away from him and he looked down at her feet.

"I think you should tie it," he said. "You are a bit clumsy tonight. You will probably trip over it before you get home."

"So . . ." she said with a slight shrug, "Does it bother you?"

"What? That you might trip and break your neck before you get home? I guess that would bother me a little," he facetiously said.

"No, I mean . . . Well, never mind what I mean," she said, thinking that maybe it was knots vampires could not leave untied and not something like a shoe lace. Perhaps if she put knots in the laces . . . But, no, she was just getting crazy now. She shook her head as if to clear it, and then she began walking away.

"What are you doing?" he called after her. "Stop and tie your shoe."

She did stop, but it wasn't to tie her shoe.

"So, it does bother you," she said.

He did not readily answer her. He paused long enough to fold his arms across his chest, and then he chuckled softly.

"No," he dryly said. He shook his head. "And you think I am strange," he then added.

Well, darn!

"Emry!" an anxious voice from the house suddenly called into the night.

"Oh, crap!" she said. There was no longer a question about tying her laces. She needed to run home and Victor was right. She would probably trip and break her neck. She threw herself down onto the grass and then she snatched up her shoe laces, hurrying to tie them. She fumbled with it while her father called for her again and Victor cast an anxious look in that direction.

"You must hurry," he said just as she finished tying the

shoe.

He reached down and pulled her to her feet and she took off, running toward the house.

While he stood there a shadow fell across him. He wasn't concerned. He knew it was Artemus without even looking.

"Did you hear all that?" he asked.

"Yes. We should have known. He always chooses a high population area. I considered that he might be in Orange Park or Jacksonville, but his scent is all over this place."

"It is because of the girl."

"Too bad he got wise to us before we did him."

"Yes, but we should have known it would not be easy." *It is never easy.*

"Uh, what was all that about there at the last?" Artemus asked, referring to Emry.

Victor chuckled. "She thinks I am a vampire."

"Oh. Well, she did not seem too worried — or afraid."

"People are not afraid of vampires anymore. Hollywood, you know."

"But still . . ."

"Yes, you would think they would have better sense."

"So what was she trying to prove?"

"She was testing me. You know the legends. People would carry a pocketful of rye seeds to scatter if they encountered a vampire. They thought it would give them time to get away because he would have to stop and pick up every one before he could follow. They did not know he is so quick he could pick up every one and still catch them before they could get away. The same thing with knots and strings. It is an obsessive compulsive thing."

"You should indulge her."

"Yes. I have considered that."

They both smiled into the night.

"Well, your job is a lot more fun than mine, I can see," Artemus said, teasing him. He gave him a slap on the back before turning away. "Just be careful, brother. She might be more dangerous than Hugo."

"You may be right. I have considered that, too."

At Victor's serious reply, Artemus dropped the smile and turned around so that he could look squarely at him.

"Are you alright? I could take this tonight and you could go with father and Marius. It might be a healthy change."

"No, I am fine with this. Besides, you are better with Marius than I am."

"If you say so," Artemus said but he was reluctant to leave. "Where are your weapons?" he asked.

"There," Victor said, pointing to the gate. He didn't mention the silver knife hidden between his shoulder blades, the haft at easy reach near the nape of his neck or the small caliber gun strapped to his ankle. Artemus was referring to the more formidable ones, the wooden sword that was so uniquely made that it looked like tempered steel or the M-14 with its specially crafted bullets. All their weapons were of their own making and made with one purpose in mind — to destroy Hugo and his kind. He walked to the gate and lifted a bundle that included a dark shirt as well as the weapons.

Victor fastened the belt around his slim hips and then he pulled the shirt he was wearing over his head, throwing it to the ground with some force. He all but faded into the background.

"I am going wide tonight," Victor said, referring to the perimeter he had set in guarding their property. "There is someone out there. He has been coming closer every night and I think it is time I stopped him."

"Do you want help?"

"No, I can handle it."

"Is it Emry he is after or is he curious about us?"

"Us, I think, but I do not want to take any chances."

"Yes, she is quite an appetizing little morsel." He looked at Victor again. "Are you sure you can handle this?"

"Yes. No problem."

There was a moment of silence that Artemus finally broke.

"You know what will happen if you get involved with her," he quietly reminded him.

"Yes, I know. It will not happen."

"Besides, she is Thomas' great granddaughter."

"I said it would not happen," Victor snapped, his voice bitter and on edge. "Trust me, I have weighed the consequences. She is well in hand."

Artemus solemnly looked at Victor. "I am sorry, brother," he said. "I really am."

Victor shrugged. "They will be waiting for you," he said, meaning his father and Marius. "And I need to take a turn around the property."

"I am going," Artemus said.

As he turned, he heard a sound that was not unlike that of sails catching the breeze, the stiff sound of canvas billowing out and popping in the wind. It was followed by a rustling and then silence. He looked where Victor had been, but there was nothing there. His eyes looked up and he frowned. A dark spot crossed his vision and then floated silently behind the trees, and then the night sky was empty. Victor was gone.

Chapter Eleven

"Who was he?" Stefan asked.

Victor had come in at dawn with news. His shirt was ripped from shoulder to waist and he had exhausted all his ammunition. But he had come out better than his rival who was dead and burned in the woods behind their house.

"I have never seen him before, but he was not just a minion. He knew what he was doing. He took my bullets and came on as if he was immune."

"Which ones did you have with you?" Artemus asked, greatly concerned. He was the one who had made the bullets for the guns they all carried. They were special and of ingenious design. The ones Victor had were both silver and wood.

"The madcap," he said, using Artemus' name for the style.

"It did not even slow him down?"

"Maybe a little. He was strong."

"He was wearing protection?"

Victor slowly shook his head. "I did not see anything unusual before I burned him."

The silver was meant to slow him down and in the case of a direct hit to the heart, the wood would stop him completely, but he had shaken the silver off as if it was nothing more than bee stings. He had been big and he had been strong. Hugo had sent one of his warriors and not just an expendable subject.

"I was lucky," Victor explained. "I caught him off guard and that is all that saved me."

"From now on, we should go out in pairs," Stefan said. "Artemus, tonight you will stay with Victor and Marius and I will follow Hugo's trail. We are close. I will send for you when we find him."

"I do not need him to stay with me," Victor said. He pulled the shirt over his head and threw it at the trash can in the corner. It hit with precision and fell to the bottom. A bright red streak ran from his upper arm to his waist, but it was already fading, disappearing as it quickly healed.

"How many does this make, Victor?" Marius asked. "Three?"

"Four if you count the one at the church," Artemus answered when Victor said nothing.

"It makes you wonder . . ." Marius mused, his words drifting off as he thought. They quickly regained strength. ". . . exactly what it is Hugo has on his mind. Maybe your first thoughts were correct, Victor, and Emry is his focus. You know how he is. He can wait forever for revenge and he never forgets a slight."

Victor visibly flinched and Artemus cast a concerned look his way.

"My point is," Marius went on, "he may be testing our strengths and our strategies. If you want to keep Emry safe, then two of us here would be wiser than just one — at least until we see what his plan is."

Victor glanced at Artemus and then back at Marius.

"You are right," he agreed. "But will *you* be safe?" He meant Marius and Stefan, alone, hunting Hugo.

"Obviously we are safer than you. We have seen nothing to engage in battle and you have killed four."

"Three," he corrected him. "Joseph killed the one at the church."

"But still, you see my point."

"I understand you got a lead last night," Victor said, purposely turning the conversation in a different direction.

"Yes," Stefan answered. "But there are so many people at the mall; we are at a great disadvantage. Hugo was not alone, either. He had six with him last night."

"So, where did he go when he left there?"

"South, but we lost them on Blanding Boulevard. They abandoned their car and disappeared before we caught up with them."

"I would look north then," Victor said. "If they went south, it is because they wanted to misdirect you."

"It does not matter. With so many people living there, we could search for weeks and never find him."

"Follow his trail. Follow his scent."

"Easier said than done. You know how clever he is at hiding even his scent. The ones with him were plainly marked, but he seemed to disappear on the wind."

"Which is probably where he did disappear," Artemus said, knowing that Hugo could change, making his human form into that of night animals — or simply smoke. "He took to the air and then there was no following him."

"We may have to rethink our strategy," Marius said. "Let us just take him in the crowded mall. The job would be done and we could leave, disappearing as if we never existed. The police could never catch us, much less hold us."

"How many people do you think would die if we did that, Marius?" Stefan asked him. "One? Five? Perhaps ten or twenty?"

"At this point, I would say they are acceptable losses."

Stefan shook his head. "No. Besides, Hugo has tempted us so before if you will remember. And still he got away."

He was remembering the carnival in Whipshire over a hundred years before when just such a scenario played out. People had died all around him. It had been a blood bath that sparked a feeding frenzy that ended in such sanguinary chaos that nothing could be done. The next day, the good people of Whipshire were ready to burn them all at the stake. All except Hugo. He was gone and had been gone since the beginning of the disturbance. It took them twenty years to find him again.

"He is smart — and lucky. His luck cannot hold out forever, though."

"I agree. But our best chance of getting him is to catch him at his most vulnerable time — daylight — when he has to sleep. No one will get hurt, no innocent bystanders, nor any of us. We have tried the direct approach. We have tried engaging him in battle. All of these have failed. Now, we will take our time and we will do it right. He will never expect this. He knows how the light affects us . . ."

"If he does not leave first."

"He is not leaving," Victor said. "Not yet."

"And you know this — how?" Marius asked.

"I have a feeling."

"Now you have Joseph's gift as well as your own," Marius mocked him. "Indeed, that does not surprise me."

Marius wasn't always diplomatic and the fact that he was just the least bit jealous of Victor didn't help his attitude. The youngest of the Balfours was the most adept and powerful member of their sect. Brother Cavanaugh had said so himself. Little did Marius know, Victor had never aspired to this greatness and would gladly have given Marius his gifts if he could have. He did what he did the same as the rest of them, without giving it an inappropriate amount of concern or thought. And that too provoked Marius.

"That is enough," Stefan said, not without kindness. "We should rest now. I too have a feeling and, I imagine, that will not surprise you as well, Marius." He paused to wryly smile. The smile vanished and he continued. "This is winding down. We need to be at our peak, so let us not lose anything now that will weaken us later. Get your sleep and remember; we are a team — and brothers." He looked from Marius to Victor. "Remember that."

"We do," Marius said, realizing he had been out of line, but his eyes silently strayed to Victor and they were not entirely free of ire. "I would have given Lorna my name if things had played out to our advantage, but now I have taken hers," he said. "I consider myself your son and these my brothers." He indicated Artemus and Victor. "I made my choice and I have never regretted it."

Stefan affectionately gripped his shoulder. "We feel the same."

"Yes, brother," Artemus said and Victor nodded.

"Brothers," he said. But to say he had never regretted his choice would be a lie he could not say. He had regretted so many things through the years but none so completely as now. He wanted Emry Winters — wanted her more than anything.

His eyes quickly scanned the dimly lighted room, taking in every member of his family in one glance. They were all content in their pursuit. His father was the patriarchal judge, consumed by his desire to wield justice, and Marius, like Stefan, was passionately taking his revenge and considering it to be a rectitude. Artemus was simply the warrior, born to fight, the love of battle in his blood, but amazingly, he was the most diplomatic of them all. He was quiet and reserved with an air of peace about him that often brought a heated argument to an end before it could blossom into a real concern. They had no desire outside the life of the Strangers. They were well placed and content.

But Victor was not like them. He struggled with human vices and human desires. It was something that caused him to take respite when he could, often indulging himself for months in a profession where he could be quietly settled, living the life of a normal human being if only for a little while. He had been many things during these times, but the thing he had enjoyed the most was operating a small crossroads tavern. He had maintained that simple lifestyle longer than any of the others, liking the nighttime hours the job required. He had stayed with it for two years before need pulled him back into the game. He always felt better after such a respite and would return to The Strangers renewed in interest, his focus sharp once again, and his energy multiplied by the months of rest.

The trouble was, there had never been a girl who had so completely attended his thoughts and his desires as Emry Winters had suddenly done. He had known many women, beautiful women, in fact, and he was sure they were much more beautiful than she, but for the life of himself, he could not think of the first one.

But then, he was quick to remind himself that in the scheme of things, Emry was no more than a child. He had been no older than she when all this had begun, but somehow, she seemed so much younger than he had been. It was the years that stretched behind him that made him feel this way — that and the polished and urbane women he had known through the years. Emry was nothing like them, and with a start, he realized he was glad she was nothing like them. She was young and naive and she lacked the social poise and worldly experience of the women he had known. It caused him to pause in wonder at his unshakable desire for her. He had never had any trouble simply walking away from a relationship before this. It was dangerous — much too dangerous for him to become involved with a woman and until now, it had not mattered. Besides, she was Thomas Winters' great granddaughter. He owed Thomas a debt that ruining Emry's life would do nothing to repay, and unfortunately, it would ruin her life.

Well, when she learned what he really was, the problem would be solved.

It was time to start failing her tests — gradually, of course. He did not want to scare her away too soon.

Chapter Twelve

Stanley was standing at the door when Emry ran inside and to say he blew his top would have been an understatement. Maybe it was the result of the argument he and Maggie had been having or maybe it was the information Jim fed him on a daily basis, or maybe it was a combination of it all, but Stanley was ready to explode.

He raked Emry over the coals and when he was finished, she went to her room thoroughly convinced that he was unreasonably treating her like she was nothing but a child. She felt a rebellious spirit coming upon her and she did not even try to shake it off. She was angry and a little disappointed. Stanley was not himself and had not been for some time. She longed for the days when things were normal in their family.

Sometime in the night, Emry finally fell asleep. When she awoke, the house was astir and for a fleeting moment everything seemed normal again.

It was Sunday, and they always went to church on Sunday. When they got home, Ellen made sandwiches for their lunch. She usually had a huge meal ready and waiting for them when they came in, but not today. That was the first indication that things were not quite back to normal.

Stanley was unusually quiet and he did not smile — not even once. He had a faraway look in his eyes, and Maggie never stayed in the same room with him very long. Emry could see something was still brewing between the two of them and then, she supposed, he was still upset with her, too.

This has been the weekend from hell, Emry thought, and for the first time, she was glad for Monday morning and for school.

It was her turn to drive, so she and Crystal jumped into the old Buick and picked up Casey at his house. He looked good this morning and Emry gave him more than a casual glance. He was a really cute guy. Maybe she should see what would happen if she tried to make herself seriously like him.

He looked at her as if he had read her mind, and she felt her face flush.

Maybe not, she immediately thought. She quickly put the car in gear and took off.

Lunch at school was a harrowing experience. Once you made it through the line where you picked up your food, there was almost no time to eat it. This week, things seemed to be better. The kinks in the system were getting worked out and Emry actually had time to sit down for a few minutes. The trouble was, there was no place to sit in the crowded room they called The Commons. She looked around and began to aimlessly wander around, hoping to see someone abandon a table so she could take it.

She saw something across the room that looked hopeful and she had just taken a step in that direction when the girl at the table next to her spoke her name.

"Emry?" she tentatively asked like she was not sure she had

the name right.

Emry had seen her in one of her classes. Kendra, if she remembered right, a black girl with skin the color of milk chocolate. She was one of those girls that no matter what she wore it looked like she had stepped out of a fashion show. She could wear jeans and a tank top and it looked classy. Today she was wearing a short skirt and a double layered blouse, and her black hair was pulled back on one side while the other side arched down to her chin in a graceful curve.

"Wanna sit here?" she asked, and Emry quickly accepted.

She and Kendra had Calculus together but they crossed each other's paths off and on during the day. Soon they were waiting at strategic points just to walk together from one class to the next, even to the ones they did not share, and after that, they always had lunch together.

Maggie got the job she was after and went to work. Stanley fell deeper into depression. Emry could see him going down. Ellen stayed very busy. She was no doubt trying to stay out of their business, but Emry could see where it was taking its toll on her, too. Suddenly Friday night was not the only night she, Lois and Eunice spent together. Their outings were becoming more and more frequent. The atmosphere in the house was tense and inhospitable, and just like Ellen, every chance she or Crystal got anymore, they were out of the house.

Emry still jogged, but it was not the same. Every time she passed the Balfour's gate, she looked at it, halfway expecting to see Victor standing there waiting for her.

Of course, it never happened. He never came out in the

daytime, but she looked anyway, imagining him standing there, leaning carelessly against the wooden post, just like he had that one night. Crazy or not, he was one good looking guy and she sighed, thinking it was such a waste that he was a Balfour.

September was soon upon them and school had its first holiday. Labor Day gave them a long weekend and even Maggie had the day off from work. They were going to have a cookout at Jim's so Monday morning; Ellen was in the kitchen making baked beans and some kind of fluffy dessert that took a ton of whipped cream and a pan of pudding to make. Emry tried to help, but she felt she was in the way more times than not, so she finally gave up and went out.

Stanley sat at the kitchen table looking outside, not saying anything. Emry was beginning to worry about him. He had always been smiling and happy. This was so foreign to his personality that he seemed like a stranger.

She could smell the charcoal burning even before she left her yard. Jim was in the backyard, setting up the grill, and Betty was in the house, nervously bustling around her kitchen.

They set a chair by the grill for Stanley and he and Jim chatted while the steaks sizzled. Betty, Ellen, and Maggie worked in the kitchen, gossiping with whispers and laughter as they worked. Casey turned on his PlayStation and he, Emry and Crystal played games.

Everything seemed almost normal that day, but then the cookout ended and Emry went home, and the same old depressing feeling settled over the house. She hated this! It was almost as if she had stepped into the Twilight Zone and this was not even her house anymore or even her real family. It was a scary parallel universe where everyone was the opposite of their true selves. She wondered how she appeared to the others. Was she different, too? Somehow she had to find her way back to reality, but in the meantime, the easiest way to cope was just to leave, which is what she did at every opportunity.

Kendra lived in Palatka, in the old section of town and near the river. Their house had been beautifully renovated, an older house that showed no signs of its former self. It was now very modern with stucco siding and a Mediterranean look that fit the Florida landscape perfectly. Her father was a doctor and her mother was an instructor at the college. They lived much higher up the social scale than Emry ever had or probably ever would, but they were neither condescending nor snobbish. Emry was invited to visit and to swim in their pool and soon she was spending more time at Kendra's than anywhere else.

Unfortunately, she and Kaylee were drifting apart and it was not something Emry particularly planned or wanted. It just happened. Then one day as Emry walked with Kendra to the parking lot after school, Kaylee called out to her, and ran to catch up with them. She looked at Kendra as if she suddenly understood things she had been wondering about. *So this is why I never see you anymore*, quietly spoke itself through her eyes.

"Emry," she began. "Got a minute?"
"Sure. Oh, this is Kendra. Kendra — Kaylee."
"Hi," they both said.
"We have chem together," Kaylee said and Kendra nodded

an agreement. She turned back to Emry and went into her reason for stopping them.

"My birthday's comin' up," she said. "I'm having a party and well, it'll be just a small event, but . . ."

She seemed to be struggling.

"I was hoping you'd come," she managed to get out.

"When?" Emry asked.

"Friday at seven."

"Yeah. I'll ask my dad. You know how he is about curfews these days, but if he'll let me, I'll be there."

"You too, Kendra," she carefully said, then with more enthusiasm she added, "Honest, it'd be great if you'd come."

"Can I bring my boyfriend?" Kendra asked.

"Sure. The more the merrier."

"I'd love to," she said and Kaylee became all smiles.

After this, the three of them began hanging out together all the time. It was like it had been back in Charlotte when Emry, Stacy, and Heather had been the best of friends, but when she allowed herself a moment of honesty, Emry had to admit, it was better than that. Kendra and Kaylee were so much more. It was almost like a kinship rather than friendship. They did everything together and shared their secrets — well, not every secret. Emry could not tell them about Victor. She was bound to a certain amount of secrecy and there was no way of telling Kaylee about him without exposing Victor for what he was.

Well, what was he? She still had not figured that out, but she was giving it a lot of thought. Nevertheless, she could not tell Kaylee anything that might break the confidence he had in her.

Two weeks passed, and Emry came home one day to find her dad whistling. He was in his room, but she was so amazed to hear a happy sound coming from him that she walked to the open door and looked inside.

He was standing next to a new computer that he and Ellen were in the process of setting up. Ellen was on the floor and he was standing there whistling while she fished wires up to him.

"Hey, Emry," he said when he saw her standing there.

"Wow, daddy. You've got a new computer. That's really cool."

"Yeah, I'm kinda excited."

He looked it, too. He was smiling for the first time in weeks.

"Here," Ellen forcefully said, beating the cable against the wall as she tried to get him to take it.

"Let me get down there, grandma," Emry suggested. "I can do that."

They traded places and Ellen took Stanley's job of retrieving. She was really quite mechanically minded and it was she that actually got the computer up and running and not Emry nor Stanley.

When it was done, Stanley sat down and faced the flat screen that was the monitor, looking at it with pride and excitement. Then he turned and gave Emry a concerned look.

"I bet you're wondering why I bought a computer when we don't have the money for anything else—"

"No, daddy. You've done without more than anyone. I'm

glad you've got it."

Mostly she was glad he was happy again. If it took a new computer to bring him back to life, then she was all for it.

"I had to get one," he explained. "I've got a job and I'll be working online."

"Oh, daddy!" she exclaimed, understanding a few things at last. He had been feeling helpless and more than likely useless, too. When Maggie got her job, it probably only intensified all these feelings, but now he could put it all behind him. He was the bread winner again.

Maybe everything else would go back to normal, too. Emry certainly hoped so.

She had been invited to Kendra's again, so she went upstairs to put on her bathing suit. Her favorite one was in the laundry. Ellen had been busy with the computer and hadn't gotten to the wash, so Emry had to make do with the skimpy bikini she never wore. She didn't know why she had even bought it. It embarrassed her to see herself in it, although, even she had to admit, she had the figure for it. Well, it would be only Kendra and Kaylee who saw her, so she supposed she could endure that — as long as Kendra's boyfriend, Jason, didn't drop in.

That's why they make cover-ups, she told herself and she immediately began rummaging around looking for the old terrycloth one she knew she had. She found it in the back of one of her dresser drawers and pulled it out, holding it up, critically examining it before throwing it on the bed.

She pulled a pair of khaki shorts on over the bikini, then

she stuck her arms through the cover-up and her feet into flip flops. She grabbed up a towel, keys, and her books and then she hurried out the door. The day was getting away from her.

She picked up Kaylee from her house on River Road and the two of them rode to Kendra's house together.

It was quiet and pleasant on the river. The three girls lay around the pool after taking a short swim, did their homework, talked, and made plans for the upcoming weekends. When the sun touched the horizon, Emry knew she had to be getting home. The thought was not as odious as it had been the day before. The sight of her daddy that afternoon had given her hope that life at home was going to be tolerable once again.

She pulled on her shorts and grabbed up the old terrycloth cover-up, throwing it across her arm instead of putting it on and then, she and Kaylee left together.

Kaylee had been a little more quiet than usual that whole day, and when they stopped in the Miller's driveway, she hesitated before getting out of the car.

"I'm concerned about Abby," she said after some effort on her part. "Something's really wrong with her."

"What?" Emry quickly asked.

"I don't know for sure." She paused, struggling with her thoughts. "I think she's doing drugs," she finally said.

That set Emry back. She couldn't imagine Abby being so stupid and she said so.

"I never thought so either, but she's changing, becoming belligerent, not doing her school work and hanging out every night with a group of kids that scare the daylights outta me."

"What happened to Van?"

"He's still around, but he won't come to the house anymore. He makes her come to him and she does it every night without fail. It's like she's as addicted to him as she is to the drugs."

Drugs! Well, that could be the common denominator in this whole crazy scenario. Van could be a drug dealer and Victor and his family were — what? DEA? Or were they drug czars and this was some kind of territorial dispute or drug war?

The idea left Emry breathless. She'd almost rather Victor was a vampire than some drug lord or member of a crime family.

Emry looked for Abby's car, but it was gone.

"I don't see her car."

"Yeah, she's gone and we may not see her until tomorrow. Mama's ready to put her out."

"I'm so sorry, Kaylee," Emry said, placing a consoling hand on her shoulder. She didn't know what to say or to do at this point. She desperately wished to come up with the right words, but she simply didn't know how.

"Thanks for listening," Kaylee said. "It helps just to talk about it."

Emry wondered why she hadn't said anything to Kendra, but she didn't ask. Kendra didn't know Abby or Van. Maybe that was the reason.

"Should I come in and let you get everything off your chest?"

"Nah, I'm good. Your daddy's gonna freak as it is," she said with a weak smile.

"Yeah, he is," she agreed. "But I'm so tired of his silly restrictions I could scream."

Emry had been pushing the limits of her curfew lately and Stanley had been so preoccupied that he hadn't seemed to notice. This wasn't the first time she had stayed out way past sundown.

"I'm almost eighteen years old, for crying out loud, and he has me on the curfew of a ten year old."

"Mama's almost as bad. She's been talking to your grandma, I think, and she's almost as spooked as your dad. And this Abby thing isn't helping any."

They commiserated for a few minutes and then Kaylee opened the door.

"I'll see ya' later," she said and got out. Emry waited until she was safely in the house and then she backed the old Buick out of the driveway.

The road was dark in both directions, but when she turned onto Palmetto Bluff Road lights appeared from out of nowhere and a car pulled right up behind her. It rode on her bumper and Emry looked in her rear view mirror, trying to make out who it was. She couldn't determine either the make or the model of the vehicle nor who was sitting behind the steering wheel, but it unnerved her for him to ride so closely behind her. She wondered why he didn't just go around her. She drove along, wondering if she should speed up or slow down, and praying the whole time that the old Buick wouldn't conk out on her.

Just as she reached the reduced speed limit sign on the

edge of Bostwick, the car went around her. It was a blue jaguar — Victor!

He pulled in front of her and deliberately slowed down, but then, his blinker came on. The only road up ahead was the one to the Catholic Church. It was a deserted road. Nothing was down there but the church, the rectory, and the cemetery.

"He wants me to follow him," she said to herself, and her heart began pumping furiously.

Or maybe I'm imagining that, she thought. *He's probably just going to the church to . . . to . . . well, whatever drug dealers - slash - syndicate families do at church on Friday nights.*

This was no time to be funny. Even if he did want her to follow him, she told herself, she wasn't sure she wanted to. Well, that was a laugh. She thought about him all the time. The desire to see him was greater than Emry's curiosity which at this moment was off the scale. She knew she was going to follow him even before she flipped on the blinker.

She followed close behind him, right into the parking lot near the church. He went to the end of the pavement, the farthest point from the church itself, and pulled into a space that overlooked the cemetery. It was a spooky place and for just a brief second, Emry considered making a u-turn and driving right out again.

He stepped out of the jag and into her headlights, and that was all it took to remove the one rational and sane thought she had had. She pulled up beside him and unlocked the doors. She turned the key in the ignition and the Buick went silent and

Emry pressed the button that released her seat belt.

He was quick to get into her car, sliding inside with that same graceful ease that came so naturally to him. He looked at her and his eyebrows raised ever so slightly as he took in her skimpy attire. He quickly closed the door and the light that briefly illuminated the inside of the car, went dark, but not before Emry saw the flattering look he shot her way.

"Hello, Emry," he said, just like she expected him to. There was a hint of a smile on his lips and appreciation in his eyes. She moved restlessly under his gaze, wishing for the terry cloth cover-up lying on the backseat. He was a little too crazy to be looking at her that way.

"I was swimming at Kendra's," she said, feeling it was necessary to give him an explanation. Her heart was pounding so hard, she could hear it beating in her ears.

"So I see."

"What do you want?" she asked, hoping she didn't sound rude, but she was getting nervous. Why had she even stopped? *I must be crazier than he is.*

"I have been looking for you," he said. "But you have not been around." He moved the armrest just as he had done the last time he had been in her car, pushing it up so that there were no barriers between them.

"It's been crazy at my house," she said, eyeing the space between them and wondering why he wanted the armrest out of the way. "I've been spending a lot of time at Kendra's."

"Your friend in Palatka?"

Now, how did he know that?

"Yes," she warily answered, then she quickly added. "Was my information useful? Did you find Van?"

"It was useful, but Van has gone into hiding. I was wondering what Abby had to say about it. That is why I was looking for you."

"Oh," she softly sighed, remembering her conversation with Kaylee. "Abby's acting real weird right now. Kaylee thinks she's on drugs."

"Not drugs," Victor said. He knitted his brow and his eyes burned as if with fire. "What have you heard?"

"Kaylee said Abby's hanging out with a bunch of bad kids. She's not doing her school work and she's stayin' out all night. Mrs. Miller's ready to put her out."

He shook his head, a pain in his eyes she couldn't understand. Maybe he was in love with Abby, after all.

"I was afraid of this," he sighed. He leaned back and looked out the windshield of the car, staring toward the stars as if there was an answer in the cosmos.

Emry felt let down at his reaction. She told herself that every boy wanted Abby and that Victor Balfour was crazy, anyway, but her ego was deflated just the same.

"I've gotta go," she said. "Daddy isn't letting me out at night anymore. I'm AWOL right now."

He turned his head and looked at her. The pensive mood had left him and he smiled. "Why? Have you been a bad girl?" he jokingly said.

"No. Jim's been tellin' daddy all sorts of things and has him all worked up," she said. "He makes us come in before dark now."

"What kind of things?" he asked, the smile gone as quickly as it had appeared.

She shook her head. "Strange things. People dying — murder, I think. A regular epidemic to hear Jim tell it."

His brow wrinkled again and he cast a glance toward his car. Emry figured that meant he was ready to leave. Well, so was she.

"We need to set up a time to meet again," he said. "Will you meet me Monday evening?"

Emry's mind told her to say no, but her mouth opened up and she said, "yes." She immediately repented, but it was too late.

"Pick me up at the end of our road," he said without hesitation. It appeared he had already thought this through. "On the corner near the park. Eight o'clock, Monday night."

He immediately turned and reached for the door handle.

"Are you leaving?" she asked and he stopped.

"Yes," he simply replied, but he made no move to leave now that she had stopped him.

"Before you go, will you tell me something?" she asked and he carefully eased his hand away from the door.

"If I can," he said.

She hesitated while she built her courage.

"What are you — really?" she asked.

He sat very still for what seemed to Emry a very long time, but when he moved, she was surprised by the direction he took. He leaned toward her and he put his arm on the back of the seat so that he could almost touch her.

"What do you think I am?" he solemnly asked.

His voice was low and soft but Emry was not fooled. There was something menacing about his posture and she did not want him to lull her into a state of apathy with his voice.

"A magician, maybe — or a hypnotist — or something . . ." Her voice trailed off into nothing.

"Go ahead and say it," he said when she failed to complete her sentence. "I know what you are thinking."

"No, you really don't."

"Shall I guess? I will get it right on the first try."

He was giving her a very intense look but then his eyes slowly moved, first down and then up. He leaned back in his seat and sighed heavily.

"Why did you stop tonight?" he asked.

She had asked herself the same question, and with the same results. She had no answer. There was just something about him that made her want to see him — want to be with him. She knew it was crazy, but the very sight of him thrilled her.

"I don't really know," she admitted.

His head turned and he gave her a pondering look. He had such beautiful eyes, but right now, they were as dark as six feet under.

"You think I am a vampire," he casually stated.

She wanted to say something profound but a slick tongue was not her forte. She shook her head.

"No, I really don't believe that," she insisted, quite ready to convince him once he had said the word — not that she didn't *think* it. "I know that's crazy. It's obvious you aren't." She looked at him and she would have been lying if she said she wasn't just a little bit concerned at this point, but she smiled, trying to pass it off as a joke. "No bite marks," she facetiously said. She tilted her head back, and her unblemished neck turned up to him.

His eyes fell to her neck and very slowly something changed in his look. A stillness came over his countenance that gave him a deadly calm expression. It was a feral look, a hungry look, and Emry dropped her chin and covered her throat with her hand as if that would protect her.

She wondered if seeing the artery pulsing in her neck or feeling the warmth of her blood as it pushed through every vein in her body had triggered a desire that until that moment he had successfully kept under control. But then she asked herself why he would want to control it to begin with. If he was some inhuman maniac, why would it matter?

He moved and every muscle in Emry's body tensed.

"Come here, Emry," he said and her breath stilled in her throat. She didn't move so he repeated his demand. "Come here," he insisted and at the same time, he took her by the arm and pulled her across the seat to him.

She gasped as much from surprise as from fear, but there was no stopping him. She made a feeble attempt anyway, but he effortlessly dragged her to him. Funny, her hand was still shielding her throat as she came to rest beside him.

He moved it aside and not gently either.

"No, Victor," she weakly begged but he was not listening to her.

At this moment, she honestly expected him to grow fangs before her very eyes and sink them into her bare throat, but instead he grasped her left arm and lifted it away from her body, turning it so that the inner part of her upper arm was exposed.

"Lesson one," he darkly said. "This is where you look."

Her eyes jumped up to his in astonishment. What was he saying? She looked down at her arm and right back into his eyes. He was not smiling. He was all too serious. "If I was going to bite you, I would do it here where the marks would not show." She began to tremble. There was no question about it. There was no hesitation in his voice. The facts flowed out so freely that he surely knew what he was talking about. "That way, feeding can take place over a period of time because there is less chance of breaking your neck."

She stared at him. Shock was written all over her face. She tried to pull away, but he held her tightly. She winced and he slowly loosened his grip. The dark mood gradually left him as his passion died. Very carefully, she pulled her arm out of his hand and this time, he didn't try to stop her. She folded her arms and held them close to her body while she thought about moving back to the driver's side of the car. She wondered what he would do so she sat very still beside him, afraid to move.

"Do you understand what I am saying?" he asked after a few seconds of silence. "If I wanted to keep you alive, I would not go for the neck." He touched her arm again and she tensed.

"It would be here," he said. "—or here," he then added as his hand dropped to her bare leg. She gasped and caught at his hand, but he did not appear to have any ignoble intent in mind. He paused, however, at the touch of her anxious hand.

"Let me show you," he said, his voice quiet, but insistent. The warmth of his hand ignited a fire within her and she didn't trust herself. Very slowly, though, she loosened her grip and as she did, his hand carefully moved.

"Here," he said, indicating her leg with a smooth stroke of his hand. He withdrew his hand but his eyes held hers. "And tonight, you would make it so easy for a vampire."

Or a man, he immediately thought.

Emry didn't know what to say. She stared at him with eyes gone wide and emotions running wild.

He slowly leaned back. "Lesson over," he said.

It took Emry a full minute to compose herself. "Are you a vampire?" she breathlessly asked once her voice came back to her.

"No," he answered without any hesitation. In fact, his answer came quickly, maybe too quickly.

Emry was silent for a brief moment as she considered him. He really was crazy. Of course, she knew that and she shouldn't have been surprised, but she was.

"But, you can't come out in the daytime," she insisted.

"It isn't that I *can't* — it's that I *don't*. There is a difference," he said, speaking with the contractions he seldom used.

He leaned forward again and she instinctively drew back.

He smiled with wry humor and reached for her hand, but she quickly withdrew it. His smile broadened as he considered the challenge this presented. It would be no effort on his part to ensnare that retreating hand, but he didn't want to overpower her. He had frightened her enough, he was thinking, and he didn't want her to leave tonight feeling completely overwhelmed by him. He still needed her. He mentally grunted at the double meaning taken on by that thought.

"Give me your hand, Emry," he said. "I only want to show you something."

She considered that while her curiosity consumed her.

She gave in and he wrapped his hand around hers. Very carefully he brought it up to his chest and he pressed it there right where his heart should be. She felt his heart beating steadily under her hand.

"That is my heart beating. Vampires do not have a heartbeat."

She felt the steady, even rhythm in his chest. His body was warm, too, and she imagined that if there was such a thing as a vampire, he would be as cold as ice. She spread her fingers out from the fist she had made and with a smile of relief, she gently touched him. It was a wonderful feeling and even though his hand continued to hold hers, it was no longer necessary in order to keep her hand against him. Her hand stayed there by choice.

If only . . . she thought.

"And — I am not obsessive compulsive," he suddenly said, his voice full of dry humor. The tension between them broke.

Emry wanly smiled. "You know, you really scared me," she said as she wilted beside him.

"I thought you were not afraid," he said.

"I lied," she admitted.

"Not afraid now?" he asked.

"Well, maybe a little," she truthfully said and he smiled.

"I promise, I will not hurt you."

His arm had encircled her when he had pulled her to him. It could have been a lover's embrace and they both seemed to come to that conclusion at the same time. They moved simultaneously. Emry gently eased her hand out from under his and he moved his arm, placing it on the seat behind her. Even at that, it took Emry a full minute to calm her racing heart again.

Her throat had gone dry and she cleared it before she spoke. "Will you explain that again — and this time not quite so graphically?"

He smiled at her request, but as he gave it thought, the smile wilted and a frown creased his brow. He looked down in contemplation.

"Yes," he said. He looked up at her again. "I did not want to tell you this. You provoked me."

She nodded as if she understood. "I was too frightened to grasp what you were saying," she admitted. "I need to hear it again."

"That is where a vampire would feed if he did not want to kill you right away," he said without any further hesitation. "You see, it is easy to break someone's neck when you are as powerful as a vampire."

"How would you know that?" she asked.

"I have seen it," he simply replied.

"Are you a vampire?" she asked again.

"No."

"But, there really are vampires."

He smiled derisively and looked down. "That is why you have been following me around, is it not? Because you think I am a vampire."

She didn't say anything, so he added, "And you still are not convinced."

"Well, you seem to know so much."

"I have to know so much," he said. "Otherwise, I would have been killed long ago."

"How long ago?" she asked, wondering about his age.

He turned his head and looked down at her. "I said, the lesson is over. And, anyway, you are forgetting your curfew. You should go home."

He lifted his arm from the back of the seat and brought it down at his side. At the same time, he opened the car door. The lights inside the car immediately came on.

"Wait," she said, reaching for his arm and he stopped.

He turned at her summons and looked over his shoulder.

For the first time, Emry was looking at Victor in the light. He squinted his eyes and frowned a little, but there was nothing he could do that could take away from those handsome features. Emry looked into his face and anything she had been about to say was immediately forgotten.

"You better let me go, Emry," he said. "I may not be a vampire, but right now, I am a very dangerous man."

She knew what he meant. She was struggling with feelings she had never had before and it was not fear, but desire that prompted her to hang onto him. She couldn't trust herself to do the right thing, so she was glad he, at least, could walk away without hesitation. Little did she know that he was very close to throwing reason to the wind. In another minute, he would close the car door. She had no idea how much trouble she would be in if he did that.

Very carefully, she mentally pried her fingers off of his arm. Slowly, her hand let go of him.

He hesitated only a few seconds, looking at her with contemplation, and then he stepped out of the car.

"I will see you Monday night," he said and he closed the door.

She found it hard to move, but finally, she slid across the seat and got under the steering wheel. Her hand was trembling, but she turned the key in the ignition and when the car fired up, she dropped the gear shift into reverse.

He was standing there and she waited before taking her foot off the brake. She wanted him to open the car door and get inside again, but instead he pointed to the door and said, "Lock it."

She did and then she slowly backed out, hoping all the time that he would stop her, but he didn't.

He waited until she drove away, then he pulled the cell phone out of his pocket and made a quick call.

"Emry is coming home. Will you see she gets in safely? I have something to do."

He casually dropped the cell phone into his pocket. Letting Emry leave just now had been the hardest thing he had ever had to do and he didn't know if he was disciplined enough to do it again under these same set of circumstances.

He turned his attention to the rectory. It was dark, but he knew Joseph was there and that he would be awake. He glanced once in the direction Emry had gone and then he walked away. He needed to talk to someone and no one would understand him better than Joe.

Chapter Thirteen

"You're distracted today," Kendra said.

Emry was staring across the cafeteria, methodically chewing her food. She hadn't said a lot because her mind was miles away in the past.

She had thought of nothing since Friday night except what had happened between her and Victor. He had actually frightened her — really frightened her — but he had done something else to her, too, something that made her blush with chagrin. She kept replaying the evening in her mind and it was the sensual touch of his hand that occupied her thoughts and not the thing that should have scared her into reason. She told herself she was messing with things that could get her hurt but scolding herself did absolutely no good. There was obviously a reason for the old tales about the Balfours. She should have paid more attention.

"I am distracted," she admitted to Kendra.

"Things any better at home?" she asked, trying to find the reason for the distraction.

"Yeah, since daddy went to work again, things've been a lot better."

"I take it, that's not what's on your mind then."

"No. I'm just kinda daydreamin' today. You know how it is."

"Who is he?" Kendra asked, smiling smugly.

Emry stiffened and then she slowly relaxed as she realized that Kendra was only fishing. She didn't know anything.

"I'm still considering," she said, playing along with her, and redirecting her own thoughts at the same time. "I wonder if I can get past the whole *I feel like he's a cousin* thing with Casey. He's so cute."

"It wouldn't be a problem for me," Kendra assured her. "If I were you, I'd be doin' more than just considerin'. I'd be findin' another ride to school for Crystal. It's a long way from Bostwick to Palatka. A lot can happen."

Emry laughed, but inside she was thinking, *Yeah, right! Like I really want that to happen.*

"Don't look now," Kendra suddenly said, "but Johnny Patton is coming our way."

Emry looked up and sure enough, Johnny was weaving through the maze of chairs and tables, walking as straight toward them as the furniture allowed.

He pulled back a chair and sat down as soon as he arrived.

"Well, would you look at this," Kendra said, glancing at the watch on her wrist. "I have to be goin'. I'll talk to you later, Emry. See ya', Johnny."

She got up and left and Emry smiled across the table at him. Funny, but she had given very little thought to him after that day at the beach.

"I've called your house a few times, but you're never there," he said.

That was strange. No one had told her he had called. It

must have been her daddy taking the calls. He didn't want the boys calling or hanging around. She said as much.

"It *was* a man I talked to," he said, but then he went on. "I wanted to know if you'd go out with me. Maybe to a movie or something."

Emry didn't have to think too long on an answer. She had already made up her mind to look seriously at an active social life. She obviously had too much time on her hands. Otherwise, she wouldn't be plotting and scheming with Victor Balfour.

This past weekend she'd given a lot of thought to him. His Friday night lesson had upset her in more ways than one, so being objective had become a hard thing. She told herself he was a seriously disturbed man and she had to quit seeing him, but somehow, the words rang hollow in her mind. The trouble was, she didn't want to stop seeing him.

At the same time, the very idea that she wanted to see him so badly brought her to the conclusion that she should abruptly stop seeing him. She remembered the look on his face when he had told her he was a very dangerous man, and even though she was taking it out of context, he was right. She had lost control where he was concerned and that was what made him so dangerous to her. She had to put him back into perspective. He was a Balfour, she told herself, and they were all insane. The trouble was, the thought of not seeing him again hurt like a drug addict without drugs. She couldn't just taper off. She had to go cold turkey or she'd never be able to do it. She was supposed to meet him at eight o'clock that night and with great difficulty, she decided not to do it. Seeing Johnny somehow made that decision easier to handle.

"I'd love to," she told him and he smiled with genuine pleasure.

"How about Friday night? We could go to Orange Park, grab a bite to eat and catch a movie."

"That sounds great," Emry said. Whether it did or not, she was determined that it was going to be.

They made plans and then he left and Emry went to class. After school, she faced the dilemma of telling her dad. She knew he wouldn't be happy. When they lived in Charlotte, he never liked it when Jeff came by. He watched him like he thought he was going to abscond with the family silver or something. She'd only gone out with him on double dates and with groups of friends and her daddy had freaked even then. She could only imagine his reaction to her going with Johnny, alone, all the way to Orange Park and back.

She decided to wait until Maggie was home. In the meantime, she helped Ellen in the garden and when they were finished there, they went into the house and started preparing supper. Somewhere in the course of the afternoon, Emry told her grandmother about Johnny and Ellen sort of laughed.

"Don't let Stanley intimidate you," she suggested. "He's gonna try, you know."

"Yes, I know. I thought I'd wait until mama got here before I said anything."

"Don't ask if you can go," Ellen said. "Just tell him. Not rude or belligerently, mind you," she added. "Just tell him Johnny asked you out and you're goin' with him Friday night.

He'll chew on it awhile, but he won't tell you you can't go."

"Okay. And thanks. I'll do that."

They were making spaghetti for dinner — Ellen's famous recipe. Emry helped put the sauce together and then she set out the vegetables for a salad. She was thinking that while the meal had Stanley softened up, she'd make the announcement about her date with Johnny. That made her think about the date she had with Victor that very night and she cringed at the thought.

Curiously, it wasn't the idea of seeing him that made her cringe. It was the thought of not seeing him. She could imagine him standing in the shadows by the park, waiting for her. She wondered how long he would wait before he gave up and if he would be disappointed. More importantly, what would he do when she didn't show up?

She didn't imagine it would be any great disappointment to him, and she shrugged apathetically, but apathy was actually the last thing she was feeling.

The sensible side of her brain told her she was being reasonable and smart, but the other side made one excuse after another as to why she should see him one more time. He needed her help — Abby was in trouble and she was letting her down. And then the real kicker — what would she do if she never saw him again?

That was the problem.

He's a Balfour . . . He's a Balfour . . . He's a Balfour . . .

It wasn't helping anymore.

Emry made her announcement during dinner and Stanley laid his fork down with a loud thump.

"Who is this guy?" he quickly asked.

"Johnny Patton. He's a friend of Casey's."

"I wanna meet him."

"You can meet him Friday night when he comes to pick me up."

"No, I mean before Friday night."

"Daddy, don't do this," she said with a sigh. "It's not like I'm asking to go out with one of the Balfours or something."

He gave her a curious look and then he picked up his fork.

"You bring a Balfour in here and I'll skin you," he said.

Well, that was interesting. She looked at him with a million questions on her mind.

"Why?" she asked, curiosity overriding her better judgement.

He was chewing again and he didn't say anything until he had swallowed. He gripped the fork in his fist and rested it on the table in the upright position.

"I think the answer to that's obvious," he said. "But it's a moot point — isn't it?"

"Sure it is," Emry said. "I'm just curious why you feel that way."

"Like I said, the answer's obvious."

"Is it because they're descendants of axe murderers? I'm sure I could dig up some unfavorable history on the Winters if I tried real hard."

He was chewing again and he took his time. You could see he was thinking real hard about his answer.

"I don't like the Balfours. That's the main reason. But

they're a dangerous bunch of men and I don't trust any one of them to come into this house.

"And just because I'm crippled doesn't mean there's anything wrong with my hearing either," he went on. "I hear what everyone's sayin' about them — especially the women. They're good lookin' men, and I can't deny that, but I'm afraid they have no scruples, and would take any advantage they could."

"What makes you say that? Have they done something?"

He shook his head. "No," he said and then he looked suspiciously at her. "Why do you care?"

"I don't care," she lied. "You made me wonder, so I was playing the devil's advocate."

"Well, I hope you won't let what I've said make you do anything foolish. I know how you can get a bee in your bonnet sometimes."

"Oh, Emry already knows one of them," Crystal spoke up, waving her hand carelessly. Emry shot her a startled look. "We saw him at Hall's one night. He was talkin' to her at the gas pump."

"What did he say?" Stanley demanded.

"Hello," Emry dryly remarked. "It's called being courteous."

Stanley relaxed. "Don't get any ideas," was all he said, and then he went back to eating.

Emry sat there for a few minutes before collecting her thoughts. It seemed the Balfour subject had been successfully closed so she wisely left it and went back to the original one.

"Daddy, I'm not goin' to let you intimidate me about this date. I hope you'll be nice to Johnny. He's a nice boy."

"Of course, he will," Maggie finally spoke up. "We just expect Johnny to come in Friday evening and introduce himself before you leave, is all. No blowing the horn and you running out to his car and leaving, understand?"

"I understand — and he will. You'll like him. He's nice."

"And cute," Crystal added. "Real cute!"

Ellen winked at Emry and then she began talking about the garden and other domestic things and the subject was left behind.

It was interesting how easily Emry could move on past the subject of going out with Johnny, but she wasn't able to let go of the one about the Balfours. Stanley's reaction had caught her completely off guard and the fact that Victor would be waiting for her in less than an hour, set her to thinking of nothing else. Her eyes went to the clock so many times she realized she was counting the time in seconds rather than minutes.

Eight o'clock finally came and she watched as the minute hand on the clock slowly moved until it slipped past the hour. She told herself she had won the battle, but there was no feeling of victory. In fact, she felt awful.

She kept imagining Victor waiting for her, looking down the empty road while he stood there. Would he be angry or would he simply shrug it off and move on?

She went to her room and opened the blinds. The yard was dark, but the tiny light at the Balfours shined through the gloom just like it always did. She quickly snapped the blinds closed and turned away from the window.

I'm not going to dwell on this, she thought. *I'm going to think about Johnny and not Victor. And I'm letting go of Victor before I become as insane as he is.*

That's what she told herself, but she could no more stop thinking about Victor than she could stop breathing. By morning she was sure there was something wrong with her. What girl in her right mind would be thinking of him after what he had said and done? There was definitely something wrong with her. She even regretted her choice of not seeing him the night before and began plotting how she could rectify that.

Without even knowing of the war that was raging in Emry's mind, it was Ellen who actually brought some quiet to her struggle.

She liked to talk while she worked in the garden and Emry was an avid listener. Every afternoon after school, she was there beside Ellen, learning what she could about growing things, and at the same time, listening to the local gossip, of which her grandmother was extremely knowledgeable.

A dark cloud arose while they worked and Ellen nervously looked up at the sky. When her eyes swept past the Balfour's property, she saw a light burning from a window. This was a curious thing since it was only late afternoon.

It caused her to comment and then to expand on that until she was reciting local history. She began by telling Emry that Stanley was right to caution her about the men who lived in that old house. They were a weird family and more than just peculiar. She honestly believed there was insanity that ran in the family and affected all of them. Why else did they behave in such an odd manner?

And it was no different than their ancestors that had lived there years before, she pointed out. Stanley's grandfather had befriended them, and had been the caretaker for the old place until he mysteriously died. There was also the story of the young girl, Clara Kent, who had believed she was all but engaged to one of them and then, she too, had turned up dead.

Then, of course, everyone knew about the murder of the stranger who had dropped into Bostwick from the car of a freight train one night — sadly, to his demise.

She ended her story by saying, "If it hadn't been wartime, I suppose they'd 've found and punished him, but things were different back then. He got away scot free. It's quite strange that such a fine looking family could be so evil."

Emry gave the Balfour's property a long and careful study before congratulating herself on her wise decision to put Victor out of her mind. Every time she thought of him, she simply replayed Ellen's words. Soon the thoughts of him were just white noise — static in her mind — that she tuned out with surprising success.

Now, if only he would stay out of her dreams, she would have this thing licked.

But he didn't.

Chapter Fourteen

Johnny arrived at five o'clock and just like Emry predicted, everyone liked him — even Stanley, although he wouldn't admit it.

They went to the Orange Park Mall and bought tickets for a movie and then they went to the food court and got something to eat.

Johnny talked easily but not excessively and he showed himself to be quite the gentleman, opening doors and carrying her tray to a table. He guided her gently with his hand as they turned corners and always let her go before him. While watching the movie, he held her hand, and when they arrived back at home, he walked her to the door where he kissed her with a nervous, but adequate kiss.

She thanked him for the evening and they talked about doing something again sometime, and then he left.

Maggie was waiting in the living room when Emry came in. She was watching her Friday night shows on television, but Stanley limped out of the kitchen to join her, anxious, you could tell, to make sure everything had gone well.

"I had a great time," Emry said at their questioning looks. "We're goin' out again sometime."

Stanley suddenly took her in his arms and hugged her.

"What was that for?" she asked when he turned her loose.

"Can't I hug you without a reason?" he asked, but he sounded pretty emotional. Emry hadn't realized how hard it was for him to let go and let her grow up.

She hugged him back. "Of course you can, as long as I can return the favor."

"Deal," he said.

The phone rang and it was Kendra wanting all the details of the evening.

"I can't talk now," Emry said, looking around at the audience. "I'll call you later."

She got as far as the top of the stairs and the phone rang again. It was Kaylee.

"Tell her I'll call her tomorrow," Emry shouted down the steps.

"She says it's important," Maggie said.

"Oh, alright. I'll take it up here."

She ran to her room and threw her things down; then she picked up the phone. The extension in her room was a compromise. Since they couldn't afford cell phones for the girls, Stanley and Maggie had put extensions of the regular phone in their rooms. They had just gotten them installed the week before.

"Hello," she said as she flopped down on the bed.

"Emry," Kaylee's voice came over the phone. "How'd it go?"

"Uh, good. It was a lot of fun — but I just walked in. Can we talk tomorrow?"

"Well..."

"What is it?"

"Can I come over tonight?"

"What's wrong?"

"It's Abby. She and Van are here — and I'd like to leave. Could I just spend the night there?"

Emry pushed herself up to her elbows. "Van's there — right now?"

"Yeah, and I'm weirded out. They're both strung out on something, I think. They're actin' real strange. Look, if this ain't a good time."

"No, it's a good time. Of course you can come and stay as long as you want to, but what about your mother?"

"She's still at work. I think they'll be gone by the time she gets here."

Mrs. Miller had taken a second job, waitressing at a new restaurant in Palatka. On weekends, they were open until eleven o'clock and she never got home before eleven-thirty or twelve o'clock. Kaylee sounded a little frightened.

"Come on over," Emry said.

"You sure you don't mind?"

"No, of course not."

"Well, I'll be there in about thirty minutes."

"See ya'," Emry said and quickly hung up the phone.

She ran to the window and jerked the blinds open.

"How do I get in touch with you?" she said into the night. Her eyes scanned the dark yard looking for Victor, wishing he would magically appear, but he was nowhere to be seen. Probably he was off on one of those nightly trips they took.

The light in the old house winked through wind caressed

branches, and Emry focused on it, a plan forming in her mind.

She walked to her desk and pulled out a piece of paper. Quickly she scribbled a note and stuck a strip of transparent tape to the top of it. Her hand was shaking, but she wasn't sure whether it was from excitement or fright. She was dealing with both to an unusual degree.

Quietly, Emry left her room and slipped downstairs. Maggie was still in the living room — Stanley and Ellen were in the kitchen. She didn't know where Crystal was, but the door was closed to her bedroom. She was probably there. Emry moved on tiptoes to the French doors in the dining room and carefully opened one of them. She stepped outside and eased the door closed behind her; then she walked to the edge of the porch and jumped to the ground.

When her feet hit the ground, she began to run.

Tripper barked from Jim's yard. It made Emry run even faster. She ran away from the house and didn't slow down until she was next to the fence that enclosed the Balfour's property.

Everything was dark and the wind was blowing just enough to shake the leaves, making it hard to hear well. It sounded like movement in the brush and Emry probed the darkness trying to see if there was someone there. She couldn't see anything.

She began to run again and soon the old gate at the northeast corner of the fence was before her. She put her hand on it and prepared to climb over when a sound that was different from the others made her pause. She looked up and she imagined she could see someone standing in the dark path — a vague outline that hadn't been there a second before.

"Victor!" she called in a hoarse whisper. The shadow moved and a moment later it reappeared as a man just a few feet in front of her.

From his looks, he could have been a corsair. His mustache was a tiny, thin line, so perfect, it looked like it had been drawn on his face. Likewise, his beard was a narrow strip that followed the contours of his face, running along the jaw from ear to ear. His hair was dark and swept back as if the wind had caught it and his face was wide of brow and his eyes sharp and focused. You could almost imagine him standing on the deck of a ship, the wind in his face and the sea rolling beneath his feet. He was a remarkably handsome man, but there was a stillness in his features that gave him a stern look.

"No — Artemus," he said. "What is wrong?"

"I'm lookin' for Victor. Is he here?"

"Uh, no." He sounded reluctant. "He just left."

"I've got to talk to him. It's urgent!"

"Tell me," he demanded, taking a step closer. "I am his brother. I will get the message to him."

"Van is at Kaylee's."

He didn't seem to comprehend. He stared at her as if he couldn't understand.

"I just talked to Kaylee on the phone. She said Van and Abby are at her house right now! I've got to tell Victor."

"Oh, damn!" he cursed. He jumped the fence and slid his cell phone in his hand as his feet hit the ground beside Emry. "Come! I am taking you home," he said, grabbing her hand as he trotted in that direction. Emry had to run to keep up.

He hit speed dial on his phone as he pulled her toward the house, but when no one answered he began to angrily talk to the phone. "Oh, come on! Pick up — pick up the phone. And stop acting like a damn fool!"

He suddenly ended the call and punched in another number. As it rang, he stopped and pointed toward the house.

"Go," he said. "Run home. I will watch to see you are safe — oh, hello? Marius? — go!" he demanded as she hesitated. "How soon can you get here?" he asked into the phone, but Emry wasn't listening. She was running home as fast as her legs would carry her.

Chapter Fifteen

Emry paced the floor until it was a wonder there wasn't a trench from one end of her room to the other.

She walked to the window and then to the door, and then she turned and did it all over again. The only thing that stopped her was Kaylee's arrival. She entered Emry's room and threw her bag in the corner and her pillow on the bed.

"Are you sure you're alright with this?"

"Yeah, I'm sure."

"You look upset."

"It's nothing to do with you comin' over."

"Johnny?" Kaylee tentatively asked.

"Oh, no," Emry said, looking up with a shocked expression. "That went great. He was a lot of fun."

"I've got to know," she said as she fell across the bed and stuffed the pillow under her body. "Did he kiss you?"

"You expect me to kiss and tell?"

"I certainly do!"

"He did."

Emry didn't care much for this kind of exchange. She was a private person and found it hard to reveal personal things about herself — even little things like this. Besides, she was more than curious about what was happening at Kaylee's house, so she quickly steered the conversation in that direction.

"What about Abby? Tell me what's goin' on at your house."

Kaylee rolled over with a sigh.

"Oh, Emry," she moaned. "I don't know what's goin' t' happen next. It's like I've stepped into a parallel universe."

Emry knew the feeling. She'd been there before.

"Abby has lost her mind!" she continued.

"What about Van?" Emry quickly asked.

Kaylee pulled the pillow around and rolled back onto it before answering.

"You know," she said. "He's being really good to her in spite of the fact she's actin' rude and hateful. But there's something about him that when he looked at me tonight scared the daylights outta me. It was as if he was starin' right into my mind and readin' everything that was there."

"Were they still there when you left?"

Kaylee nodded. "Yeah. Van kept talkin' about waitin' for some friends to arrive. He said he was expectin' comp'ny."

Emry jerked as if she'd been stabbed with a knife. Who was he expecting? The Balfours?

She turned to the window with her heart in her throat. Had she set up something that was going to get Victor hurt — or killed?

The thought was unbearable. She felt her breath coming quick and shallow but she couldn't stop it. Kaylee was talking, but she couldn't hear her either. All she could do was stare at the empty window and worry about Victor.

Suddenly her head felt light. Everything seemed small and out of focus.

"Emry! Emry!" she heard Kaylee shouting but she was so far away she couldn't get back to her.

Rough hands shook her and the next thing she knew, Emry was sitting in the chair at the computer, her head between her knees and Kaylee commanding her to breathe.

"What happened?" she asked when she was able to sit upright again.

"You almost passed out," Kaylee said. She was on her knees beside the chair, looking at Emry with anxious eyes. "I think you hyperventilated."

"Good grief!" she sighed. "I've never done that before."

"What's really wrong, Emry?" Kaylee anxiously asked. "There's something on your mind tonight and it has nothin' t' do with Abby or Johnny. What is it?"

Emry shook her head. "Nothing," she insisted. "I didn't eat much tonight with Johnny — nervous, you know. Maybe my blood sugar's too low."

She rallied her strength and stood up. "Let's go to the kitchen and raid the frig."

Kaylee laughed. "Sounds good."

She took a shaky step toward the door and Kaylee took her arm for support, but her strength came back quickly. By the time she was downstairs, she felt almost normal again.

"Uh, Kaylee," she said. "Let's not say anything about my little episode upstairs, okay?"

"Sure — whatever."

"I just don't wanna worry daddy. He's so overly protective, if he hears what happened he's apt to call 911 or somethin'."

But that wasn't the real reason. She didn't want to be reminded that Victor could be walking into trouble, and all because of her. In fact, she didn't want to think about him at all.

"You wanna hear about Johnny?" Emry asked and at Kaylee's enthusiastic response, she smiled. That should do the trick. She'd tell Kaylee every detail of her date and then rehash it as many times as it took to remove Victor from her mind. This should be easy.

But it wasn't.

Chapter Sixteen

"Three days! You have been gone three days!" Artemus exclaimed. "And for what reason? Because the little girl next door kissed a boy good night!" He paused for only a second. "I thought you had everything under control."

"I do now."

"Well, it is a little late. We lost Hugo again. If you had been here we might have caught him."

"He was waiting for you — hoping you would go to him. It was a setup."

"You do not know that."

It calmed him down, though. Victor was probably right, but it didn't redeem him completely.

"If that is true, you know what it means," Artemus said. The stillness of his voice caused Victor's eyes to jump up to his. "He knows Emry has a connection to us, or he was testing her to see. Either way, your girl may be in serious trouble."

"I told you we should not drag her into this," Victor stated, his voice hard and low.

"She was already in it. Better that she was working with us rather than on her own. She is too much like Thomas for her own good."

Victor had to agree. She had a personality very much like her great grandfather's and it was sure to get her into trouble just like it had him.

"She came here looking for you," Artemus said, his voice suddenly calm. It wasn't without sympathy either. "It was black dark, but she sneaked out of her house and ran all the way over here with a note in her hand for you."

Victor clenched his teeth.

"She was climbing the fence when I saw her. I think she was planning to stick the note to the door if she could not find you."

"I'll tell her not to do that again. We will set up a signal of some kind."

Artemus gave him a curious look. It was a study that considered the failure of getting her to meet him the last time. He wondered what she was really thinking about all this.

"If she is like Thomas, she will be able to handle the truth. If you want her to cooperate, you need to tell her everything."

Victor was silent, but his thoughts betrayed him. His eyes swung away from his brother and a look of anguish settled onto his face. One of two things would happen at that moment and he wasn't sure he was ready for either one. She would either calmly accept everything he told her and embrace the truth or she would leave him completely. There were consequences to either conclusion that were serious beyond imagination. Either way, he would lose her in the end. If only he could delay that — just a little longer to be with her, then maybe he could endure the years ahead without her.

"I'll tell her when the time is right."

"Very well," Artemus said, but the look he gave Victor was

dubious.

"Tell me where we are with Hugo," Victor said, and Artemus' attitude and countenance completely changed. It smoothed out and calmed down and suddenly he was the warrior again.

"When I could not get you I called Marius. He and father came as quickly as they could, but when they arrived, Hugo was already gone. We arrived at the Miller's residence about twelve-thirty and the mother was just getting home from work. She was being watched but Marius took care of those guys."

"I guess that made him happy," Victor interjected and Artemus grunted a slight laugh.

"It improved his personality one hundred percent."

"What was the idea of them watching her?"

"I think they may have been left behind to report back to Hugo about us, but that is one communication he will never receive."

"Did you follow his scent?"

"We did. He had the girl with him so he could not just blow away like he usually does."

Victor felt the excitement grow as the possibility of victory skirted his consciousness.

"Right to a house in Orange Park," Artemus continued. "The next day, we entered the house at noon, but although we found four vampires asleep and helpless, Hugo was not one of them. He and the girl had slipped away at some point and we lost them completely."

"Well, at least Marius got some satisfaction. Maybe we can

stand to live around him again."

Artemus looked gravely at Victor. Marius took too much pleasure in his work and he had entirely indulged himself that day, leaving the house in ashes when he was finished.

"It is too late for the girl, Victor," Artemus solemnly pointed out. "She is almost turned."

It was a process to become a vampire, one that could take weeks to complete. It involved the exchange of blood, and often it was accompanied by sensual pleasures that included a variety of vampire vices. According to his inclination, the vampire could prolong the ritual for weeks or simply do the job and have it over with timely precision. Hugo always preferred a long courtship before completing the ritual, prolonging the moment for maximum satisfaction, so while the process was taking place, Abby would be sick, weak from loss of blood, but feverish with new desires. She would be unpredictable right now and possibly dangerous just like Lorna had been.

It had taken Lorna two weeks to make a transformation that could have been done in three days. It looked like Hugo was doing the same thing to Abby.

"I know," he simply said.

"We will treat her no differently than any of the others."

"Yes. No different," Victor agreed.

"Victor?" Artemus said, his voice calling for attention. "If Hugo even *thinks* you have a desire for Emry, he will take her."

Victor didn't say anything, but his face turned ruddy and his nostrils flared with emotion.

"And you know what he will do to her."

Victor's body trembled ever so slightly. "And then we will have to kill her, too," Victor said.

"Can you?"

His eyes swung back to Artemus and they were full of fire.

"Yes. And then you can kill me, too!"

Chapter Seventeen

Kendra arrived at ten o'clock Saturday morning and Emry had to go over the details of her date with Johnny one more time. She was tired of it by then and hoped every time she went out with him it wouldn't require a recital like this.

He called in the afternoon and asked to come over. Kendra went home, but Kaylee stayed and as evening approached, Johnny arrived.

Brad and Beaker were at Casey's and when they saw Johnny's car, the three of them came over. Johnny was disappointed, but Emry found relief in their company. After the repeated telling of her date with him, she was glad she wouldn't have anything to tell.

Jessie arrived a few minutes later. Casey had called her, much to Emry's astonishment, but then she really wasn't all that surprised. After the trip to Anastasia Island, they had been paling around together more than before.

It was like an impromptu party. Brad went to Hall's and came back with drinks and chips and Maggie suggested they order pizza for dinner and everyone stay and eat. Tony's Place was a little Italian restaurant in Bostwick that did delivery and when they arrived with the pizzas, everyone left the porch and went into the kitchen.

Ellen's music was playing on the computer and Beaker

gave her library an intense study.

"Hey, you've got some good stuff here," he commented as everyone ate pizza. "Could I make a playlist?"

Ellen waved a careless hand. "Sure," she agreed.

Soon he had music playing that was to his liking. It was a combination of old and new, classic groups and Alternative music and when he was finished eating, he took Kaylee by the hand and pulled her to her feet, swinging her out into the room for a dance. He and Natalie had already broken up, but the thing between him and Kaylee was just friendship.

The adults quietly slipped away as the teenagers took over the kitchen. Everyone stayed until almost ten o'clock and then one by one, they said their goodbyes.

Kaylee was the first to leave. Mrs. Miller called when she got home early from work and asked her to come home. It was the thing that started the exodus. Brad and Beaker left, then Casey took Jessie home. Only Johnny remained but he left soon after everyone else.

Emry walked to the door with him and she could tell he wanted her to go outside, but she didn't. She stayed at the open door until he was in his car, and then she waved and closed the door.

"That was nice," Maggie said as Emry walked past the living room. The television was on and she and Stanley were watching a movie on DVD.

"Yeah, it was — and unexpected," Emry added.

"Sometimes planning ruins a perfectly good party," Stanley said and Emry smiled.

She looked at them sitting together on the couch, Stanley's arm lying comfortably across the back and around Maggie's shoulders. This was the way it had been before their last argument and the way it should be. She was so glad. It made her feel secure and relaxed, and, she thought, it was the way she wanted her marriage to be one day.

It prompted a thought that suddenly erased the wonderful feeling. With someone like Johnny, this could be her in twenty years, but what about with Victor? She could see nothing when she thought about the future with him. It was like a dark tunnel in her mind and there was no end to it. It just went on forever and forever, a dark abyss that fell into nothing but more darkness. There wasn't even a pinpoint of light in that thought.

It saddened her, but it didn't surprise her. Victor was like an imaginary friend, the ghost in the closet or the playmate that no one could see but her. He wasn't really real.

So why could she do nothing but think about him? She sighed with the weight of this burden. It worried her and she worried about him, but the worrying did her no good. She neither saw nor heard from him the whole weekend. It was enough to drive her crazy. Monday came and school gave some respite to her constant thoughts, but not enough for relief, especially when Kaylee told her that it looked like Abby had left for good. She and Mrs. Miller hadn't seen her since Friday night.

Kaylee was upset, but she wasn't distraught. She seemed almost relieved, but Emry knew that wouldn't last. When things calmed down, she'd feel the loss. Right now, the hurt was just too fresh.

Every evening Emry stood at her window and looked into the night. The moon had begun to fill and the yard was lit up again with images of swans and golden crowned princes. She actually thought she saw her daydream come to life one night as she sat on the floor in front of the window. In this position, the window sill was just high enough she could rest her arms on it, so she folded them and laid her head there, her face turned to the outside.

She must have drifted off, fallen asleep there on the window sill. She saw the swan prince as he landed in her yard, wings stretched wide. His dark head changed to a man as his feet touched the ground and his wings disappeared. He took a few steps on the lawn and his eyes lifted to her window.

And then he was gone and she was waking from the dream and staring with searching eyes at the empty yard below.

It was funny. He had looked like Victor. She probed the darkness of the Balfour's property but all she saw was the lonely light that burned every night from the same window in the old house. She wondered where he was, and she told herself it was because she was worried about him. She had sent him into a situation that may have gotten him hurt, that was all. Curiosity was a great factor, as well. She didn't know what had happened — if anything — with the news she had given Artemus, and she desperately wanted to know.

If only she had met Victor that last time!

But then, there was no use crying over spilled milk. What was done was done, she told herself.

She got up from the window and closed the blinds. She had school again the next day so she took a shower, brushed her teeth, and went to bed.

The next morning, it was raining. It rained all day and then a cool front came through. By Friday morning, the temperature was down in the low fifties. This was Emry's favorite time of year, especially when the cool weather made it feel like fall.

She and Johnny went out again Friday night. When they returned, he stopped the car in the shady part of the driveway, away from the brightness of the moonlight, and when she reached for the door handle, he stopped her.

His hand wrapped around her elbow and he gently pulled her to him. She knew what he wanted and what to expect. He kissed her and with more passion than he had on the porch the weekend before. She returned the kiss, but not with the same enthusiasm. After a couple of minutes, she pulled away and with a nervous laugh, she reminded him that her dad would be coming out with a shotgun if she didn't get inside.

Reluctantly, he opened the door and got out.

When they walked inside, Stanley's eyes went immediately to the clock on the wall. Emry knew what that meant. He had been timing her. She wondered how long was too long to sit in the car before he would come out and get her. Maybe she'd test it one night just for the fun of it.

Crystal met them at the door with a reminder that the community center was hosting a dance for the teenagers again on Saturday night. She wanted to know if Emry would take her. If so, she wanted to invite some friends.

"Sure, I'll take you," she said and then she turned to Johnny. "You wanna come?"

"Yeah," he said without even knowing what he was agreeing to.

"There's just one little problem," Crystal said, screwing her face up as she talked. "Mark needs a ride. Could you *please* go get him? Please!" She prayerfully folded her hands before her.

"Mark Baskins? I thought he was history."

"Are you kiddin'?"

"Well, let me ask daddy. He may not let me go all the way to West River Road late at night and if I pick him up, I'll have to take him home."

"I'll pick him up," Johnny offered. "I drive right past West River Road on the way here."

"Would you? Oh, that would be so cool!" Crystal exclaimed.

"Yeah." He shrugged indifferently. "Why not?"

The high on Saturday was only in the low seventies, but the weather report said the cool snap was only temporary. The temperature was expected to start climbing again on Sunday. Ellen had opened all the windows in the house days before, taking advantage of the cool breezes, but on Saturday she found it necessary to close most of them. Emry didn't close hers. She loved having one less barrier between her and the outside even if it was a transparent one. She stayed in her room nearly all day, cleaning it, then doing homework, and finally just sitting at the computer.

It was an unexpected thing to her that she would be so easily distracted from her old friends. She hardly ever thought about them anymore. She and Stacy kept in touch, but most of the others had drifted into a quiet place in the back of her mind. She thought today would be a good day just to make contact with them, if for no other reason than to keep them alive in her memory. When she finished with that, she looked at the time and realized she should be getting ready for the dance at the community center.

She needed a shower, but Crystal had completely taken over the upstairs bathroom. Emry banged on the door a few times, but Crystal was barricaded inside, preparing herself for the meeting with Mark Baskins, and nothing or no one was routing her out.

Ellen walked to the door of her room and looked down the hallway as Emry exploded a fist on the door.

"Use the downstairs bathroom," she suggested.

"All my things are up here," she complained. She realized how much that sounded like Crystal's whining, and immediately she sighed and then chuckled. "Sure," she said. "I'll use the downstairs bathroom."

"Well," Ellen drawled, looking toward the bathroom as she talked. "Tonight's important to her. She wants to look her best."

Emry walked toward Ellen. "Yeah, but she doesn't need to do anything. She's pretty already."

"Yes, she is," Ellen agreed. "But this boy seems to be special."

"She's only fourteen," Emry pointed out. "No boy was that special to me at fourteen."

"Everyone's different."

Ellen tilted her head and gave Emry a quizzical look. "No boy's that special at seventeen either, I think."

Ellen was thinking of Johnny, but Emry's thoughts went immediately to Victor Balfour. She shrugged one shoulder.

"Maybe not."

She looked past her grandmother and saw that her usually painfully neat room was stacked with old boxes of varying sizes and shapes.

"You gettin' ready for Christmas?" she asked. Ellen turned and followed her line of sight.

"No. Those are some old things I'm goin' through. I thought I'd clean out the downstairs closet and it turned out to be a bigger job than I expected."

"What's in them?" Emry asked and both she and Ellen walked into the room. She looked from one box to the next, fingering the items gently.

"A lotta junk, I think, but some int'restin' things too. I found a whole bunch of old pictures. Most of 'em belonged to your granddaddy's family and I'm sorry to say, I don't know who a lot of the people are in the pictures."

Emry picked up a picture of a woman and a baby. The woman was wearing a dark dress with a long waist and buttons down the front. The dress fell below her knees and she wore stockings and black leather shoes. Her hair was short with finger waves in it.

"Who is this?" Emry asked, seeing that the picture was very old.

"I think that's your great, great grandmother holding

Thomas Winters — your great grandfather. He was my father-in-law."

"Wow!" Emry exclaimed. "This is awesome — Who is this?" she quickly asked, holding up another picture.

"Uh, let me see. I'm not sure. That could 've been Thomas' sister, Belle."

"Oh, Grandma! This is a treasure. I want to look through every one of them."

Ellen chuckled. "That's what slowed down my progress with cleaning out the closet. I've been diggin' through all these pictures all afternoon."

"You should write on the back of them who they are," Emry said as she flipped a picture over and looked at the back side.

"I have with some of them," she said, pointing at the desk in the corner. "I've been takin' 'em over there where the light's better and where I have the desk to press against. I've got a stack for identified and one for unidentified."

Emry looked through them. They were faces to names she had heard spoken of and some that she'd never heard before. She sifted through the stacks and after a few minutes she sat down and made herself comfortable — the shower she planned to take completely forgotten.

Stanley called up the stairs, and Ellen went out to see what he wanted, but Emry continued to flip through the pictures.

She was enthralled. This was history, but more importantly, it was *her* history. After a few minutes, she began to recognize the once unfamiliar faces. This is Margaret Winters, and this is her children, Belle, Thomas, and Martha —

and this is Thomas again — and here he is with his cousins, Ben and John.

And here is Thomas again.

And then, there was a picture, an old picture of two young men. The caption scribbled across the bottom border said, *friends*. It was not Ellen's handwriting — maybe Thomas' own hand, but that wasn't what caught Emry's attention and held her in shock and silence. It was the men in the picture. She knew them. She had seen both of them. They were Artemus and Victor Balfour!

Emry came to her feet and the chair scooted across the wood floor, making an awful sound.

"My God!" she exclaimed. "It can't be."

She turned the picture over and on the back was a date — March 26, 1944. Quickly she turned it over again. She had to be sure she hadn't imagined what she saw, but no, there they were, both of them looking just as they had the last time she had seen them.

"There has to be a reasonable explanation," she said. The Balfours had been here in the forties. Everyone knew that, so this was Victor's great grandfather and great Uncle or something, she told herself. And it was just a freaky coincidence that he and Artemus looked exactly like them.

But Emry couldn't make herself believe it. It was Victor. It looked just like him — and Artemus — the man even had the same tiny beard outlining his perfect jaw line.

Ellen returned just then, walking into the room with a hearty laugh.

"Still at it?"

"Grandma," Emry quickly said. "Who 're these men in this picture?"

Ellen looked and then she shook her head. "Don't know," she said. "It could be those Balfour brothers, seein' as they're good lookin' men." She squinted, and moved the picture to different angles like she was trying to catch a better light. "I never knew anyone had a picture of 'em, though. They were shy about sunlight and pictures, so I've heard." She stopped and chuckled, holding the picture at arm's length for better focus. "Well, I declare," she finally said. "This is somethin', but it's no wonder they got into so much trouble around here. I never saw such handsome men."

Ellen handed the picture to Emry and began talking about other things, but Emry wasn't listening. She was thinking that if this was Victor then he would be eighty or ninety years old now, and that was just impossible.

Not if he was a vampire.

Emry looked down at the picture.

But could you take a picture of a vampire? she asked herself. It wasn't likely. They weren't supposed to reflect an image, and if that was true, then how could film capture their likeness?

No reflection! Huh! Why hadn't she thought to check for Victor's reflection when she had him in the car with her? Come to think of it, she didn't seem to recall seeing even his reflection in the windows.

So, how did Thomas Winters get a snapshot of them?

"You're goin' be late," Ellen said. "Hadn't you better be gettin' your shower?"

"Oh, my shower," Emry sighed.

"You can have the bathroom!" Crystal called out. Emry heard the door to her bedroom bang as she closed it behind her.

"I'm not puttin' 'em away any time soon. You can look at the pictures later. Go get ready for the dance."

Emry nodded and reluctantly laid the picture down. She wanted that picture. She wanted to show it to Victor and ask him who the men were that looked just like him and Artemus. She wanted to hear his explanation.

But, at the same time, she didn't want to hear his explanation. He had explained vampire etiquette to her already and he had done it just a little too expertly.

Emry took her shower and when she went down for dinner, Crystal rushed her through the meal until she hardly ate anything. She was in a hurry to get to the community center, so Emry pushed away from the table and went to her room. She dressed in jeans and a long sleeved blouse, and then she grabbed up a thin cotton jacket before going out.

They arrived at the community center a few minutes later, and Emry was surprised that the parking lot was already lined with vehicles. She pulled in beside Brad's Ford pickup truck and parked. There was no sign of Johnny's car so they had made it ahead of them, much to Crystal's relief.

"Hurry up," Crystal demanded as Emry looked around. She didn't wait, but walked ahead, but Emry caught up with her when she stopped by the main entrance. They walked in together and each paid their dollar and then Crystal went in one direction, and Emry in the other.

The same group of kids was there as the last time, but the seating arrangements had changed. Casey was with Jessie, and Brad was actually giving Kaylee a lot of attention, sitting next to her and picking at her with friendly teasing. Natalie and Ann were at another table all together, and Courtney was with a boy Emry had never met before. His name was Jake. Cindy wasn't even there.

Johnny and Mark came in together a short time later and Courtney made room at their table for Johnny — just as Emry expected.

The music was playing and the lights were low. Couples were dancing, but mostly, everyone was sitting around, talking.

Emry danced once with Johnny and seeing they were together, no one else asked her. They had walked back to the table and were just sitting down when the door swung open and Father Joe walked in. Emry had been expecting him. She knew he always came to these functions.

He made his entrance and the ladies at the admission's table greeted him just as they had before. He smiled politely and clasped his hands together as he slowly walked into the room. Her eyes were following him and that was why she didn't see the door open again.

It swung wide and a man stepped inside, pausing as his eyes adjusted to the new light. One of the women at the admission's table said something and he turned to her, paying his dollar without a word.

His eyes swept the room, but when they fell on Emry they stopped. It was just then that she looked up again.

It was Victor and he was standing at the front of the room, looking at her. He had a pleasant look on his face and he even smiled when their eyes met, but then his eyes slipped past her and floated around the room. Emry wondered what he was looking for.

She glanced around too, but she didn't see anything different than what she had expected. She quickly looked back at Victor and this time, she didn't take her eyes off of him.

He stood there for another minute and then he walked to the side of the room where Father Joe was standing. Emry immediately noticed how smartly he was dressed. It seemed he was dressed differently every time she saw him. There was no pattern to his style. Tonight was no different. He was wearing dark pants and a shirt with a jacket over it. His hair was parted on one side and a few wisps of it fell across his wide brow, almost touching his restless eyes. Emry thought that he had never looked so handsome. She suddenly wished she had taken more care in choosing her own outfit.

She wasn't the only one looking at him. He was attracting attention without even trying, but then Emry had always imagined that he would do that very thing. He was like Abby in that respect. You just couldn't help but look at him.

He was talking to Father Joe. Emry could see his mouth move and his head nod in conversation, but he never really looked at the priest. He watched the room, his eyes falling often on Emry.

But it seemed that Kaylee was his main focus. Emry looked at her, wondering what had made her so popular tonight — first Brad and now Victor.

Kaylee and Brad were laughing when Emry glanced her way. They were grabbing at something on the table, first one person snatching at it and then another. It passed from Kaylee to Brad and then Beaker took hold of it only to lose it to Casey. It flashed silver as his hand closed around it and Emry saw that it was just the metal ring from the top of a soda can. Kaylee leaned across the table and grabbed Casey's fist, but he pulled away and passed the tab to Jessie who held it up like a prize.

Emry smiled at their game and when she looked back at Victor, he was smiling, too.

He seemed to feel her eyes on him, or maybe it was just time for him to look her way again. He did it on a regular basis, but this time, he gave her a lingering look.

She wondered why he had come tonight and what the meaning of his expression was just then. More than anything she wanted to walk across the room and ask him, but she couldn't think of an excuse to do that — although she tried.

One of the women from the admissions table approached him and Father Joe, and Victor's attention turned to her. She said something to the priest and then she shook Victor's hand. Emry had always thought the woman was a little odd, flirting with the priest the way she did. Didn't she understand what holy man of God meant?

And she was much too old for Victor, Emry thought, even though she was giving him the same overly friendly greeting that she had given Father Joe. But then, maybe the woman was just trying to make him feel welcome, and Emry was misinterpreting her motives. She skeptically watched her anyway.

When the woman walked away, Victor's eyes swung back to Kaylee and then carefully slid down the table to Emry. Father Joe said something to him and he nodded in response. She wondered what they were talking about.

The tempo of the music changed, noticeably slowing down and Johnny asked Emry if she wanted to dance again. She felt self-conscious while Victor was watching her, but, of course, she wasn't going to tell Johnny that. Instead she told him she was enjoying hanging out with everyone right then so he let it drop. A minute later, he came to his feet and said something about getting a coke. He stalked off, offended, it seemed.

Father Joe began his usual touring of the room, but Victor didn't go with him. He stood there alone and Emry felt a moment of sorrow for him. No one approached him, although he didn't seem to care.

He was relaxed, carelessly leaning against the wall, but as she watched, he suddenly pushed away from the wall and walked toward the door.

He was leaving.

A feeling of panic hit Emry. She should have been glad he was leaving, she told herself, but she wasn't. She wished she had gone to him and invited him to join her and her friends — wished she had introduced him, let him know she was glad he was here, but she hadn't.

But he didn't leave. He made a turn and walked back into the room, directly toward her. Emry almost held her breath as she watched him approach. He was so cool — so completely composed, but she was beginning to hyperventilate. She took a deep breath and let it out just as he stopped beside her.

"Hello, Emry," he said, just like she knew he would.

He was looking at her, but so was everyone else. All conversation around her had ceased and now, it seemed, everyone was holding their breaths while waiting for her to respond.

"Hi, Victor," she shyly said.

"Will you dance with me?" he asked, and Emry immediately came to her feet.

"I don't dance very well," she warned him as he led her to a spot where the furniture had been pushed back to clear the floor for dancing.

"Neither do I," he said. "But it does not matter. It is just an excuse."

He lied. He was a good dancer. Occasionally, he took a step or two that gave it away, but mostly he kept pace with her, simply moving with the rhythm of the music so she wouldn't feel awkward.

It didn't much matter. She was so stunned by his sudden and unexpected appearance that it took her a while to get her thoughts together. Once it was done, though, all the worrying and wondering she had been doing about what had happened with Van and Abby caused the questions to start tumbling out of her before she realized what she was even doing.

"What happened last week?" she anxiously asked. "Did you find Van? Was he still at Kaylee's? No one got hurt, did they?"

"Sh-h-h-h!" he softly cautioned her, pulling her a little closer and with low voice adding, "Someone will hear you."

She glanced around. Almost everyone in the room was looking at them, including the couples that were dancing right beside them, some of them bumping into each other in their eagerness to watch Victor and Emry.

"Now is not the time to discuss that."

"Then what're you doin' here?" she hoarsely whispered.

He chuckled softly, amused by her directness.

"I came here to annoy your boyfriend," he said with a teasing smile. "It is working, too."

She looked across the room. Johnny had returned to the table and he was staring at them, as stunned as everyone else, it seemed.

She looked back at Victor. "No, really," she said. "What are you *really* doin' here?"

He took a few steps in time with the music before answering. "We need to talk," he said. "You have not made it easy, you know."

She cringed, thinking about the night she had stood him up.

"Sorry about the other night," she apologized, moving closer to him and whispering. "But I've been dying to find out what happened last Friday night."

He pulled her closer, letting his face rest against her cheek so that he could speak softly to her. His warm breath touched her hair and played across the sensitive area around her ear. She wondered if he had any idea what that did to her.

"Nothing. Nothing happened."

Emry didn't realize she had tensed every muscle in her body until they suddenly relaxed. She even sighed with relief.

"Listen to me, Emry," he said. "Never do what you did that night. You know, running out at night to get in touch with me."

She pulled away from him and looked up at his face, hurt in her eyes. "I did it to help you. I thought you would want to know."

"I did, but not at risk to you. That is one of the reasons I am here. If you need me — if you hear anything — call me. I am giving you my cell phone number."

She nodded.

"Here," he said. He reached inside his coat and pulled out a piece of paper that he stealthily slipped into her hand. "You can call anytime, even after we leave."

"You're leaving?" she asked.

"Van is gone. We have to go, too."

"When?"

"Tomorrow night, I think."

Emry felt like someone had just opened a valve that released everything inside her. It drained out and she was left empty, standing there in stunned silence, her mouth open in surprise.

"It has been good," he said and Emry felt his grip relax. He was going to leave.

"Victor!" she said, speaking louder than she had intended.

She wrapped her fingers around his hand, keeping him there. "Please . . ." She begged.

He raised an eyebrow in surprise, but he made no move to leave.

"Please, what?"

"Please don't go without explaining a few things."

He smiled, but his eyes dropped for a second before he looked up again, squarely into her eyes.

"You know, the less you know, the better for you."

"I don't care."

"Well," he hesitantly said. "I am leaving tomorrow."

"Tonight then? Meet me tonight?"

He looked at her as if he couldn't believe what she was saying, but then, she could hardly believe it herself.

"Tonight?"

She nodded.

He didn't answer right away and Emry felt the courage draining out of her, along with everything else that had just spilled out. His eyes were alive with thought and he stared at her with an intensity that caused hers to drop.

They were standing apart, no longer dancing, but he pulled her to him again, and held her very close.

"Very well," he whispered into her ear and her whole body trembled even though she gripped him tightly to steady herself. "You won't change your mind later and not show up?"

She winced at the reminder of standing him up. "No, I promise," she said. "If I can't come, I'll call you."

He was silent again, taking a few steps in time with the

music before speaking.

"I'll wait for you outside your house," he finally said. "After everyone has gone to bed, meet me at that big oak — the one near the back gate."

"Okay," she said, but she was so breathless it was hardly more than a sigh.

He lifted his head and looked behind her, and as he did, a smile crossed his face.

"Your boyfriend has decided to claim you. Here he comes."

Sure enough, Johnny was walking toward them and his face was as dark as a thundercloud.

"I will save you some grief," Victor added. "I was leaving anyway. I will go before he gets here."

"Thanks," she said and he smiled again, this time just for her.

"I will see you later."

Those words pierced her heart. It provoked a sense of anticipation that was full of anxiety, as well. She nodded and he walked away. Johnny arrived only a second behind him and his eyes followed Victor, alive with both victory and contempt.

"Emry," he said, an edge to his voice. "What was that all about?"

She sighed and shook her head. "I'm sure I don't know."

Chapter Eighteen

If she thought she had questions to answer after a date with Johnny, Emry hadn't known anything. Everyone quizzed her about Victor — even the boys.

Kaylee was the first to ask — no, insist on knowing everything. She took Emry by the hand and dragged her to the ladies room and once there, she plied her rapid fire with one question after another.

It hadn't escaped anyone's notice that he was one of the Balfours so when Emry returned to the table, the questions started all over again.

Emry lied — smoothly and easily. She scolded herself, thinking she had picked up a bad habit, and one she was going to have to break one day, but tonight, she assured herself, was not the night to begin. So she lied, deflecting every question as carefully as she could.

Crystal was the last to put her through an interrogation, waiting until they were going home before saying anything. She took advantage of the fact that Emry was behind the steering wheel, driving home, and unable to get away from her. The second the car door closed and the engine roared to life, she began.

"Ohmagosh, Emry!" she exclaimed. "That Balfour guy danced with you tonight! Wasn't he the one we saw at the gas station?"

"Yeah, I think so."

"Well, you're awfully cool after bein' picked out of a crowd — the only one chosen to dance with him."

Emry laughed.

"You're crazy," she said.

"No, you are. What did he say?"

"I don't remember — nothin' much."

"He was doin' a lot of talkin'. I was watchin'. He didn't stop talkin' the whole time y'all were dancing. You were doin' your share of talkin' too."

"I don't know, Crystal," she said with great exasperation. "Lovely night — nice people — you're a lousy dancer — things like that."

"Well, I believe the last part anyway."

"It was small talk. Who remembers small talk?"

"Okay," Crystal said, but she didn't sound convinced. "He knew you. He called you by name."

That got Emry's attention. How many other people would wonder about that? Crystal was the only one to point it out.

"We all know *his* name even though we don't know him."

"I didn't, but you did."

Emry flashed a concerned look at Crystal. This girl was too smart for her age, Emry was thinking.

"Oh, come on. Everyone knows his name."

"No. He's just one of the Balfours. That's what everyone says, but you not only knew his name, but he knew yours. Are you sure there isn't something you want to tell me?"

"Like what?"

"Like how the two of you know each other. Uh, Emry, would you tell me if you were seeing him?"

"No," Emry answered, the first truthful thing she'd said all evening, it seemed.

"Well," Crystal suddenly mused. She stared straight ahead as if thinking. "I wouldn't blame you if you were, but I would be concerned."

"You're crazy!" Emry repeated, wishing she could think of a good argument with which to shut up Crystal.

"You know how everyone says the Balfours are vampires? Well," she said, without waiting for an answer. "He looked like a vampire — all dark and mysterious — and sexy. Did he frighten you? I was a little afraid."

Emry gave Crystal a curious look. Why did she have to ask so many questions?

"No, he didn't frighten me. He's just a guy, Crystal."

Emry turned the Buick into the long driveway and brought it to a stop in its usual spot.

"Uh, Crystal," she said as her sister opened the car door. "Do me a favor. Don't tell daddy I danced with Victor tonight. It'll only upset him."

"You know why, don't you?"

"Yeah, he told me. He doesn't like the Balfours and he doesn't trust them."

"No, that's not it. His grandfather was murdered by one of them."

Emry jerked with surprise. "What? What 're you sayin'?"

"Casey told me. The story goes, he was workin' for them, takin' care of the place after they left. You know, they had to leave in a hurry because Mr. Balfour chopped the head off of some hobo that dropped into town off a train one night." She paused to take a breath and then went on. Emry just stared in stunned silence. "Anyway, he was found dead in their yard — somewhere near the greenhouse. It was believed that Mr. Balfour came back and killed him because he was a witness to the murder of the hobo."

"Why would he do that? He was already gone and they couldn't catch him."

Crystal shrugged. "I don't know, but both witnesses to the murder died shortly after the Balfours left and in the same way."

"Both?"

"Yeah — Clara something or other."

"Kent?"

"You've heard the story."

"No. I was told she was a fiancée to one of the Balfours."

"I don't know about that."

"How did they die?"

"Well, that's the strange thing," Crystal said. "Our great grandfather had cuts and bruises on the inside of his upper arms and Clara had them on her arms and her thighs. The arteries were severed and they had bled to death."

Emry couldn't move. She stared at Crystal in shock and horror. Wasn't that how Victor had explained to her that vampires actually feed?

This was no coincidence. Victor had firsthand knowledge of the method of murder used to kill two people who died back in the nineteen forties, and Ellen had a dated picture from the era of someone who looked just like him.

The piece of paper he had given her with his phone number on it suddenly felt as big as a basketball in her pocket. Involuntarily, she laid her hand on it and pressed against it.

"But that's not the interesting thing," Crystal went on. "Their arteries were cut and they had bled to death, but guess what?"

"There was no blood at the scene."

"Ah, you know," Crystal moaned. "Spooky, huh? Well, I'm goin' in. You comin'?"

"Right behind you," Emry said. "But hold on! You won't say anything, right?"

"My lips are sealed," she promised.

"Thanks."

"Yeah, well, you know it'll cost you. I'll eventually ask for payment."

"Fair enough," Emry said.

It was definitely going to cost her. Emry knew that, but it wasn't Crystal's price that concerned her, it was Victor's. Sooner or later, Emry had a feeling she would find the cost was too high. She hoped it wasn't tonight.

Chapter Nineteen

Emry was having second thoughts.

As one by one, everyone said good night and went to bed, she lost her courage.

More than once, she looked at the tiny piece of paper lying open on the desk beside her, the number written in Victor's own hand, and the daring spirit that had provoked her to set up all this failed her.

She paced her room and wrung her hands, and more than once, she considered calling the number that stared up at her from the paper.

It was long distance. That was the only thing that stopped her. She had no idea how she would explain calling someone at an 828 area code. Where was that anyway?

Ellen was the last one to go to bed. She stopped by Emry's room and spoke to her through the closed door and then she walked down the hallway to her own room. It was time for Emry to start a countdown.

She turned off her light and sat down in the darkness to wait. She was all jumpy inside. The clock on her desk glowed, showing off its red dial. The numbers seemed to get bigger and bigger as time went by.

The wait gave her time to think, and Crystal's story did nothing to ease her anxiety. She knew she should take in account all the evidence against Victor and simply make the call that would end this madness, but Emry struggled with something that was no longer just black or white. It wasn't even gray, anymore. It was complicated.

The very idea of Victor Balfour waiting for her in the darkness was a sensuous thought, and one she couldn't readily get rid of. She knew what was right and she knew what she should do, but she also knew she wanted to see him more than she feared the outcome. It was a sobering thought. She was being driven by desire and need — and she needed to see Victor one last time.

Thirty minutes passed and Emry came to her feet. It was time to either call Victor or sneak out of the house and meet him. It wasn't even a question anymore. Emry picked up her jacket and walked out of the room.

She had never realized how many squeaking boards there were in the house until she tried to walk quietly over them. It seemed like every other step brought a squeak or squawk or some other loud, annoying sound out of the floor. She held her breath and slowly made her way to the front door.

Once outside, she stopped and listened. Far away in the distance, she heard a train whistle and nearer at hand, the sounds of traffic on highway 17, louder at night when everything was still and quiet. The chorus of frogs in the cypress pond sang softly in the cool of the night and an owl hooted from the top of a tree in Jim's yard. When she stepped onto the grass, it crunched under her feet and swished with each step. She never noticed the sound in the daytime, but it was remarkably pronounced in the night.

The moon was bright, but Emry couldn't see under the shadow of the oak tree. Was Victor there? She imagined him leaning against the trunk of the tree, his arms folded across his chest and his dark eyes watching her while at the same time his perfect lips turned up into a crooked smile, but when she stepped under the spreading limbs, he was nowhere to be seen.

Emry was disappointed, and then she was scared. The night was suddenly a frightening place.

She never heard his footsteps, only his voice as he spoke from behind her.

"You came," he said, and Emry turned with a little gasp of surprise. It was the first time he had failed to address her with his usual greeting. "I did not believe you would."

"I almost chickened out," she admitted.

"I am glad you didn't — chicken out, I mean."

He cautiously looked over his shoulder and then without another word, he took her hand and began leading her away.

"Where're we goin'?" she asked.

"Someplace you cannot be seen from the house. Just in case someone looks out."

He walked as far as the back gate and then he stopped. Beyond the fence and about thirty feet away, Emry could see the shiny outline of his Jaguar.

"This should do it," he said.

He leaned his back on the gate and Emry did the same.

"So," he began, "Did your boyfriend forgive you?"

"For what?"

"For refusing him and then dancing with me."

How did he know that?

"Johnny has no legal claim to me. I can dance with whomever I please."

Silence.

"So, did he forgive you?"

"Yeah, he forgave me."

Silence again.

"Well, Emry," he said after an awkward minute, "What was it you wanted?"

Now, that was a loaded question. She imagined he didn't want to know what she really wanted. But then, she didn't know what she really wanted either. She knew she had wanted to see him before he left. She knew she wanted to know what had happened at Abby's the week before and she wanted some answers to who and what he really was, but she wanted something more from him and she was too confused about her feelings to put it into words.

She shivered. The night was chilly and the breeze even chillier. She wrapped her arms around herself and wished for a warmer jacket.

"Some answers," she said. "And I've been wantin' to know what happened about Van and Abby."

He seemed to contemplate that, not saying anything right away. His head was down, his chin very close to his chest, but he looked up before answering. She could see his face quite clearly in the moonlight and she thought he looked angry. Why, she couldn't imagine.

"Nothing happened. When they got there, Van was gone."

"They?" she asked. *As opposed to we?* Perhaps this was the reason her question upset him. "You didn't go?"

"No," he simply said.

She considered that, thinking of all the trouble she'd gone through to get word to him.

"Why not?"

"I was not here. I had gone — away," he said, stumbling over the last of his words. "I had something to sort out. It took me a few days."

"Business?"

"No, it was personal."

What does that mean? A girl, perhaps?

Well, why not? He was so handsome; surely he had a girl somewhere. Curiously, Emry didn't like the way that thought made her feel. She beat it out of her mind, stuffing it with mental fists and then stomping it, mentally drop kicking it to obscurity.

She shivered again.

"Are you cold?" he asked and she nodded. He was wearing the same clothes he had worn at the dance, but he seemed perfectly comfortable.

"Aren't you?"

"No. I don't get cold."

"Not ever?"

"No."

"Why not?"

"I just don't," he said. He gave her a careful study as if

trying to decide what to do with her. He pushed away from the gate and stepped in front of her, taking her hands in his. The move filled Emry with expectations. His hands were warm and they touched her with a caress that was more than just testing the temperature. He ran his hand up her arm and he laid it against her cheek.

"You are cold," he stated, plainly surprised.

Not any more, she thought. She was clearly on fire.

"I don't want you to catch a chill," he said. He brushed a loose strand of hair away from her face — the same one he always found. He had one too — one that fell across his wide brow, almost touching his eye. She wanted to move it back, run her hands through his hair, and test the temperature of his skin just like he did hers, but she lacked the confidence. She actually felt afraid at the very thought of reaching up to him.

Not that she was afraid of him. She'd gotten past that. She was afraid he wouldn't like it. She wanted him to like it, but she was afraid he wouldn't.

"What are you thinking?" he softly asked and she lifted her eyes up to his. There was something extremely pleasing about the tone of his voice, something that set her heart to racing.

When she didn't answer he smiled. "You looked like you were a million miles away in thought."

"I was," she said.

"Tell me what you were thinking."

She experienced a second of panic. To hide it, she nervously laughed. "I'm curiously wondering about you and your family," she said — not entirely a lie. "Before you leave, will you tell me what you are — what you really are?"

"What do you think we are?" he asked. He'd asked that question before, but this time it wasn't scary or threatening. It was just a simple question, but he hovered nearer and she felt his presence — so warm, so tangible. It caused her to shiver again.

As she paused in thought, he softly chuckled.

"So, you still think I am a vampire," he said.

"If you can read my mind, why did you ask me what I was thinkin'?" she asked and he laughed.

"I cannot read your mind per se, but it is obvious what you are thinking."

"It's what I'll continue to think until you give me another explanation," she said.

"I tell you what," he said, dropping his hands from her face and taking her by the wrist.

She anxiously looked up as he pulled her to him, but his intentions weren't what she had thought — or hoped. She saw it in his eyes, knew what he was planning, even before he said it.

"I will see to it that you simply forget all this and the problem will be solved," he said.

She jerked her hands away from him like he had burned her.

"No," she said as she wrenched herself free of him. "Don't do that. It's what you did that night in the park, isn't it? You made me forget — somehow you made me forget." She took a step away from him and he made no attempt to stop her. "I was in the park with you and the next thing I remember I was waking up in my room, in my own bed, and my broken car was in the driveway, running perfectly."

"I took you home," he said, admitting it, at last. "I saw you as far as your door and then I waited until I was sure you were safely inside . . . And Marius fixed your car. He is a good mechanic."

"Why don't I remember?"

"Because I did not want you to remember. We had a scuffle with vampires right in front of you and I did not think it was wise to let you remember."

"You should've wiped my whole memory clean then."

"No," he said, smiling derisively. "I did not want to do that. I wanted you to remember . . . me." He turned and put his back to the gate again. "My mistake."

Neither of them said anything for what seemed like a long time. Emry felt the awkwardness of the moment and wished she could ease it someway.

"Well, if that is it," Victor finally said, "I have a lot to do."

He pushed away from the gate. It looked like he was ready to go.

"You haven't explained a thing," Emry said, shivering again.

"You are cold. You should go home."

She looked around. "Could we sit in your car?" she asked. "Out of the wind, it'd be warmer."

He cast a glance over his shoulder. The jaguar was a dark outline on the overgrown path.

"And you did promise me a ride," she reminded him. "It'd

be the next best thing."

He smiled. "So I did," he admitted. He turned completely around so that the path to his house was before him. "We can do that — even though my better judgment tells me to send you home."

He helped her over the old gate and then he vaulted it with one easy movement. They walked side by side as he led her to the car.

"Wow," she said as she stood beside it. "This is a beautiful car."

Casey had told her it was a XJL Supersport, available by special order only. He also went into details about the 510 hp engine and other technical things she didn't quite understand. He had spoken with reverence and awe. All she knew was, it was one heck of a nice car.

Victor opened the door and she quickly sat down inside. No lights came on inside or out except at her feet. The treadplate illuminated in Phosphor Blue, which was a little eerie. At first, Emry couldn't see anything, but as her eyes adjusted, she looked around.

The seats were leather and separated by a fancy console with wood trim and as she half expected, not a thing was out of place. There was something lying on the back seat, but she couldn't see what it was. It was long and dark, a tight bundle that took up half the seat. Overhead was a panoramic roof that she looked through all the way to the sky.

Victor opened his door and gracefully slid inside.

"Is this better?" he asked and she nodded even though she

was still a little cold. He touched a button that reclined his seat just a little and then he turned and looked at her. Emry felt self-conscious again. When he looked directly at her, it always disconcerted her. "Well, Emry. Now is your chance," he said when she didn't say anything.

"Is it?" she asked, surprised that he hinted he would answer her questions.

"Yes," he said. "You want to know who I am. I will tell you. I am really Victor Balfour, and the others are really my family. Stefan is my father. Artemus is my brother and Marius is my adopted brother. We are who we say we are."

"Not who you are, Victor — what you are. You can't be human — you aren't human," she tentatively added. "I know it."

He gave her a curious look and she dropped her eyes, unable to look at him.

"What makes you say that?"

"Well, you aren't, are you?"

"Not anymore," he admitted. "But I am curious how you know it."

"Well, for one thing, I have a picture. It's of you and Artemus. You're sitting in a room with books on a shelf, like a library. My great grandfather took it March 31, 1944."

At first his eyes narrowed and she thought he was angry, but then he smiled, and then his smile turned into a laugh.

"Why, that sneaky fellow," he said. "I thought I destroyed all his film. I guess I missed one."

"So, you *were* here back in the forties." She squinted into the darkness of the car, trying to see him better. "How old are you? A hundred?"

"No," he quickly answered, just like he always did when she felt he was lying to her.

"But it *is* you in the picture."

"Yes."

"Then you're what — eighty? Ninety?"

"No," he quickly said again. He wasn't smiling anymore and Emry could see he didn't like the subject. "I am more than two hundred years old," he finally said, answering her question even though it was plain he didn't want to. "I was nineteen when I became one of The Strangers."

Nineteen? Yes, he looked it. He must not have changed at all since then.

"The Strangers?" she said.

He chuckled again. "Yes. You have at last brought me to the truth," he said, his voice full of irony.

"But what is that?"

He glanced across the car at her. Suddenly he wanted to tell her. It would be a relief to say it — to get it out in the open. Besides, he could take care of it later. When she left to go home, she wouldn't remember a thing. He would see to that.

He reached forward and put his hands on the steering wheel.

"We have been called many things — prophets and wizards — sometimes angels. I have even been called the devil, and maybe that isn't so far from the truth."

He sounded weary — tired to the bone, but he was talking, telling her at last.

"I am one of the Peregrinias — one of The Strangers. I will never belong anywhere now, no matter where I go. It is part of the curse."

Emry felt herself tremble. She was suddenly afraid — not of him, but for him, and for herself. With every word he said, she saw clearly what she had suspected all along. He was the elusive fantasy, the boy in a dream world, the boy who couldn't be a part of her life no matter what. He didn't seem real — maybe he wasn't real.

"What does that mean?" she asked, her voice hardly above a whisper. He glanced at her and then away again, over the steering wheel and down the dark path that led to the gate.

"It means, my life has one purpose and one purpose only. I cannot deviate from that course, no matter what." He briefly paused. "Are you afraid of me, Emry? You have come here tonight, alone, in the dark, to meet me, but aren't you at all afraid of me?"

"Sometimes," she admitted.

"Sometimes?" He chuckled softly. "Are you afraid of me now?"

"Should I be?"

"You should have some fear in you — or, perhaps, I should say, caution in you. It can be a dangerous thing to be without it."

"You've never tried to hurt me."

"No," he said with a little shake of his head. "But I could. That is the thing — I could." He looked back at her. "I know you have probably wondered, but I have not been stalking you."

"I haven't wondered. I never thought that."

"I have been looking out for you. Whether you want to believe me or not, Emry, there are things in this world that no one can save you from but me."

"Vampires, you mean."

He gave her his full attention, looking straight into her eyes. "I know you do not believe me, but, yes, vampires — now, do not give me that look," he said as she sighed heavily.

"No, I know," she said, thinking how she would have scoffed at this just a couple of months before. She had sighed only with the weight of this information. "I don't understand, but I believe you." She anxiously looked at him. "And you — tell me the truth. You're one, aren't you?"

He became very still and Emry waited for his answer, her heart in her throat.

"Unfortunately, I had to become what I destroy in order to destroy it. But, no. I am not a vampire — not anymore, that is."

"I don't understand. You *were* a vampire?"

He turned in his seat again, the leather making a noise as he shifted position.

"Something like that," he evasively said. "I had to have the power to kill my enemy. That is what this is all about. I am hunting a vampire — a specific vampire. He has gone by the name of Hugo Von Norrington. You know him as Van Norris."

Emry nodded. She knew that was what Victor was going to say. "Abby's Van," she flatly stated.

Victor nodded. "Yes. She is not the Abby you knew anymore. There is no hope for her now."

"You mean . . ." Her voice trailed off as she considered exactly what Victor was saying. It was so bizarre she could hardly comprehend — but she did. "That explains everything, doesn't it?" she sadly said.

"It does."

She wagged her head in dismay. "Are you sure?"

"I am sure. I have been at this for almost two centuries." He paused to wearily shake his head. "Yes, Emry, I am very sure."

"What are you, then? A vampire slayer?"

"I am not Buffy, if that is what you think," he said. "Nor Angel, either," he added.

No, that wasn't what she thought and she shook her head to let him know.

"I told you. I am one of the Peregrinias," he said. "We are called 'The Strangers'."

"What is that? A cult? I don't understand."

"No," he said. He frowned, but it was not a frown of disapproval. It was the look of a man trying to find the right words to explain something he couldn't explain. "And you will never understand." He gave her that frank, square in the eyes look that only he could do. It was one that always made her draw back away from him. "That is why I do not want to tell you. Let us just part as friends and you remember me as the friendly — but strange — man who lived next door to you for a while."

"I didn't mean to call you strange," she said and it eased the tension for a few seconds.

"No offense taken," he said. "I am a little strange," he admitted. He looked away from her again. "That is my point," he added.

Emry looked at him with new eyes. She didn't think of him as strange, at all — not anymore, anyway. In fact, she loved him, although she was trying very hard not to admit that.

"Look, it is getting late," he said. "Let me walk you home."

For an answer, she asked, "Will you at least explain to me about Van — Hugo, I mean? He's a vampire, right?"

Victor didn't say anything. He was silent for so long that Emry moved restlessly, shifting position to ease her discomfort.

"Yes," he finally answered. "But he is not a normal vampire. He is more intelligent and stronger and he has human-like characteristics that make him very dangerous. He thinks with the mind of a psychopath but he has the power to do whatever his twisted mind dictates. That is what makes him so dangerous."

"Why is he different?" she asked.

"He just is," Victor simply answered. "And I do not want to talk about it."

"Okay," Emry agreed. "What about you? When you were a vampire, were you like Van — and how did you stop being one? I thought it was irreversible."

"It is," he said.

That took her back. Unless he was contradicting himself, then he was a vampire. She wanted to ask, but he began talking and she didn't interrupt him.

"We have finally become friends," he said, giving her a wan

smile, "And I was hoping we could leave it at that, but I see we cannot. I am going to tell you a story, and I imagine I will not have to beg you to go home once you hear it."

She gave him an anxious look, but he didn't notice. He wasn't looking at her. His attention was focused on something far away — a thousand-yard stare, as the saying goes.

"It is a long story," he began. "I had a sister once. Her name was Lorna." He briefly smiled at what appeared to be a pleasant memory, but the smile quickly faded and was gone with his next statement. "She met a man named Demetrius. We did not know he was a vampire. We did not know a lot of things back then." He sounded bitter, but maybe it was just his solemn mood. "But Demetrius was not just any vampire. He was very old and very strong and he turned Lorna just like Hugo has turned Abby." It was hard for him to continue, but he did after a short pause.

"We would probably have simply let her go if things had turned out differently," he said. "I don't know, though." He wagged his head as he remembered. "It is hard to say now what we would have done. You see, Emry, Lorna killed our mother."

Emry caught her breath, but otherwise, she did not interrupt him. It took him a minute to compose himself, but when he spoke again, it was with a kind of detachment.

"We went after them, but we were babes in the woods," he said and this time there was no mistaking the disappointment and the sorrow in his voice. "I lost four brothers over the next three years and still we did not even come close to getting to Demetrius and Lorna." He paused again and Emry patiently waited until he went on with his story.

"But it was then we found a man. He was a monk — Cavanaugh was his name, and to say he was a unique individual would have been an understatement. He was a teacher, and one of the Peregrinias — the first, in fact. He promised us that we would have our revenge and he was right. He taught us and he trained us and he put us through something that no man should aspire to, but we were full of a desire for revenge and nothing on this earth could have kept us from following him."

He looked directly at Emry. It was the first time since he had begun his story and Emry felt the full impact of his gaze. "I am what I am by choice and in all honesty, I do not really regret it."

"Are you sure?" she asked and he smiled dubiously.

"There was a time," he said, his tone wistfully pensive, "when we were invited into towns and villages, homes, palaces, and even sanctuaries. But over the years, things have gradually changed. Modern civilization has forgotten the horrors of the creatures that inhabit the night. We have become no more than legend — or fairy tale. What I do is no longer looked upon with approval, but frowned on in disbelief and condemnation. The Strangers are no longer understood or tolerated, but we continue our work anyway, even though, when I kill a vampire, I am a murderer and not a savior. Sometimes I regret that."

"Are there others like you?"

"A few. Far too few to be effective, I am afraid."

"Are there a lot of vampires?" she asked, suddenly curious about the balance of power between the two factions.

He shrugged. "Enough to keep us busy," he said.

She looked outside the car, scanning the dark yard. She was afraid and she had never been afraid of the dark before.

"Do not worry," he said as if he could read her mind. "They are gone. What we do not kill usually pulls out of an area very quickly. Vampires are transient, moving a lot. They have no feeling of permanency so they do not feel the need to defend an area. When threatened, they usually just leave."

Emry considered that and thought that it sounded just like Victor and his family. They moved constantly. They felt no permanency, either.

"So where is Van and Abby?" Emry asked and Victor shook his head.

"We do not know. We have lost him again for the hundredth time." He sounded angry—no, bitter. "His luck cannot hold out forever, though. One day, I will get him."

"So, that's why you're leaving. It's all about killing Van."

For a moment he said nothing. Emry wished she could see his face, study the expression in his eyes and possibly read something there, but she couldn't.

"What can I say?" he finally answered. "It is my raison d'etre."

"What does that mean?" she asked, unfamiliar with the phrase.

"It is what I was created for — my reason for being."

"So, you were created to kill vampires?"

"Yes. That basically sums it up."

"But if you were a vampire . . ."

"Yes, then I had to begin with myself," he said. "But enough has been said. No more tonight, Emry."

"But your heart beats," she said. "I felt it — unless it was some kinda trick."

"It was no trick. It beats and if it stops beating, I am dead, but that is all I am going to say."

"But—"

"No more, Emry. Drop it."

The tone of his voice set her back although it was full of impatience rather than harshness. It hurt her just the same.

She jutted out her bottom lip in a little moue of offense and Victor was quick to respond.

"Now, now," he said. "Don't take offense. I just cannot say anymore, understand?"

She made no attempt to speak so he reached across the car and cupped her chin in the palm of his hand. Very gently, he ran his thumb across her protruding bottom lip.

"Do not pout," he said. "Let us not part on a sour note."

That did it. The mention of him leaving caused her to pull in her lip and anxiously look at him. She didn't want him to go — not ever.

"We need to say our goodbyes," he went on to say, "and you need to go home and forget we ever met. That is the safe thing to do."

Forget him? Emry knew she would never forget him — unless he made her.

"You keep trying to get rid of me. I guess that means you didn't really want to meet me tonight. You're just humoring me."

He chuckled softly, but derisively. "What I want, Emry, does not matter. What I do is what I have to do, but, saying that, I will say, yes, I wanted to see you."

"Will you ever come back?" she asked.

"Not likely."

"What about the old house? Will you sell it?"

"No. I imagine we will keep it. It is a good base."

"Then you might come back."

He clenched his teeth. Emry saw the outline of his jaw as it tightened, then his eyes slowly moved to hers and when he spoke, he was looking right into her eyes.

"Not in your lifetime," he carefully said, the meaning stark and plain.

Emry began to shake. She knew what he was saying. He would live forever, but she would grow old and die, and he had no intentions of coming back until after she was gone.

"Oh," was all she could say. She trembled again. It was cold — she was cold, but she wasn't sure if it was from the weather or from his icy response.

But Victor saw her shiver and he carefully touched her again, testing the temperature of her skin with the back of his hand.

"You are freezing," he scolded her. "You should have told me."

He put his foot on the brake and then pressed a button that brought the Jaguar to life. Immediately, the car filled with music and Victor quickly turned the volume down before reaching for the heater controls.

"Sorry," he apologized while adjusting the dials. Emry's seat began to radiate heat and a blower at her feet pushed warm air that drifted up to her.

"Better?" he wanted to know and she nodded.

"What are you listening to?" she asked, meaning the song that was now only a whisper in the background. It was actually a rhetorical question. She knew the song. It was a group that played Indie music. She just couldn't imagine him knowing it. "I'm surprised. I didn't expect you to listen to that kind of music."

"What kind did you expect me to listen to — Gothic rock?"

She laughed.

"Bach . . . classical, I guess."

He touched the media system. Immediately the song disappeared and changed to soft piano — Arabesque by Debussy.

"You mean like this?" he asked, and Emry smiled again.

"Yeah. Just like that."

The music brought an immediate change to the atmosphere inside the car. They could've been just two normal people sitting together, enjoying each other's company. Emry imagined that's the way it was and she smiled with the thought while she listened to the music.

"I like this," she said. "I've always wished I could play the piano, but I never wanted to do the work required to learn. I guess I really didn't want to learn that badly."

He turned his head. "It is a commitment, but one well

worth doing."

"Do you play?"

"Not the piano," he said, but he offered no alternative instrument.

"But you do play something?"

"I took violin lessons for many years," he said and Emry looked at him with raised eyebrows.

"I'm impressed. And surprised. I love the sound of the violin."

"Really? I didn't expect you to listen to that kind of music," he said, mocking her, and then they both laughed.

Emry did not have to imagine anymore. At that moment they were just two normal people — a boy and a girl, sitting alone — together in his car, listening to music in a very normal way.

"Let me play something for you," he said and he changed the player again. A song began. It was a haunting tune, full of minor notes, played by a violin and accompanied by a piano. He turned up the volume and the music seemed to fill Emry. She laid her head against the soft, embossed leather headrest and closed her eyes.

It was a beautiful song that began subtly and grew in expression. Soon the violin and the piano were joined by drums. It affected her deeply, stirring up an emotion in her that left her with a strange longing and at the same time, a contentment. She opened her eyes and looked up at the sky. She couldn't explain how she felt. It was overwhelming but at the same time, delicately suggestive like the gentle touch of a lover's hand.

"Beautiful," she whispered as the song ended. "What is it?"

He shrugged. "Just something a friend recorded for me."

"Oh?" She lifted her head and looked at him. "It's not you, is it?"

He chuckled. "No," he adamantly said. "It is not me."

She laid her head back again. "Play it again." she whispered.

He did.

It all seemed so normal . . .

The song ended and Emry turned her head so that she was looking at Victor. His seat was partially reclined and his head was resting against the headrest. He was looking up to the dark sky above with a wistful expression.

"So, Victor," she said, prompted by his appearance. "You've talked about obligation and responsibility, but what do *you* want?"

His eyes widened as if her question startled him and he raised his head as he turned and looked at her. An amused smile touched his lips and he laid his head down again.

"Hmmm," he mused, his eyes squinted in mock concentration. "World peace, of course."

Emry laughed.

"That is my unselfish, unmaterialistic desire," he lightly said. "A yacht would be nice — very materialistic, though — not a real big one, just one large enough to be comfortable, but small enough to handle alone."

"Alone? No room for guests?"

"One guest," he amended.

It was a romantic idea. Too bad she couldn't do it even if she was invited. She had a fear of deep water and she got seasick at the drop of a hat — or an anchor.

"You're full of surprises," she said. "I never pictured you as the sun loving type."

"Have you ever seen the moon as it rises out of the water, casting a line of silver light across the surface of the sea? It is beautiful — and peaceful. Who needs the sun?"

"Oh," she said, and he cast a glance across the car at her.

"But I can tolerate the sun. It will not hurt me," he said. "Even if I do not like it."

"Oh," she said again, wishing she had something better to say in response.

He reached across the car and touched her cheek with his hand. He was testing the temperature of her skin and this time he seemed pleased with the results.

"All nice and warm," he lightly said, but then his voice changed and with a more serious note he added, "Time for you to go home."

She threw a startled look across the car at him. She didn't want to go.

"A minute more," she begged, and he smiled, but it was a wry smile. There really wasn't any humor in it.

He leaned across the car and for just one breathtaking, heart-stopping moment, Emry thought he was going to kiss her. But he didn't. All signs of normalcy were suddenly gone.

"There is no reason to put it off," he said, speaking softly, almost in a whisper. "The time has come for you to go home and for you to forget all this."

"Don't make me forget," she begged him. "I won't tell anyone about you."

He studied her face. His mind was working. Emry could see it in his eyes.

"Well," he finally said as if humoring her, "we will talk about it at the gate. Come on. I will walk you home."

Reluctantly she got out of the car. He turned off the Jaguar and got out too, walking to the front of it and standing there while she dragged her feet about leaving. She wished she could think of an excuse to stay with him a little longer. She looked behind her at the dark spot that was the old house and she wondered if she could talk him into taking her inside.

"Victor..."

"What?"

"Could I see inside your house? I've always wanted to."

"Inside my sanctuary?" he facetiously asked, giving her a grin. "I do not think that is a good idea."

"Why?"

"Just trust me. It is not a good idea."

"Do you sleep in a coffin or somethin'?"

He laughed out loud. "No. I sleep in a very large bed with down pillows." The tone of his voice suddenly changed. "And maybe that is the reason why it is not a good idea."

He took her hand and pulled her down the path, hurrying her along.

"You let my great grandfather in," she reminded him, in

spite of his oddly suggestive statement.

"Yes, well, he was not a pretty young girl now, was he?"

They were at the gate by then and without warning, he swept her up in his arms and bodily set her over the gate. She gave a little shriek of surprise, but she was on her feet before she had time to appreciate the moment. He vaulted the gate and came to stand beside her.

"It is time, Emry," he said, and she knew what he meant. It was time to forget.

"Not yet," she begged and he sighed.

"You have to go," he said. "And it is better this way."

She didn't say anything and he patiently waited.

"How do you do it?" she finally asked.

"What?"

"Make me forget. How do you do it?"

"It is one of my gifts."

"One of them?"

His body jerked as if her question was a pin that had pricked him. "Or one of my curses," he said.

"Why do you say that?" she asked. "It would be wonderful to have magical gifts."

He put his hands behind himself and leaned back on the gate against them. She heard the sound of old wood taking his weight.

"If I could give them up and the world be normal, I would," he admitted. "I do not regret my decision to be one of The Strangers, but at the same time, it would not make me unhappy to be just a normal man." He turned to her. "It will never happen. As long as there are creatures like Demetrius and Hugo, I will be glad that I am here to stand between them and the innocent." He touched Emry's cheek as if he meant her.

"Could you if you wanted to?" Emry asked.

"What? Go back? Be what I was before this? No. There is no going back."

She could see his face in the moonlight. He looked sad — or maybe just wistful. She was not quite sure.

"I had a dream about you," she suddenly said and his head came up in interest.

"About me?"

"Yes. You were one of the swans in a childhood fairytale my mother once read to me."

He chuckled as if that amused him. "The ugly duckling?" he asked.

Ugly? Him? He had to be kidding.

"No," she said. "It's a story about seven brothers who were cursed by a wicked witch. During the day they were beautiful swans, but when the sun set, they became men again."

He carefully looked at her, very quiet and very severe.

"I dreamed you were a black swan and you flew in and landed right over there on this lawn and as your feet touched the ground, you turned into a man again."

"You dreamed this?" he asked.

Emry had expected him to laugh or at least to chuckle, but he was serious as if the dream had meaning to him.

"Yes. I fell asleep with my head on the window sill and I dreamed I awakened and I saw a swan fly into the yard and land. When he looked up at my window, he looked like you." He did not say anything so she carefully added, "I thought you'd be amused."

He looked at her. "I am," he said, but he did not sound as if he was amused. He sounded troubled.

"Well, it was only a dream," she said with a shrug.

He looked away and suddenly Emry felt an odd barrier come up between them. She didn't know why, but the subject of her dream seemed to have built an impregnable wall between them — or maybe it was just all the information they had been sharing. Emry supposed that was more likely. Each piece of information had been a brick laid into a growing wall that was now so high she could hardly see over it. Soon he would be completely cut off from her and that was the thing that frightened her — that, and the fact they were as far apart on an evolutionary scale as people were from ants.

It made him rather untouchable, even without the wall. There was something sacrosanct and inviolable about him, but curiously, that made her wonder why he had teased her and flirted with her all along. From the very beginning, he had touched her with premeditation and had spoken using words with inflections that were meant to provoke her. Even as naive as she was, she could read the signs.

Maybe that was how demigods amused themselves, she thought.

She knew that was all she could be to him — an amusement or a temporary distraction. He knew it too — better than she did — but she figured he didn't have anything to lose like she did. He would amuse himself and move on — live forever, perhaps, and have a million distractions like her, but she would fall in love, get a few broken hearts here and there, and then, she would grow old and die — if she was lucky.

She heard the wood of the old gate release Victor's weight and she gave a start, knowing what was coming, but not ready for it. She took a step away from him and he reached for her, pulling her back.

"Walk me to the tree first," she begged him.

"Here — there — what difference does it make?"

"I don't know, but I feel it will make a difference."

He ponderously shook his head back and forth, clearly amused with her.

He was smiling and when he smiled, he was so very attractive. He held her by the wrists, holding on as if he thought he would lose her otherwise. He had pulled her very close to him, and she was looking up, thinking that it would be so easy to kiss him. All she had to do was push up to her toes and tilt her head back and she could kiss those perfect lips before the opportunity was gone forever. It didn't matter to her at that moment whether or not she was just a distraction. She wanted to do it more than she wanted anything. She felt her whole body tighten with anxious anticipation, but, oddly, tonight, she was not too afraid to do it.

She eased forward, her heels leaving the ground as her weight shifted to the balls of her feet. She seemed to grow taller and his face grew closer to hers, his lips within easy reach.

Her lips touched his, but he did not kiss her back. In fact, he stood as still as a statue. His grip tightened around her wrists, and then very carefully, slowly even, he pulled her away from him.

He shook his head. "No, Emry," he hoarsely whispered. "I cannot do that."

He couldn't — couldn't what? Kiss her, love her — make love to her? What?

She felt foolish — embarrassed too. Why did he flirt with her and tease her if he had no intentions of going any further? His words struck her with curious effect. She was thinking more about them than she was the humiliation she felt at his rejection.

She didn't know it, but he was struggling with something much larger than their tiny wants and needs. He knew he had provoked her to this and now he regretted it. It was just that his feelings had provoked him, as well, and he had not always been able to restrain his temptations. He knew, though, that if he gave in to her, even the slightest bit, it would prove to be his undoing. He could not just kiss her and walk away — but he had to walk away. He had to let her go. He could not — would not kiss her.

"Oh," she sighed and his hands slowly released her.

"It is time for you to go home," he roughly said. He sounded angry and she did not want to leave him this way — angry at her — or on a sour note, as he had put it.

"Don't be mad at me," she said. "But if you expect me to say I'm sorry — well, I can't."

"No," he said, more compassionately. "I am not angry with

you. I opened that door. I should not have."

Yes, he had, but what did she say to that?

He suddenly smiled. "I'm glad you kissed me," he said. "I really am. If things were different . . . well . . . they are not," he sadly added. "Maybe now, we can move on."

"Okay," she said, but she did not regret what she had done. Even if he had not kissed her back, it had been a wonderful thing to place her lips on his. At least she had that memory — if he didn't take it away from her. "I guess I'll go home then," she said, resigned at last.

"Good," he said, but oddly, it was he who hesitated. After a brief pause, however, he began walking, pulling her along toward the big oak tree, hurrying once he had begun moving.

He stopped at the edge of the shadow cast by the moon. The tree limbs were just above his head and he paused there, pulling her forward until she was completely under the outstretched arms of the old tree.

"Look at me, Emry," he softly said. She had her head down, her countenance grim as she waited for him to erase her thoughts of him, but when he spoke, she looked up and into his eyes. "Everything is going to be fine. I want you to trust me."

She nodded. "Okay," she mechanically said.

He paused and Emry read the hesitation in his expression. His hand was touching her. She had always imagined he needed the contact to make his magic work, but for the first time, she realized that he was actually reluctant to make her forget.

"Let me remember you," she whispered as his grip tightened.

"I will," he promised.

He said something else, but Emry didn't quite hear it or maybe she just didn't understand. She closed her eyes, tensing with expectation, waiting for the feeling of flight to come over her.

But she didn't feel as if she was flying. In fact, nothing was the same as it had been before when he had made her forget. She opened her eyes and saw that Victor was not even looking at her. She felt his body tense as a branch in the old oak tree began to tremble.

Something growled overhead and he pushed Emry, turning to shield her even as the limb shook and something leaped forward, screeching as it escaped.

It was only the barn cat. Baby did not like Victor. His appearance under her resting place had upset her and sent her into flight, but not before she had arched her back and with a hiss had screeched like a banshee, jumping from the limb with such energy that the whole branch had violently shaken.

Both Victor and Emry quickly realized it was only the cat, but even as they recognized her for what she was, a chain of events had been set into motion that they could not stop. Victor turned, pushing Emry as he put himself between her and what he had imagined was danger. Emry stepped back, losing her balance as Victor made his turn and she stumbled over the root of the tree. She clawed at the air, reaching for anything that would keep her from falling and it was Victor's jacket that she finally got a hold on.

It did not give her the support she needed, but instead, it

pulled away from him, causing her to continue to fall.

It all happened in a split second. The cat jumped to the ground and ran away and Emry fell. Victor was not a second behind her.

They lay very still for a stunned moment and then, they both began to laugh.

A mild expletive escaped Victor's lips. "That stupid cat," he exclaimed. "Shit! She scared me."

They lay with their backs on the soft dry grass, laughing as they looked up through the tangle of tree branches, but it was Victor who first stopped laughing. The humor went out of the situation and he pushed himself up and turned on his side, looking down at Emry. He was struck with a deeper feeling than he cared to admit. She was very appealing lying there beside him — no, she was more than appealing. She was irresistible. The memory of her kiss was suddenly a fuel that fed his desire. He told himself to get up and to pull her to her feet, but he was tempted beyond reason. He didn't want to get up and he definitely didn't want her to get up. He did not even call on his reserves for resistance. They were spent, anyway. There was no more reasoning power left either, but at that moment, he didn't really care. Every reason abandoned him and he simply threw caution to the wind.

Emry felt the change in him. His desire was almost tangible, radiating out from him with such force that she could feel it, too. She was no longer laughing. She looked up at him and he touched her face with a caressing hand.

"Oh, Emry," he sighed as if apologizing. He brushed her

hair away from her face and then he kissed her.

It was not a tender kiss like the one she had given him, but a violent kiss full of so much passion that it set Emry on fire. There was a great eagerness in him and a hunger, too, and Emry was sure she had never been kissed in any such manner before nor ever would be again.

It literally took her breath away, so when his head came up with a jerk, she gasped and fell limp beneath his weight, not caring that something had disturbed his passion. It took her a moment to realize that he was no longer the lover. He was suddenly the hunter once again.

It was a sound in the night that had pricked his consciousness. In his passion, he had lost the sense of awareness that kept him attuned to his surroundings, but something minute, and critically urgent, had managed to stimulate that part of his brain that was trained to be watchful and always alert.

He lifted his head and listened into the night. The abruptness of his actions caused Emry to listen closely, as well.

She heard nothing. "What is it?" she asked.

"Quiet!" he hoarsely whispered and the urgency in his voice silenced her.

He came to his feet, pulling Emry along with him, and then he began running, dragging her with him as he led her toward the house.

"What's wrong?" she asked.

"Vampires!" he hissed.

He stopped at the porch steps. "Get inside quickly! And do

not come out again tonight. Do you understand?"

"Yes," she said, nodding her head. His eyes were ablaze and his expression wild. She was afraid not to agree.

"Go!" he demanded and she ran up the steps, looking back at him as she opened the door. He was looking at her, but his head was up in a watchful position. As the screen door closed behind her, he moved and simply disappeared from sight. Emry gasped and searched the yard, but all she could see was a swirl of misty fog where he had been standing.

Chapter Twenty

Victor materialized beside the Jaguar, his phone coming into his hand before the wisp of smoke around him had dissipated.

"I was about to call you," Artemus said. "We were wrong. They did not all go with Hugo."

"There is more than one," Victor said. He was walking toward the house, scanning his surroundings as he went along.

"And Emry?" Artemus hesitantly asked.

"She is safely in her house."

"Good. You want to make a turn around the property while the rest of us get our gear?"

"Yes."

He dropped the phone in his pocket and threw off his shirt. The wings spread out from his back, unfolding, billowing out until their darkness caught the breeze and popped like sails. His countenance changed as he morphed. He was no longer Victor Balfour, but some strange, beautiful creature that might have been called a dragon in some bygone era.

He rose into the air, his vision perfect, his sight as acute as an owl's. He soared over the treetops and across the woods and it was no trouble for him to see them — four vampires, spread out, hunting, it seemed.

He watched them and his eyes narrowed as he realized

their direction. It was the Winters' property.

"The fools," he said, his voice rumbling in his chest like distant thunder.

He saw his family and he soared down to them, his wings retracting and his features changing as his feet touched the ground.

"Four," he said at their questioning looks. He quickly gave the location and the Balfours spread out.

"An even match," Artemus said.

Victor turned to take up his position beside his brother when Stefan spoke.

"Victor, we need one of them alive," he said.

The three of them looked around in surprise.

"Do you call this characteristic behavior?" Stefan questioned them. "They are not simply hunting. They have a purpose and I would very much like to know what it is."

Victor looked around, considering that. Just like he had told Emry, when the Balfours came into an area, the vampires always left — the ones that were able to anyway. Why stay and risk death or injury when there were so many other places they could be? Vampires weren't interested in defending property. They simply took their necessities and quietly left.

That's what had happened in Bostwick — or so they had thought. Perhaps these vampires had just arrived and were unaware of the Balfour's presence.

Then why the sudden move onto their property?

Victor slowly nodded. "I see your point," he said. "I will see what I can do."

He moved into the night, still naked from the waist up. It was a cool night, but the temperature didn't bother him. He walked with a steady gait, keeping his brothers in sight at all times.

Only a minute passed before Victor saw one of them. The vampire was moving quickly, running like a wild animal, sniffing at the air as he advanced.

The others came into view and suddenly they all stopped. Their heads came up and you could see them testing the air. They growled and showed their teeth while at the same time, they ran to each other, making a tight circle, back to back, preparing for the inevitable attack.

Marius wasted no time. He was always too eager, Victor thought, but sometimes it was better not to give the enemy time to think.

He pulled a gun from his side and shot into the bunch of them. A startled yelp assured him he had hit one of them, but then they all fled, running in different directions like frightened quail.

That is, they all fled except the one Marius had hit. He took five steps and fell on his face, unable to run anymore. He was stunned, but not immobile. He began dragging himself across the ground.

Marius leaped over him, landing with legs spread wide and his arm held high. Something dark came down with a sickening thud and the vampire's head rolled away from him.

One down, three to go.

The others had made well their escape, but no sooner had

they disappeared from sight than one of them unwisely decided to double back, and he fell into Artemus' fateful hands.

But as only two remained, the brothers spread wide in search, only to find reinforcements. A man and two women attacked as Stefan came unexpectedly upon them. He brought up his weapon, but it was knocked from his hand only to be lost in the deep brush. He was pushed to the ground and all three of them piled on top of him, biting with fangs and sharp teeth, tearing at him with clawed hands, and hitting him.

Marius was the first to come upon them and again, he shot first, knocking one of them away. The two remaining looked up in surprise and then he was upon them. The wooden sword took the man through the heart and he fell back, but the remaining girl attacked with such violence and power that it threw him off balance. He fell to the ground and she leaped upon him, grabbing his throat with her powerful hands and choking with all her might.

It had very little effect on Marius. He reached up and twisted her hands away only to have her fall forward, biting as her mouth came in contact with him.

He threw her away from him and she landed on steady feet equidistant between him and Stefan. He was just beginning to recover and she saw her chance to get at least one of them. Just as Marius came to his feet, she snarled and jumped toward Stefan.

She sprang into the air with leonine beauty, her body stretching out gracefully. Marius leaped, as well, moving just a little too slowly to stop her. His hands reached out, clawing at the air with fingers curled, positioning himself for the moment of contact, when suddenly her body stiffened and the sleek and easy movements that gave her the cat-like characteristics, froze in midair. Impotently, she fell to the ground. The sound of Artemus' shot rang out at the same time.

"I will take care of this," Stefan said, meaning the cleanup of the three motionless vampires. "Find the others."

It was well they decided to. Victor was alone, except for the two vampires that had him cornered. He put his back to a large tree like a wounded elk, harried by wolves, wisely preparing for its last battle. He dropped into a crouch, steadying himself for the attack.

It was a man and a woman and they came at him separately, first one and then the other. She delayed while her mate got what she thought was a secure hold on Victor and then she attacked too. He pushed them back with greater ease than either of them was expecting and so when they attacked again, it was as one, both of them coming at the same time.

Victor reached over his shoulder and pulled the silver knife from the scabbard that ran down his back. The knife was slim and sharp and balanced easily in his hand. He held it low, hoping to embed it into one of them, preferably the man who was probably the stronger. It wouldn't kill, but it would take him out of the fight until something more permanent could be done.

Neither of the vampires was afraid, or even concerned. They attacked and Victor lashed out, going for the chest where there was a larger target. The vampire caught his wrist and while he held him the girl threw herself against him, locking his free arm in a vicelike grip.

Victor dropped the knife and the grass swallowed it.

They both had a hold on Victor, grasping him tightly by his arms. They were learning, testing the limits of his physical power and this time, he found it difficult to break away from them.

What they didn't reckon on, was the degree of his other powers and contact with him was a mistake they would make only once.

"You cannot see," he told them. "You are blind . . . blind. All is darkness."

The girl screamed and turned him lose, reaching up to touch her eyes as the sight went out of them, but the man held on. He could not see, but he was not giving up. He gripped tighter and suddenly attacked, biting and clawing.

Victor pushed back, slamming him into the girl. They all fell to the ground, breaking any holds they had on one another.

The blindness had them disoriented. The girl cried out with a wail that sounded like a mournful howl, but the man picked himself up and stood poised, testing his senses.

He located Victor by scent and by the warmth that radiated from his body, attacking, only to meet with a stake in his heart. Victor had pulled the long slim weapon from the belt at his waist and effortlessly stabbed it into the vampire. He fell to the ground as if he was dead and Victor left him there while he pulled the girl to her feet.

"I cain't see!" she exclaimed, her voice strong with an

accent. The fight had gone out of her. "I cain't see nufin'," she said.

Artemus and Marius arrived at that moment and seeing the vampire on the ground with the stake in his heart, Marius casually drew his sword and lopped off the head.

"Are you going to do her, or shall I?" he asked as he sheathed his weapon.

"She is the live one father asked for."

Marius grunted derisively, but his expression was sour. He reached down and pulled the wooden stake from the fallen vampire's chest. Once his head was cut off, the wooden stake could be removed. Otherwise, if the stake was pulled from the heart, the vampire would revive.

"Let us clean this up," Artemus said. "You take the girl to father and we will follow as soon as we can."

Victor pulled her along and she was not that hard to maneuver. She stumbled beside him, the graceful poise inherent to her breed lost along with her eyesight.

"What is your name?" he asked as they neared the place where Stefan waited, the smell of burning flesh leading Victor to him.

"Mira."

They stepped into a small clearing in the otherwise dense woods. Stefan had dug a small ditch across one end of it and had placed the vampires' bodies in it. They were burning as Victor shoved the girl toward it.

"What's 'at? she anxiously asked. "What's 'at smell?"

"Burning vampire," Stefan answered and she fell to her

knees, crying.

"Get up," he demanded, but Victor had to pull her to her feet. "We want some answers."

"I knows nufin'," she said. "It wuz Gregory what knew d' orders."

"What orders?"

She cried and wrung her hands. "Ah dunno! Ah dunno!"

Victor placed his hand on her shoulder.

"Calm down," he said, "and just tell the truth."

"Ah is! Ah is terrin' d' truf," she insisted. "Ah dunno nufin'!"

"We just want to know if you were sent here and if so why?"

"Gregory knows. He knows d' orders."

"What do you know?" Stefan asked. "Just tell me what you know."

"I dunno nufin. It's jest d' orders," she said. "He got plans. I dunno nufin else."

"Who has plans?" Victor demanded although he was certain he knew.

"Hugo," she replied. "He tells Gregory and we foller — 'at's all."

"Hugo? Where is he?" Stefan demanded. Victor could see he was losing his cool.

"Gregory's de only one what knows. Only Gregory knows."

"What were you supposed to do? Were you after something in particular — a girl, perhaps?" Victor asked.

"Could be. Hugo always likes d' gurls. He takes 'em all d'

time."

"Kill her," Stefan hissed, but Victor put up his hand.

"Wait," he said. "Which one is Gregory? The one that was with you?" She nodded. "Too late to ask him anything," Victor said to Stefan.

"We know enough. Get rid of her."

Compassion was not a trait shared by the Peregrinias, but unfortunately, it was one Victor couldn't shake from his former life. He felt pity for her and he hesitated with what he knew was the inevitable.

Her sight returned as he paused in thought and she unexpectedly pulled away from him, running for the safety of the surrounding forest even as Marius and Artemus stepped into the clearing. She didn't make it as far as the edge of the woods. Artemus caught her. He pulled her arms behind her in an effort to restrain her, but she pushed back, causing Artemus to fall to the ground. It didn't break his hold as she had hoped it would. He flipped her over and drew her arms back, placing a knee on the low of her back to keep her securely on the ground.

Stefan and Marius were beside them by this time, but Victor watched from the center of the clearing where he had been when she escaped from him. Stefan pulled his sword and made a quick, smooth cut that separated her head from her body. She went limp and Artemus released her arms, slowly rising to his feet.

"I thought you wanted her alive," he said.

"Not anymore."

"It is Hugo," Victor said and they all looked toward him.

"He is after Emry."

"Why?" Marius demanded.

"I told you this would happen," Artemus said to Victor, ignoring Marius' question.

"What are you talking about?" Marius insisted, refusing to be ignored.

No one said anything for a few seconds. The time ticked by while they all stared at Victor.

"Oh, do not tell me," Marius moaned. "Not you and Emry."

Their eyes locked and neither of them looked away, but Marius shook his head and gritted his teeth.

"We will discuss this later," Stefan said. "Let us clean up and go back to the house." He looked at Victor, his expression full of exasperation. He kept his thoughts to himself and continued to be the one in charge. "You want to check around? Make sure there are no others?"

Without a word, Victor morphed. He took to the skies and gladly left them. He took his time and moved slowly, not wanting to face his family any sooner than he had to.

He saw nothing more and returned to the house after making a wide circle that took in most of the tiny community of Bostwick. He dropped from the sky and slid to a stop by the back door. The others were inside. His acute hearing could hear them talking, discussing his indiscretion. They hushed as he walked through the door, but he knew what they were saying. He had heard them plainly enough.

"Someone is going to have to stay with her," Stefan said as Victor took a seat in the large leather chair by the bookcase, the same one where Thomas had photographed him years before. "Watching is no longer adequate. Someone will have to be with her."

"I will do it," Marius said, but Victor gave him a look that would have chilled the blood of anyone else. "You certainly cannot," he added, undeterred by the warning look.

"She will be safe in her house. They cannot enter without an invitation."

Stefan gave him a quizzical look. "And how long do you think it will take before Ellen's southern hospitality invites one of them inside? When you knock at her door, the first words out of her mouth are 'come in'. If we know it, they know it, too. Who knows? Maybe they have already gotten the invitation and are just waiting for the right moment to strike."

Victor came to his feet, fear in his eyes.

"I am going to her."

"How?" Marius asked. "Have you been invited inside?"

"No, but she will let me in."

"I am sure she will, if you can get her attention without waking everyone in the house."

"He is right, Victor. Let us watch tonight. We can keep her safe, and tomorrow you can talk to her," Artemus suggested.

In the daylight? He hated the sun. It hurt his eyes and was hot on his skin, but he would've gone through a stretch of hell for Emry. It was just that he couldn't stand the idea of waiting.

"Very well, but I am going to check on her now."

When he got outside, he spread his wings and leaped into the air. He wanted to look at her, see that she was alright. He flew up to her window and hovered there. He took a deep breath and tested the smells in her room. Her scent was like a warm emollient, a flavor that stirred his senses and left a pleasing taste on his tongue. He searched for some other smell — the biting odor of vampires, sickening sweet like the blood they drank, but there was only her fragrance. He settled down to the ground and folded his wings. In a moment, he was Victor again, and he stood there, looking up at her window.

A minute later, Artemus joined him. Marius stood a long way back and Stefan was not even in sight although Victor knew he was there, somewhere in the night.

"She is fine," Artemus said, testing the scent very much the same way as Victor had done a minute before. "I am going to the other side of the house. It is going to be fine," he assured Victor. "And when this is over, we will work things out."

He gripped Victor's arm in a reassuring way before walking away.

Victor nodded, but he knew there was no way to work this out. He watched Artemus walk away and knew that better than anyone, Artemus knew what he was feeling.

Artemus had been married when he had become one of the Strangers, a husband and a father of four children. He had had no idea — none of them had any idea — what to expect when they made that fateful decision. Not even Brother Cavanaugh's explanations and training had prepared them for the reality of it. He had warned them, taught them, and trained them for a whole year before the actual act had been performed, but not even he was prepared for what had happened when the

Balfours made their transformation. They were unique and no one knew why they were, but even so, Artemus' situation had not been unique.

His wife had agreed to everything, but she could not have known as Artemus did not know what it would really be like. He lost her long before she grew old and died, and, of course, he distanced himself from the children. They did not know and he would not tell them. It was better that way.

After his wife had passed away, he never went back to his hometown. As far as anyone was concerned, he was dead, too. His children grew up and had children of their own, and they, in turn, had children who had children, but Artemus kept his distance. It was a pain he hid deep inside, knowing it was for the best to stay out of their lives, although, Victor had suspected he had watched things from afar, silently and stoically.

Unfortunately, it was a pain Victor would never know. He could never be a father, and he never realized how much that meant to him until today.

He looked up at Emry's window with both chagrin and wistful longing. He had to keep her alive and he had to keep her out of Hugo's hands. He felt sick at the thought of Hugo taking her — sick and empty.

There was no time for the luxury of the casual hunt anymore. They had to find Hugo and they had to destroy him now. Otherwise, one day he would simply come back and finish what he had started today.

Victor placed a hand on the side of the house and felt the

invisible barrier that kept him out. If a vampire entered there tonight, he would not be able to get inside. Which meant Emry might as well be on the moon for all the good he would be to her.

Tomorrow he would fix that problem. Tonight he simply had to make it through the night and as it turned out, it was the longest night he could ever remember.

When the eastern sky began to lighten and the shadows of night lifted from the trees and the buildings, the Balfours silently left their posts.

All except Victor. He waited nearby until the backdoor quietly opened and Ellen stepped outside. The rooster in the barnyard was crowing and all around, birds were singing. The dog in Jim's yard barked vigorously and a car horn blew somewhere on the highway. The sun touched the horizon and Victor faded into the background.

Later, he told himself, staring up at Emry's window from the safety of his own yard. *I will keep you safe — or I will die, too.*

Chapter Twenty-One

Jim sat up in the bed and listened. Something had awakened him, but he wasn't sure what.

He didn't hear anything except familiar sounds — the clock ticking in the living room, Tripper chasing a rabbit in his sleep, and Betty's heavy breathing.

He lay back only to sit upright again. There it was again, something not so far away. It sounded like a gunshot.

He threw his long legs out of the bed and stood up. His movements awakened Tripper whose tail began to bump furiously against the floor.

"Quiet!" he whispered, hoping he wouldn't wake Betty. Tripper stood up and walked to him. "Sh-h-h," Jim said, giving him a pat as he passed by on his way to the hallway.

Once there, he quietly walked into the kitchen and peered out the window into the back yard.

The moon was bright and he could see the yard clearly, but there was nothing there. He continued to look, feeling uneasy, but still seeing nothing.

He was just turning away when something caught his eye. Something moved in his peripheral vision, something big and dark. He turned back and jerked the curtain aside so that he could put his face right up to the window.

There was nothing there, but he kept looking. He had seen

something, but he had no explanation for what it was.

He walked to the gun cabinet and opened it, taking out his twenty-gauge, double-barreled shotgun; then he sat down in the nearby recliner, the gun across his knees. He'd seen too much lately and imagined even more. He wasn't taking any chances.

* * *

Emry was more shaken than she had first realized. By the time she reached her bedroom, she was trembling uncontrollably.

She wasn't cold, but she pulled the blanket off her bed and wrapped it around her, then she sat down on the floor beside the window and leaned her head against the wall.

All she could think about was what was happening outside. She was in shock from it all, or maybe just on overload. In the hour she had been gone, more things had happened than she could ever have imagined, even with her wonderfully active imagination.

She pulled the corner of the blinds away from the window and peered outside. The moon was bright and she could see the yard right up to the shadows beyond their fence, but there was no sign of Victor.

She sighed and leaned back.

What had happened to him at the front steps? He seemed to have simply disappeared, but she knew that was not possible — or was it? He had said he had more gifts, or curses, as he put it. Was that one of them? Could he just disappear at will?

She pulled at the blanket, repositioning it as a cold chill made her shiver.

He had kissed her . . .

She smiled in spite of herself. How could she help it with such a thought? It was the most wonderful thing she had ever imagined, but then what had she expected? He had had two hundred years of practice to perfect his love making skills.

And she? Well, she had never cared enough about a boy to let him do much. She was a novice and suddenly she wondered if Victor was disappointed. Maybe there were no vampires. Maybe that was just his way of quickly getting rid of her.

She squirmed uncomfortably.

Then, she heard the shot. It was in the distance, but not that far away.

Emry came to her feet and listened, poised like a frightened deer. There were no more shots, not immediately anyway, and she finally sat down again. When the next shot rang out, she only leaned forward and waited, expecting what, she didn't know.

She waited, sitting by the window until she fell asleep. When she awoke, she was cramped and cold and she all but crawled to the bed and climbed into it. She had no idea Victor was anxiously waiting outside, his attention acutely on her window and his senses testing the wind for any sign of danger. She had no idea he wanted to come in or that he was praying she would just look outside. She fell asleep again and didn't awaken until Crystal banged on her door and demanded she get up.

"Go away!" Emry said, pulling the sheet over her head.

"You're gonna make us late for church."

Emry groaned. "I'm not goin'," she said.

"Are you sick?" Crystal asked.

"Yes," she lied, then she quickly recanted. "No, I'm tired. I didn't sleep well last night."

"Something wrong?" Ellen asked as she passed Crystal in the hallway.

"Emry isn't goin'. She said she's too tired."

"Huh," Ellen grunted and then she walked on without another word.

When the car backed out of the driveway, Emry sat up on the side of the bed. The house was really quiet. It felt different with everyone gone.

She changed her clothes. She was still wearing the ones she had had on the night before, so when she threw them off, she carefully laid them on the bed, touching them with reverence at the memory that Victor had embraced her while she had been wearing them. She picked them up and buried her face in them, hoping to catch a scent or anything that would remind her of him. It was there — the soft fragrance of him — and she hugged them to her wishing it was he that was in her arms.

She walked downstairs and the smell of ham cooking in the kitchen drew her there. She looked into the oven through the glass panel in the door and smiled when she saw the gigantic fresh pork ham roasting inside. Ellen usually always left something cooking when she went to church. It was part of her southern heritage to want a full course meal for lunch on a Sunday afternoon, and then leftovers for supper.

Emry found a bagel in the refrigerator, behind the potato salad Ellen had made the night before. She toasted it while the coffee maker brewed her coffee, then she sat down and ate, taking her time and savoring the alone time.

The kitchen was pleasant and cozy. The smell of freshly brewed coffee and the scent of roasting ham on a cool morning gave her a feeling of warmth and security. She cradled her coffee cup in her hands and stared outside. The sun was bright and the sky was very blue with only wisps of white clouds here and there. A chilly wind shook the tree branches, sending dry leaves skidding across the porch and rocking the hanging swing. It came in gusts and then lay quiet and still until another blast set everything in motion again. Emry watched it and grew melancholy as her thoughts went unerringly to Victor Balfour.

When the car turned into the driveway, bringing her family home from church, Emry was ready for them. She didn't want to be alone anymore.

They tramped in, pulling off sweaters and jackets as they came through the door.

Maggie kissed Emry's forehead and gave her a questioning look. "Everything okay?" she asked, a concerned smile touching her lips.

"I was just tired," Emry said. "And I needed some alone time. It was great."

Stanley patted her back and then he sat down in his usual chair at the table. He gave her a look that was more than the one Maggie had given her. It was almost suspicious, but Emry thought, she was probably just feeling guilty. It wouldn't surprise her to look in the mirror and see the words, "*liar and guilty*" written in bold letters across her forehead.

After lunch, Lois and Eunice dropped in. There was something going on at the church for the senior members that evening and they were gathering to make cupcakes and sugar cookies to take.

Eunice had short white hair and a very rotund body. She was talkative and seemed very interested when she met Emry. She asked a lot of questions, but they were friendly things like who her friends were and how school was working out.

Lois, on the other hand, didn't appear to care one way or the other, although she gave Emry keen looks of interest once or twice. She had a quiet personality much like Maggie's and when she spoke, her voice was calm and subdued. Unlike both Ellen and Eunice who were dressed in Alfred Dunner slacks and blouses, Lois wore a dress and her silver gray hair was short and styled in soft waves. When she pulled off her sweater, she immediately donned one of Ellen's aprons and being an all-business type of woman, she was ready to get to work.

Heavy boots stomped across the back porch and Jim stuck his head in the back door.

"Anybody home?" he called out as he stepped inside.

"Hey, Jim," they all greeted him.

"Come on in," Ellen said. "Coffee's on the counter."

He accepted the cup that was offered to him and took it to the table.

"How's Betty?" Eunice immediately asked.

"She's fine," Jim answered.

"I haven't seen Casey lately. I bet he's as tall as you."

"Not quite."

"Well, kids grow up so fast. I can't believe Emry and Crystal are as big as they are. It seems only yesterday they were just babies."

She chatted on and Jim responded when required. He looked pleadingly at Stanley and he got the hint.

"Let's take our coffee to the living room and give these ladies some room," Stanley suggested and the two of them got up and went out.

The phone rang and Crystal grabbed it up only to have to relinquish it to Emry. It was Kendra. She wanted to get out of the house and suggested she, Kaylee, and Emry go somewhere.

Emry wasn't in the mood. She felt a need to stay close to the house — close to Victor, and she didn't understand why. He wouldn't be out, not in the daylight. If she ever saw him again, it would not be now.

"Why don't ya'll come over here?" she suggested anyway.

There was a moment of hesitation before Kendra replied.

"Okay," she finally said. "I could pick Kaylee up on the way."

They arrived just as the first batch of cookies came out of the oven. It was rather festive with the ladies bustling around in the kitchen and the smell of cookies and cupcakes in the air and coffee on the counter. Ellen's music was playing in the background and the lights were bright. Eunice suggested hot chocolate and the girls eagerly accepted even though it was toasty warm in the kitchen with the central unit piping hot air in and the oven radiating heat. She whipped it up in record time and set three steaming mugs in front of the girls.

Maggie had been helping out, but she suddenly removed her apron and made an announcement.

"Stanley has asked me out. We're goin' on a date tonight," she said.

"Wow!" Emry exclaimed, wide-eyed with astonishment.

"You go, girl!" Eunice said and everyone laughed.

Maggie walked out of the room and Crystal walked in.

"Hot chocolate!" she exclaimed — or rather, lamented.

"Comin' up," Eunice said and within minutes she had another mug sitting on the table.

Stanley and Maggie left on their date, and things became frantic as time drew near for the church function and the cupcakes and cookies were not quite ready. Everyone was helping by then, but at seven o'clock, it was decided they would just quit and leave the unfinished dough. They gathered up the boxes they had filled and loaded Eunice's car. Ellen took a shower and at seven twenty-five, she ran out the door and drove away.

That left the girls alone and they sighed with relief. They looked at the dough on the work island in the middle of the room and decided it would be good to eat some cookies, so they set out to bake them.

It began as a unified effort, everyone working together, but it ended in an adolescent contest for who could come up with the most ridiculously decorated cookie. Soon they had flour all over their clothes and food coloring all over their hands, and in Kaylee's case, all over her face and hands. They were laughing and making fun and someone turned up the music when an old, silly song began to play just so they could make fun of it.

Amid all this crazy confusion, the doorbell rang. Crystal and Kaylee were engaged in a battle that could be accurately referred to as the cookie war, so they were practically in the midst of a food fight when the unexpected summons filled the room. Emry wiped off her hands and went to the door.

She opened it, and for just a moment, she stood there in mute silence, staring in disbelief.

It was Victor. He smiled at her surprise and then graciously asked, "May I come in?"

She couldn't find her voice and when she did, she didn't know what to say. He waited patiently as she searched for her words. She couldn't get them straight because so many things were going through her mind. Should he come in with her friends here? And didn't he know, Crystal was going to tell on her? What was he doing here in the first place? And the big one was, could he come in if she said no — which she wouldn't, of course.

"Can you?" she asked to his great amusement.

"I can if you want me to," he said.

"That's a definite yes," she assured him. "Come in."

She stepped back and he crossed the threshold.

"Who is it?" Crystal called from the kitchen and then she walked to the open doorway, looking out into the foyer. She was holding a long, wooden spoon, licking the icing off of it as she looked out. At the sight of Victor, she dropped the spoon. "Ohmagosh!" she exclaimed and both Kaylee and Kendra quit what they were doing to rush to her side.

They were a sight, the three of them, standing there staring out. They had flour all over themselves, even in their hair and Kaylee's face was a variety of colors just like her hands. Victor smiled in their direction and all of them without exception let their mouths drop open in astonishment.

"We're decorating cookies," Emry quickly explained, looking down at her own hands and wiping at the flour on her clothes.

"Are you sure it is the cookies you are decorating?" he asked and everyone laughed.

"Hey, you gonna invite him in so we can meet him?" Kendra asked and Emry nervously looked up at him.

At her look of caution, he dropped his chin in a nod of confirmation.

"But what about . . ."

"Not now," he quietly said. "Later . . ."

She looked at her friends, still staring at them from the doorway. She saw his point.

"Come on. I'll introduce you."

Crystal, Kaylee and Kendra eased back with gaping mouths and staring eyes as Emry led Victor into the room. She gave them warning looks, but none of them even looked at her. They couldn't take their eyes off Victor.

"Kendra — Kaylee — and, of course, my sister, Crystal," she

said, introducing them to him. "This is Victor."

Their frozen positions melted like ice before heat and everyone greeted him, welcoming him to the kitchen. They began moving as if nothing had happened — like Victor hadn't even arrived, although they immediately began including him in the activities.

"You like cookies?" Kendra asked. "Come see what we've done."

He walked to the island in the center of the kitchen and smiled at the bizarre decorations on the cookies they had made.

"Try one," Kendra offered, but he shook his head.

"Thanks, but no thanks."

Emry gave him a questioning look. Could he eat a cookie? She suddenly wondered what his diet consisted of — blood?

"I made this one," Crystal said and everyone, including her, laughed. It looked like a Salvador Dali painting. The icing was running off in a lopsided way and the flower on top was going with it.

"Very interesting," he said. "If it was a watch instead of a flower, you might have the makings of a work of art."

They all laughed again.

"This one is mine," Kaylee said and then Kendra pointed out both hers and Emry's. They pulled the undecorated cookies over and showed him how they did it and before long, he was playing with them, making funny cookies and joining in the food fights. They were all a little zany, and Victor fit right in just as if he was a normal guy.

They came to the end of the dough and the cookies were all

decorated and quite unexpectedly, Victor pulled Emry to her feet and danced around the room with her. The song playing on the computer was a slow, old country music song about how right love feels — it was so appropriate.

Kendra elbowed Kaylee and she in turn gave Crystal a sage look. They walked out of the room, turning off lights as they went out until only two lights were left burning in the background, and then they closed the door behind them.

"Your friends have left," he whispered into her ear.

She looked around and then up at him. Her heart filled with such emotion that she could hardly contain the feeling.

He had flour on his face. She grinned, then reached up and wiped at it. It didn't want to come off even when he gave it a swipe. They both laughed. He seemed so normal!

"You know, of course, Crystal will tell my parents you were here tonight and I'll be in all kinds of trouble."

"I will make her forget, if you like."

"No," Emry said, shaking her head with resignation. "I may as well face the firing squad and get it over with."

"I have to ask," he said, taking a few steps in time with the music. "Merely to satisfy my own curiosity. Is this a normal evening for your family?"

"Unfortunately, yes," she said with a sigh.

"No, not unfortunately. You are very fortunate. I would give anything . . ." His voice trailed off and the smile left his face. "Never mind," he said, and he stopped dancing. "Sit down with me, Emry. I have news, and it is not good news."

"No one got hurt last night, did they?" she quickly asked. "I was wondering if that was why you were here."

"No," he said. "Several reasons. And also, we have some unfinished business, if you will remember."

"Ah, don't tell me you came over here tonight just to make me forget everything?"

He chuckled and pulled her toward the table. "Not entirely," he said. "Sit down and we will talk."

He pulled a chair out for her and they sat down at the kitchen table. He didn't say anything right away. He only looked at her, a look of intense study on his face.

"What?" she finally asked, feeling uncomfortable.

It broke his concentration. He reached across the table and took her hands between his, cupping them within his.

"I need you to do something for me," he said.

"Okay," she readily agreed, and he smiled, thinking back to the time when she insisted on hearing the details of his request before committing herself.

"Ask my brothers in," he said.

"Here? Tonight?"

Victor nodded. "We were wrong, Emry. The vampires have not left the area. In fact, we think Hugo is still nearby — Gainesville, maybe. We need entrance to your house so we can protect you. Otherwise, if one of them gets inside, at this point, only I will be able to come in and help you. It may not be enough."

"What are you sayin'?" she quickly and excitedly asked, zeroing in on the one point that caught her attention and letting the important fact about Hugo completely slip away. "You mean, you really couldn't come in unless I invited you?"

"That is what it means."

She was intrigued. In fact, her face took on the look of a child who has just learned Santa Claus is real, but still can't believe it.

"How does that work?" she asked and in spite of himself, he began to laugh.

"It works because you want us here. It is the power of being welcome."

"No, I mean — how does that work — really?"

He laughed again. "Magic," he said. "It must be magic."

"You're makin' fun of me," she said, embarrassed by his reaction.

"Now, do not pout," he demanded just like he had the night before. "I sometimes forget you could not possibly understand what just comes naturally to me." He was suddenly all business — serious again. "There are rules and natural laws in everything, Emry. This is the way it works. We operate under those rules just like you operate under the rules in your world."

"My world? Not, our world?"

He shook his head. "It is two different worlds, Emry. They just seem to have overlapped in our case."

That was a sobering thought.

"Well?" he asked as she sat there in thought.

"Sure," she said. "Of course, they're welcome to come in."

"I will call them," he said. He took his phone out and pressed a button that immediately rang Artemus' phone.

"Yes, well, better late than never," Victor said to the voice on the other end. Emry looked curiously at him and he shrugged. "Come to the back door — yes — she knows — we will be waiting."

He dropped the phone into his pocket and tilted his chin toward the back door as if pointing. "Come with me. They will be there in a second."

They stood up and Victor guided her to the door by a hand at the small of her back. They did not have to wait. Artemus and Marius were already there and they cautiously stepped inside as Emry invited them in.

They looked around, taking in the messy kitchen. The sink was full of dirty dishes and the work island was strewn with flour, bowls of frosting, cookies and well, more flour. Ellen would have been mortified even if it was just the Balfour brothers who were seeing it.

They were both incredibly attractive men and just like with Victor, she found herself staring at them, especially Marius. He was taller than either Victor or Artemus and he was blonde with blue eyes that turned down just a little. His cheekbones were high and sharp and his lips were full with just a hint of a pout to them. He looked like the man on the back of a magazine she had in her room — the one who advertised men's cologne for some special name brand.

Emry became only too aware of her appearance. She began to aimlessly brush at her clothes, remembering she had flour all over herself.

"Well, Emry," Marius said with his beautiful baritone voice, "It looks like you have things to do. No need for us to stay."

Was that a hint to clean up the kitchen?

He looked at Victor, a question in his eyes.

"I will follow in a few minutes," Victor said, answering the unspoken question. "I am not quite finished here."

He nodded, but his eyes betrayed his feelings. He was not pleased with leaving Victor behind.

"Do not worry, Emry," Marius kindly said, even though he seemed unhappy with Victor. "We will keep you safe."

"Thanks," she said, thinking everyone seemed overly concerned with her all of a sudden. She glanced at Victor and wondered if he was holding out on her.

Artemus had been standing quietly to the side, his stern features not entirely severe. He seemed moved by the domestic scene around him and a little saddened by it. He walked slowly to the door and the look he gave Victor wasn't critical, but apologetic. They locked eyes and then Artemus slid his gaze to Emry.

"Be careful," he said. "You are easily seen through the window."

"Okay," she said. "Thanks."

He nodded and went out, following Marius who couldn't seem to get out of there fast enough. She turned to Victor and he was looking at the door where they had gone.

"What's goin' on?" she asked, realizing there was something more than what Victor had told her so far.

His eyes jumped back to her. "Do not be frightened, Emry," he said. "But we are concerned that Hugo sent the vampires for you."

"You mean Van?"

He nodded.

She shook her head. "That doesn't make any sense. If he had shown up here yesterday, I would have gone with him if he had asked. I thought he was a friend."

"He does not know that. He might think I told you about him a long time ago."

"But why, Victor? Why would Van single me out? I've done nothing to him."

He pursed his lips as if trying to conceal an emotion that was about to escape.

"It is called revenge," he explained.

"Revenge?" She looked away in thought. Was everyone obsessed with revenge?

"Because of me," he went on to say, his voice very soft and quiet. "He knows how much it will hurt me."

She slowly turned her eyes back to him and all she could do was stare. Was he saying what she thought he was saying — what she hoped he was saying?

"Which brings me to what happened last night," he said, suddenly crushing her hopes. "There is no end to the reasons why I should never have kissed you. Van is only one of them. I completely lost my sense of direction when you kissed me, and it is no excuse, but it made me forget my place. Please understand, I *cannot* let that happen again."

He couldn't? It was actually rather a relief that he just wouldn't — not that he couldn't.

"Now, getting back to Hugo — I mean, Van — if he sent for

you, like we suspect, then we have a problem."

She gave him an anxious look. He was moving too quickly. She was still back at the reason for no more kisses and he was on the subject of Van again.

"I don't care about any of the reasons," she said and Victor flashed a questioning look her way. "None of the reasons matter. I don't care about any of them."

He stared at her for what seemed like a very long time, a look of realization coming into his eyes.

"You do not know what you are saying."

"I do know."

"No, you do not," he insisted. "This is important, Emry." Well, to her, so was this. "Your life is in danger."

Was it? His mind was so clouded with thoughts of revenge and hate and grief, she didn't think he could give an accurate account of what Van would do.

The thought had crossed her mind before, and again, she had to consider an unwanted possibility. If Van was not the bad guy, then Victor was.

"Van has never tried to hurt me," she ventured as an observation, but Victor's head came up like a bull ready to fight.

"Do not do this, Emry," he said with a wag of his head. "Do not let him fool you."

"It's just all so very hard for me to believe."

Victor nodded as if he understood, but at the same time, he was impatient. She had to understand the consequences but he had no time to waste with long explanations and carefully orchestrated reasons.

"You do not have any idea what Van is capable of — but I do," he said. "There are very few things in this world that truly scare me," he said, "But what Van will do to you when he gets you is one of them. You cannot imagine what he has planned for you. And then, when he is finished with you, he will turn you into a vampire just so I will have to kill you. It would be his coupe d' grace — the master stroke — the ultimate revenge, because he knows, I could not let you live."

"You wouldn't kill me — would you?"

"I would," he said without hesitation. "Just like I helped kill my sister and just how I will kill Abby if I can get my hands on her."

She recoiled and the sight of her revulsion calmed him, drew him back to her. He reached for her, taking her hands and speaking softly and gently again.

"Just listen to me, Emry. It will not come to that. We are not leaving. We are going to stay here until there is no danger to you. I will not let Van have you. I promise."

He was as changeable as the tides. She saw him shift from one emotion to the other and it concerned her more than she wanted to admit.

"You may very well turn out to be the instrument by which we destroy Hugo," he suddenly said.

"I'm the bait, you mean."

"It was not my plan. Hugo set the rules."

She felt her confidence in Victor waver. Van had never threatened her and it was difficult to imagine him as some dark Lord set on kidnaping and torture.

The gossip and the rumors about Victor suddenly filled her mind. He looked perfectly normal, but was he? Could he be insane just like people were saying and all of this some great fantasy he and his family were playing out in their delusion — one she was suddenly caught up in?

In all honesty, that made more sense than mythical creatures and kidnaping vampires. But then, she had to admit, she had seen evidence of unusual things, things she could never explain. He had disappeared right before her eyes only the night before, and the episode in the park was still a mystery she had not been able to entirely work out.

"What are you thinking?" he suddenly asked, and she jerked out of her daydream.

She shook her head. He didn't want to know.

But somehow, he knew. He slowly moved his hands away from her and dropped them to his side. She anxiously looked at him. The look on his face was hard to read — disappointment? Anger? Regret? Sorrow? What was it?

He looked around the room as if judging the evening's activities, accusing them for making him forget his obligations.

"Look, Emry," he slowly said, his brow wrinkled in thought. "I came here tonight for one reason and one reason only — well, two maybe. I needed to set things straight about last night."

She opened her mouth to say something, but he raised his hand as if asking her to wait so she closed it again.

"But mainly, I needed to get inside. You have given me that key so — well, now I have everything I need."

Was he leaving? She guessed so, but something about the way he made his statement caused the hair on the back of her neck to stand up. She gave him a cautious look and he returned it with a derisive chuckle.

"You still do not trust me," he said. "I thought after last night . . ." He abruptly stopped talking and then he carefully began again. "But here I am bringing up something that is better left unsaid. Come here, Emry, and let us get this over with so I can leave."

He was impatient again. Emry could hear it in his voice.

They were standing a few feet apart from each other. If it had been for any other reason, Emry would have flown into his arms, but she did not move, and right away, neither did Victor. They stared at each other and then it was Victor who took the first step.

"Don't be upset with me, Victor," she said as he took her hand. "It's just that, I'm having a hard time with all this. It's a lot to digest. And in all fairness to Van, he's never frightened me."

"But I have."

"Sometimes I think you try to scare me," she said. "Like now, for instance."

"If it would teach you to be cautious, I would frighten the hell out of you."

She didn't know what to say to that, so she didn't say anything. In her mind, though, a raucous debate was going on. She didn't want to have doubts about him, but she did. It generated a great deal of conversation between herself and herself. She walked away from him and she half expected him to follow, but he didn't. After a few moments, she wished he had and then she regretted her move altogether, especially when she saw the lights of Ellen's car turning into the driveway and she knew the meeting between them had to come to an abrupt ending.

She turned to warn him, but he was gone. She had not heard anything — not his steps to the door, nor the door opening and closing — nothing. He just was not there anymore.

Chapter Twenty-two

Monday morning came all too soon for Emry. The first person she saw as she walked through the glass doors at school was Johnny. She sighed with exasperation. He walked toward her and she waited for him, thinking the whole while that she wished she had never met him.

She told herself it was not his fault and that she should be nice to him, so she was, but at the same time, she knew she had to put their relationship into its proper place. She suddenly asked herself what was the proper place, but unfortunately, she had no immediate answer.

"Hey, Johnny," she said when he arrived.

"Hey," he replied. They began walking and he said a few things about school and some mundane things about the weekend, but Emry was silent, wondering the whole time what she was going to do about him. "Are you alright?" he asked as they stopped at her home room.

"Sure," she said, but she found it hard to look him in the eye. "I had a busy weekend."

That was an understatement!

"Hey, look," he said and he dropped his eyes, too. "We gotta talk, okay?"

"Okay," Emry said. "What's up?"

The bell rang and Johnny nervously looked up. "Later,

okay?"

"Okay," she called out to his retreating figure.

After school, when she arrived at her car, Johnny was standing there.

"Got a minute?" he asked and Emry wished she could say no, but she was waiting for Casey and Crystal and the truth was, she had no excuse. She had to say yes.

He folded his arms and leaned against her car, waiting to say anything more until she had thrown her backpack on the backseat.

"I have a friend who's in a band," he began as she slammed the back door to the car and walked back to him. "They're playin' this weekend an' I want you t' go with me to hear them."

"A band? Wow, that's cool."

He shrugged. "They're pretty good, but mainly, he's my friend and I promised I'd go hear him."

"Hey, look, Johnny," she began but he stopped her.

"You don't have to say it," he said. "I understand." He looked down at her and his eyes were full of unspoken knowledge. "Just this once, okay?"

"Kaylee would really like something like this. Could we ask her to go with us?"

He unfolded his arms. "Not this time."

"Okay."

"Does that mean you'll go?"

Emry gave it a moment of consideration. She didn't want to go. All she wanted was Victor, but she knew there was no future there.

"For ol' times sake?" he said when she didn't immediately answer him and she smiled. She guessed she owed him that much.

"Sure," she said, but even as she spoke, the thought of Victor's kiss popped into her head and she almost choked on the word. Emry could not help her feelings and as long as she felt as she did, there was no room for feelings for Johnny or any other boy. It was a crazy thought, but Emry had decided that if she could not have Victor then she wanted no one. She would live her life alone and devote her time to helping others. She suddenly wished she was Catholic because being a nun was exactly what she had in mind — a celibate life of sacrifice and devotion. She mused over the thought, wondering if Father Joe could give her some advice on the subject. Maybe it could happen even if she was a Baptist.

Johnny said something and it snapped her out of her reverie.

"What?" she asked since she had not really been listening to him.

"I was asking if we could leave early on Friday."

"How early?"

"Five? It'll take us over an hour to get there."

"Where is it?" Emry asked. She had been thinking they were going someplace in Palatka.

"Gainesville," he said.

"Gainesville? Gosh, I don't know. I'll have to ask daddy. He may not let me go to Gainesville."

"It's no farther than Orange Park," he pointed out.

"Yeah, I guess so," she reluctantly agreed. For some reason, she did not want to go to Gainesville.

"It's gonna be great," he said.

"Uh . . ." Emry wished she could find an excuse not to go, but her mind went blank on her. "Where in Gainesville?" she finally asked.

"They'll be playin' in front of a coffee shop on Second Street, but I thought we'd get something to eat first and catch the group around eight o'clock."

"Okay . . . an' you're sure Kaylee can't go with us?"

"Not this time," he repeated.

Why did she feel so uneasy about this?

It was not until she got home that it came to her. Van was supposed to be in Gainesville.

She was going to have to tell Victor and she knew what he was going to say. He would tell her to break the date.

She looked at the desk in her room and after a few seconds, she moved aside the picture frame where a folded piece of paper was hidden. She picked it up and looked at the perfectly and neatly written numbers of Victor's cell phone. She was going to have to call him.

Her heart began to pound at the idea. She was not sure if it was excitement or fear, but whatever the reason, she stood holding the paper, reluctant to do anything about it.

"I need a nice long run," she said aloud and the thought appealed to her so perfectly that she immediately dressed in jogging attire and left her room.

"Where're you goin'?" Ellen said from the kitchen as Emry

walked through it to the back door.

"Runnin'."

"You haven't done that in a while."

It was true. It had been a week or more since she had run.

"Supper's at six," Ellen said.

"I'll be finished before then."

She walked to the edge of the porch and did some warm-up stretches before jogging to the path.

She ran around the course a couple of times and then she ran back to the house. She had just enough time for a shower before dinner was ready.

It was a quiet night, one of those lazy evenings that makes one drowsy. Emry thought it was because of her jog, but everyone else seemed lackadaisical, too.

After the kitchen was clean, everyone scattered. Crystal went into the upstairs bathroom and took a long shower, Ellen went to the dining room where the jigsaw puzzle was laid out, and Stanley and Maggie disappeared into the back bedroom to watch television. Emry dried her hands and draped the dish cloth over the hook near the sink. She decided to turn in early.

She climbed the stairs and opened the door to her bedroom. She stepped inside and flipped on the light switch. The computer was the first thing she focused on and the thought was on her mind that she should send a few messages before she went to bed. She shook her head and reached for her night shirt with the big lady bug across the front of it. It was a comfortable night gown and tonight she was simply looking for comfort.

Emry heard Crystal leave the bathroom and so she took the opportunity to brush her teeth and wash her face. Once that was done, she hurried back to the bedroom, thinking that she could not wait to get into the bed.

The room was dark. She flipped on the light switch and closed the door behind her. Immediately and without warning, the lights went out again and at the same time, someone grabbed Emry, covering her mouth with his hand so she could not make a sound.

"Quiet!" Marius hoarsely whispered as she struggled and tried to scream. "Quiet, Emry. It is Marius. I am turning you loose, now," he said as she calmed down. "Just be very quiet, will you?"

"Marius!" she exclaimed in a hoarse whisper as he dropped the hand from her mouth. He smiled, appearing to get some perverse pleasure from seeing her startled face. "What're you doing here?" she demanded and then with a thought of possible trouble she quickly asked, "Is Victor okay?"

"He is. Do not worry about him. It is you that is in danger. That is why I am here."

She did not want Marius here. He unnerved her.

"I'm okay," she assured him.

"Yes, and we plan to see you stay that way. Something else has happened, Emry. Something that has us worried about you staying here alone at night."

"What?" she quickly asked.

"We think Hugo has a confederate among your friends and that possibly one of you has already invited in the vampire that will come here for you."

She caught her breath with anxiousness and then she slowly released it. What about her family? The Balfours were concerned about Emry, but she was concerned about her parents and her grandmother — and, for some reason, even more so for Crystal.

"You've got to protect my family," she said.

"Your family is not in danger — not right now, anyway. It is you Hugo wants."

"Why?" she asked with great incredulousness. "Why would he care about me? I've done nothing to him."

Marius laughed, but there was no mirth or humor in his laugh. "Surely, you know," he said.

Emry shook her head. "No, I have no idea what you're talkin' about. I hardly know Van — or Hugo, as you call him and, anyway, he and I have always gotten along fine. I think you're wrong."

Marius gave her a long and studious look before saying anything else and when he did speak, he scoffed at her. "You cannot be that naive," he said. "We know what happened between you and Victor the other night and trust Hugo to know as well. We have seen it coming and all of us have warned Victor, but he is stubborn and arrogant." There was bitterness in his voice. "He wants you and that is the problem. If he wants you then Hugo will have you no matter what — just simply to hurt him. Do you see now? Do you understand what I am trying to say?"

What was he trying to say? All Emry was hearing was that

Victor wanted her. That was all she wanted to hear.

"But Victor said—"

"Forget what Victor said," Marius interrupted her. "He will lie thinking it will protect you, but all his lies cannot change things. The fact is, Victor has crossed the line and now you have become a pawn in a deadly game. Taking you will give Hugo more pleasure than killing all of us combined, I am afraid. He knows that we know what he will do to you and believe me when I say, Victor would rather kill you himself than have you in Hugo's hands."

Emry felt herself shaking. She was afraid. Victor had told her this very thing. Both he and Marius were talking about torture or something, and Emry was the first to admit that she was more frightened than she had ever been.

"What're we going t' do?" she asked.

"This is the plan. You will come with me and I will take you to our house."

Her eyes slowly turned toward the window that looked north toward the Balfour's property. Could she believe him? She looked back at Marius and a chill ran down her spine.

The Balfours were supposed to be crazy and for the hundredth time, she wondered if they really were. With a start, it occurred to her that she would have to be crazy, too. How could she feel this way about a man who believed he was a vampire slayer? Suddenly all of Victor's explanations sounded unbelievably bizarre, and she asked herself what would happen if, in fact, they were all insane and she went over there with Marius. The answer came in the form of another question.

What would happen if they were not insane and she did not go with Marius?

"Where's Victor?" she suddenly asked. She did not believe he would hurt her even if he was crazy. If he was delusional, at least his delusion was directed at wanting her.

"We sent him on an errand," Marius said. "You understand, it would not be wise for Victor to be there tonight, not after what has happened between the two of you."

"It was just a kiss," Emry said, thinking that he was acting like she and Victor had been promiscuous.

He chuckled, but again, it was with irony and there was no warmth in it. He gave her a look that clearly said, *"You fool."*

"What are you sayin'?" she asked. "That Victor's in love with me?"

"No," he was quick to answer. "Do not be deceived. Victor cannot love you. You are like the fuzzy kitten or the playful puppy that steals your affection. You will have many such 'loves' in your lifetime, but they will live and die and you will go on to the next one."

"You're saying I'm his pet," Emry sadly said.

Marius shrugged. "Call it what you like, but I tell you, Emry. It will not turn out like you want. It cannot even if Victor wanted it to and in all honesty, he does not."

"I don't wanna go," she said and Marius sighed.

"You can stay here, but I am not leaving you. I will stand over there and watch you all night." He pointed toward the corner near her computer. "Or," he went on to say, "you can come with me and you can have your own room with all the privacy you want."

"What difference does it make where I am?" she asked. "Just give me my privacy here. I'll scream if I need you."

"If you are able to scream," he said and then he went on. "Nothing can come into our house," he solemnly stated. "Nothing — but here, well, we have no idea what can come or go. I will have to keep my eyes on you here, but there . . . You can go anywhere you like and be as alone as you like. No one will bother you."

She had wanted to see the house and Marius sounded so sincere, but somehow this didn't seem right. Maybe it was because this was not the way she had wanted it to happen. She had wanted Victor to take her there and to be there with her.

She gave it some thought. Perhaps Marius was wrong and Victor would be there. After the abrupt way their last meeting had ended, she wanted to see him more than ever, but then she had to remember, she would be a girl alone in a house with three men who, more than likely, were as crazy as loons.

Well, I should fit right in, she thought, *because obviously I'm as nutty as a fruitcake.*

"It would be safer for your family, too," he added. "Trust me on this."

The mention of her family's safety was the deciding factor. She looked around but it was not the room that focused in her mind. It was visions of her family. She could imagine them with two outcomes and one of those scenarios did not end well. If there was a possibility that Marius was right, then she could not take a chance.

"Okay," she reluctantly agreed. "How do we do this?"

"I am going to take you right out the front door," he said with a grin.

"Just like that? Just walk down the stairs and out the front door?"

"That is right."

"Okay," she said, thinking, he was crazy if he thought he could walk right past her grandmother with Emry in tow. Well, that went without saying.

"Are you ready, then?" he asked and she immediately looked down at herself. She could not see in the dim lighting, but she knew how she looked.

She was wearing a night shirt. It was not even a night gown. It was a long, short sleeved shirt with a ladybug on the front of it that was circling around a tall sunflower.

"I can't go like this," she said. "I need to get dressed."

"What for? You are just going over there to go to bed. Pull on some jeans and shoes and you will be fine."

She thought about Victor seeing her dressed this way and she shook her head.

"No way," she said, but in the end, Marius won the argument. He turned his back and she stepped into her jeans and pulled on some shoes, and then he took her hand.

"No matter what, do not break contact with me. Do you understand?"

"Yes," she said suddenly feeling very small and frightened.

He gripped her tightly and without hesitation, he turned and opened the door. They walked out of the room together and down the stairs. They passed the dining room and walked across the foyer, and then out the front door, and no one said a word or stopped them.

Once outside, Emry stopped and looked back, astonished that she had walked out of the house as if she was invisible — and maybe she was. She turned to Marius.

"They can't see you," she said and he smiled.

"No, but they can hear us. Come along — quietly."

He held her hand as they walked to the back gate and once there, he lifted her up and set her over the gate. Just like Victor had done, he vaulted it with one easy movement.

It was dark under the canopy of trees and the deeper Emry walked onto the Balfour's property, the scarier it became. Marius no longer held her hand, but suddenly, she reached out and took his and she held him tightly as they approached the house. He seemed to understand and he did not rebuke her.

The door opened suddenly and quite unexpectedly causing Emry to literally gasp. Artemus appeared in the opening, but he immediately stepped back.

"Come in," he said. Emry walked into the room. The door closed behind her with a thud and she stood very still, afraid even to move.

It was dark in the room. A single candle made a circle of light on the nearby table, but that was the only source of light Emry could see.

"It's dark," she said, nervously looking around.

"Come with me," Artemus said. "We do not really need the light, but Marius has worked on the old generator and got it going again. It powers only part of the house. I will take you there."

He picked up the candle but before Emry followed him, she looked over her shoulder at Marius.

"Thanks, Marius," she said and he lifted a careless hand in response.

"No problem," he said. "I will see you in the morning."

The old house was strange and frightening. In fact, it was downright scary. Emry had the feeling she had seen this scene before. It was from an old black and white horror movie she had once seen and it gave her no comfort to imagine that.

She caught a handful of Artemus' shirt and she held on tightly as he opened a door and went through it. They went down a hallway and then he opened another door and they went through it, too. He stopped and then he turned on a switch and the room filled with light.

It was the most beautiful room Emry had ever seen. She gazed at it in awe, her mouth falling open in surprise.

"Ah!" she heard herself exclaim as the breath left her lungs.

It was a very large room with a wide winding staircase in the middle of it. The floor was marble and there was a chandelier that must have been ten feet in diameter hanging in the center of a high ceiling.

There were smaller fixtures all around the room and dark paneled cabinets with beveled glass and mirrors. It looked like a ballroom, but it was the grand entrance to their home.

Artemus paused a moment to let her look at the room, but then quite abruptly he began walking up the stairs. "This way," he said and she followed him.

The base of the stairs was fifteen feet wide, growing narrower as it wound up to the next floor. The steps were marble, just like the floor downstairs, but when they reached the top step, Emry stepped onto a hardwood floor that ran in both directions for at least forty feet.

"I am turning off the lights downstairs," Artemus said. "I brought you this way because Victor thought you might like to see them on."

"I did," she said. "Where is Victor?"

She was following Artemus down the long hallway as they talked and he stopped before an open doorway before answering.

"He is not here," he answered and at the look of disappointment, Artemus added, "Do not be disappointed. There are some things that are better left alone, Emry, even if it is painful. Victor is realizing this and he has removed himself from this situation. He is sorry if this hurts you. He told me to tell you so."

Emry felt tears sting her eyes, but she did not want to cry before Artemus.

"I guess that means we can't even be friends," she bitterly said, almost choking on the words.

"Can it be just friendship?" he asked and then he shook his head. "I do not think so."

"If that's the only way, then it can be."

Again he shook his head.

"You think you are in love with him, but you are young and

you will think you are in love many times before you really are. He, on the other hand, cannot love you or anyone."

Emry's eyes jumped up to Artemus' face. That was basically what Marius had told her, and come to think of it, it was what Victor had tried to tell her, too. It was just that she did not want to believe it.

"Come inside. See your room," he said, and not unkindly, either, as if he understood.

She did not want to. She just wanted to go home and in her misery, it did not matter anymore if Hugo killed her or not, but she did as Artemus suggested and she walked into the room.

It was like the rest of the house, large and beautiful. There was a huge bed against a wall between two tall windows and a dressing table to the right of it. The carpet on the floor was a deep burgundy in color and the spread on the bed was burgundy and gold. The chandelier had hundreds of crystals lighting up the room and showing off the rich wood and the velvet curtains. It was not a modern room. The decorations were from a bygone era, but it was so tastefully done that its style was timeless.

There was an open doorway at the left of the room and Emry could see that it was a bathroom. There was a tub with claw feet and a white enamel sink. The floor was made up of small black and white octagon shaped tiles and the walls were painted white. Large luxurious towels hung on glass rods and more were neatly folded in an open cabinet in the corner. The room smelled fresh like lavender and vanilla.

"It's beautiful," she said and Artemus smiled.

"Marius will take you home in the morning before sunrise, so you may want to go right to sleep," he said. "If this works out, we will do the same thing tomorrow night. Is this agreeable with you?"

She nodded. She did not really care. Anything at this point was okay.

He put his hand on her shoulder. "Make yourself at home, and Emry . . . do not be sad. When this is over, you will get back to your normal life and none of this will matter. You will forget . . ."

Yes, she would, and she knew why. Victor would make her forget.

Artemus turned to leave, but Emry caught his hand and stopped him.

"I'm a little afraid," she admitted.

"Nothing is going to hurt you — I promise."

She nervously looked around. "Can I leave the light on?"

He walked to the bedside table and flipped on the lamp.

"How about this? I will turn off the overhead light on my way out."

She had followed him to the lamp, still holding onto his hand and she didn't turn it loose.

"Do not worry, Emry," he said. "I will be just down the hall if you need anything, but I assure you, you are in no danger here."

He gently pulled his hand out of her grip and she let it go.

"Get some sleep," he told her. "Marius will take you home in the morning and he will stay there with you until the sun rises. You are going to be just fine."

He walked to the door, but he paused there, looking back into her room before turning off the overhead light.

"Good night," he said and then he backed out, pulling the door closed behind him.

Emry stood by the bed just looking at it. She touched one of the pillows — down. Well, Victor was not lying, she supposed. Maybe he did sleep in a very large bed with down pillows. And then, she wondered if this was actually his bed. Had he given up his room so that she could have a place to sleep? She picked up the pillow and breathed in the fragrance of it. Yes, it reminded her of him. Suddenly, she didn't mind to sleep in this bed. In fact, she was anxious to get into it. Quickly, she pulled off her shoes and stepped out of her jeans, and then she carefully, almost reverently, climbed into the bed.

For just a moment she laid there, the covers pulled up to her chin and the pillows to her back. Even with the lamp on, there were shadows in the room and dark corners. Slowly she looked around. As the momentary thrill faded, she again became uneasy. Everything had a shape that made her look once and then twice at it. She was sure she would never be able to go to sleep. That was what she told herself, but when Marius touched her shoulder and awakened her the next morning, she was surprised that she had slept the whole night without awakening even once.

He went with her as she walked home and just like the night before, no one saw them. Once in her room, Marius sat in the chair at her computer until the sun was well above the horizon and then he quietly left.

That night, he was there waiting for her long before the hour she could actually leave with him. She walked into her room just after sundown and there he stood, frightening the daylights out of her.

"What're you doin' here?" she whispered in exasperation and he grinned at her reaction just like he had done the night before.

"It is sundown," he said in answer. His eyes shifted to the window and then back again. Emry's did the same.

"Oh," was all she said. She understood his simple gesture.

Everything played out the same as the night before except that Crystal seemed somewhat more bothersome. She seemed to cling to Emry. Everywhere Emry went, she turned and her sister was there.

She supposed it was always like this, but she had never noticed it until now when more than anything, she did not want Crystal following her.

Emry avoided her bedroom and after dinner she found herself in the dining room with Ellen. A thousand piece jigsaw puzzle was laid out on the table. It was the picture of a folk art painting, the scene of an old barn with hay in the doorway and pumpkins on the ground. There was a hill with cows on it and in the distance, a white church with a steeple. An American flag flew from the top of the barn and Ellen pointed out that the man who painted this always had at least one American flag in his pictures.

Crystal soon joined them and the three of them chatted

quietly as they sought out the pieces to the puzzle and slowly put them together.

"Well," Emry said as she looked up at the clock, "it's time for me to get ready for bed."

"Me, too," Crystal agreed. "I almost fell asleep in Comp today."

The telephone rang and Crystal ran to catch it. She came back a moment later and told Emry it was Johnny.

"Oh, shoot!" she exclaimed, remembering that she had forgotten about their date on Friday. "Tell 'im I'll call 'im right back," she said, coming quickly to her feet.

She found her dad in the kitchen. He and Maggie were sitting at the table drinking coffee and talking.

"Dad," she said, "Johnny's asked me out Friday night. He has a friend who plays in a band and they're going to be playin' outside a coffee shop in Gainesville."

"That sounds like fun," he said. "Okay, but just be home by midnight."

"Are you sure? I mean, you don't mind? Really?"

He gave her a curious look. "I don't mind."

"Okay."

She walked toward the phone, thinking all the way that she still had to tell the Balfours. They were not going to like it.

She rang his number and when he picked up, she noted the peculiar note in his voice. "Hey, sorry," she said. "I had to ask my dad about Friday. He's okay with it." There was silence on the other end. "Hello . . . Hello . . ."

"I'm here," he said. "Where were you today?"

"At school."

"I didn't see you," he said.

"Well, I was there."

He was sounding much too possessive — and even a little belligerent. What was going on with him, anyway?

Emry imagined she knew. He had not been the same since Victor had danced with her at the community center.

"I'll look for you tomorrow, okay?" she said and they said their goodbyes. When she hung up the phone, she pondered over their conversation for a moment before walking away. Had she been invisible to Johnny? Well, that was an interesting subject to pursue. She looked up as if looking into her room, knowing that Marius was there waiting for her.

Or was he? She nervously looked around. He could be anywhere and she would not know it. He could be following her around the house and she suddenly felt that was exactly what he was doing.

"Okay, Casper," she said aloud but just soft enough for only someone nearby to hear. "I know you're here. See if you can beat me to my bedroom."

She ran up the stairs and into her room, slamming the door closed as she entered it. She heard a chuckle in the corner and she turned to face Marius.

He was standing there smiling with amusement.

"How did you know?" he asked.

"I just figured," she said and then with some exasperation, she added, "You know, that's very creepy."

"Well, I *am* one of the Balfours," he said. "Besides, I had to keep an eye on you."

"It's okay," she said. She sat down on the side of her bed. "I gotta talk to you about Friday."

"Yes, I would say you should already have talked to me."

"Yeah, I know."

"You are going out with Johnny — to Gainesville?"

He did not sound as upset as Emry had expected.

"Yeah. I didn't think daddy would agree, but, well, you heard 'im."

He took a step toward her before speaking. "I wondered how this would happen," he cryptically said. "But fate will play out no matter how much we doubt it. Perhaps Johnny is the deus ex machina in this scene."

Emry looked up at him. "What does that mean?" she asked.

"I knew you would go to Gainesville sooner or later. I just did not know how or why, but Johnny has intervened and he may well change the course of events."

"Then, you aren't upset?"

"No. What must be, will be."

"Oh," she sighed, thinking that there was no use to try to understand him. "I'll get ready to go," she said with resignation.

An hour later, she was walking into the Balfour's mansion. Artemus was standing just inside the door, eating an apple. It surprised Emry so much that she stopped and stared.

"Want one?" he asked, but she simply shook her head and followed him.

He led her down the corridor and into the grand entrance. Tonight he did not turn the lights on, though. He just walked up the stairs, holding the candle so she could see.

She had been better prepared. Knowing what to expect, she had made a small bag of things she wanted to bring along and when she got into her room, she threw it down on the nearby chair. She had not made the bed before she had left that morning, but it was neatly made. She told herself it was probably an obsessive compulsive thing and she simply shrugged as she pulled the spread back and rearranged the pillows.

There was nothing to do but to go to sleep, so she stepped out of her jeans and turned off the light. Just like the night before, she got into the bed and left the lamp on. And just like the night before, she looked around with apprehension. She wriggled down and pulled the sheet higher under her chin and then she quietly fell asleep.

Sometime during the night, she awoke. The lamp was still on but the quiet house was not as quiet as it had been. Emry heard music playing softly and very far away. She listened intently. It was a violin and it was playing the song Victor had played for her in his car.

The difference was, it was a single violin. There were no other instruments accompanying. It was just one single violin playing alone, perfectly and without missing a note.

Emry sat up and trained her ear in the direction from which the music came.

"Victor," she whispered into the room. Almost as if her voice had broken some enchantment, the music stopped and silence once again filled the house. She waited, straining to hear more, but not a sound came from anywhere.

The next night, Emry felt more confident. She didn't dread the walk to her room nor feel uneasy once she was safely inside it. She actually felt snugly secure. She laid her bag on the chair and pulled a nightgown out of it, laying it on the bed as she looked around. The room was painfully neat and she wondered again if it was Victor's room.

She pulled off her shoes, stepped out of her jeans and then she pulled the nightgown on over her head. She climbed into the bed and without giving it a thought, she reached over and turned off the lamp.

The room went dark and Emry momentarily froze in place. It was an unconscious act that had turned the lamp off. She had done it without thinking, but once it was done, she didn't turn it on again.

The heavy velvet curtains were pulled back with a sash and only sheers covered the windows letting in a soft light. As her eyes adjusted, Emry saw the outline of now familiar objects. The shadows were still there, only deeper, but she was not apprehensive anymore. She lay in the bed looking around and listening with all her might for sounds in the night. There was nothing, not even the ticking of a clock. The house was as still and quiet as a tomb.

By Thursday night, the trip to the Balfours had become so routine that Emry was actually comfortable with the arrangement. She walked into the Balfour's house and without any help, she picked up the candle and went alone to her room. The only unusual thing was the appearance of Stefan. He was with Artemus when she arrived and he greeted her with a formal but adequate graciousness. There was still no sign of Victor. She wasn't surprised.

Emry threw down her bag and snapped on the lamp at the bedside table. As she unbuttoned her blouse, she walked to the door and flipped the switch that turned off the overhead light and then she walked back to the bed.

She pulled off the unbuttoned blouse and threw it on top of her bag. Her shoes came off next and then her jeans. The room felt chilly tonight and she quickly pulled the nightgown on over her head. She hurriedly jumped into the bed and pulled the sheet up to her chin, and then she snapped off the lamp.

The room went dark. It always gave Emry a momentary pause, but as the pale light from the window began to give form to the things in the room, she settled down and snuggled deeper under her covers.

She fell asleep but unlike the other nights, tonight she was restless and awoke repeatedly throughout the night. In the wee hours of the morning, she awoke with a start and sat upright in the bed, thinking she had heard something.

The night was very still and at first, she didn't hear a thing. But then, very slowly, her eyes turned toward the door. There was a slight stirring and then she saw him. Someone was standing there.

Emry gasped and then she spoke softly into the room. "Marius?" she said. "Artemus?"

The figure moved toward her and as he drew near he spoke.

"Hello, Emry," he softly greeted her and she recognized him. It was Victor. He came right up to the bed and Emry's heart began to pound.

Victor put a finger to his lips to caution her. "Sh-h-h," he said when she opened her mouth to speak. He reached for her and she went to him without any hesitation, coming to her feet to stand beside him.

He wrapped his arms around her in a tight embrace and she did the same to him.

"Is it really you?" she asked after a few moments.

"No," he said. "You are dreaming. I am only a dream."

She smiled. What a wonderful dream.

"Where've you been?" she asked and he relaxed his hold so that he could look down at her.

"Out," he simply said. "My family thinks it is unwise for us to be together." He smiled. "And they are right."

It was chilly in the room and she shivered.

"What?" he facetiously said. "Cold again?"

"I can't help it," she said and his smile broadened.

"Back into the bed," he said. He pulled the covers back and she reluctantly climbed in again. He tucked the sheet around her and then he pulled the spread up. She anxiously looked up at him, thinking he was leaving. She didn't want him to leave.

"Don't go," she begged him.

He paused as if he was uncertain, and then he glanced at the door.

Emry had seen that look before and she knew what it meant. He was going to leave. She inhaled with a slight gasp.

"Please!" she softly pleaded and he quickly turned his attention back to her.

He hesitated only a moment before taking off his shoes and pushing them aside. Emry breathlessly waited as he carefully lay down beside her. He was on top of the spread, and she was under it, but he slipped his arm under her shoulders and gently drew her to him. Emry pushed the sheet aside so that her arms were free and when she did, he embraced her. His lips brushed gently across her cheek and his breath touched her ear with pleasing effect. She took a deep breath and let it out and then she wrapped her arms around his neck.

"Oh, Emry," he sighed with that same apologetic tone he had used before. It made Emry smile.

"I'm so glad you're here," she softly whispered.

"I am not here," he said. "You are dreaming. Remember? You are just dreaming."

And then, he kissed her.

Chapter Twenty-three

Friday afternoon, Johnny arrived just a few minutes before five o'clock. He was dressed in jeans and a blue, long sleeved t-shirt and he was wearing sunglasses that reflected everything like a mirror.

He was rather quiet. Emry imagined he was still mad at her. He had not been especially friendly since the night Victor had danced with her at the community center, and, too, he knew this was probably the last time they would go out together.

Johnny drove to Palatka and took State Road 100 to Melrose, coming into Gainesville on the northeast side of the town. They went directly to Satchel's restaurant on 23rd street. There were colorful lights strung all around and a hippy van parked out front. It was a popular eating place, especially on a Friday night, so there was a long wait to get seated. Johnny gave his name and cell phone number to the hostess and then he and Emry wandered around, looking over the place. It was easy to pass the time. Behind the restaurant were a gift shop and a junk museum. There was also a room where a live band often played. There were tables there and people were eating pizza they had gotten as a take-out from the restaurant. Some of them were just drinking beer or tea or in some cases, Cheer Wine.

Before Emry knew it, the restaurant was ringing Johnny's cell phone, telling him their table was ready. They walked back to the front and the hostess seated them inside at a table near a wall with local art on it.

The fare was mostly Italian. Johnny ordered a slice of pizza and Emry got a calzone. It was the best she had ever eaten, but the largest, too. She sorrowfully left half of it behind, regretting the fact that she couldn't take it with her.

The evening was warm. The temperatures, true to the Florida climate, had climbed back up into the high seventies and tonight it was comfortably warm.

They drove downtown and began looking for a parking place. They found a lot with metered parking, but it was full. A minute later, Johnny parallel parked on the street just a block away from the coffee shop. As they walked up the street, Emry could hear the band playing.

It was an Irish band and they were better than Emry had expected. A girl was playing a pennywhistle and another girl was keeping time on the bodhrán. All the other members of the band were boys. A short guy with blonde hair was playing a violin and a man with a head full of curly brown hair and a full beard was playing a concertina. He occasionally put down the concertina and picked up a banjo, alternating between the two instruments as the songs required. Once he even traded those instruments for a guitar which he played as admirably as he had the concertina and the banjo.

There was an empty table near the curb and she and Johnny sat down at it. His eyes immediately scanned the crowd and then came to rest on Emry.

It was odd that Johnny had not warmed up to her. He was still very quiet, almost sullen, and Emry was beginning to be more than indifferent on the subject. Not entirely, though. After they had gotten a cup of coffee and they were listening to the band, she asked him about it.

"What's wrong, Johnny?" she asked. "You aren't yourself tonight."

After the sun had completely set, he had taken off his sunglasses, but he squinted now as if the street lights hurt his eyes. Emry took a closer look at him. Was he on drugs?

"Nothing," he said. "Aren't you havin' a good time?"

"Yes. The band's really good. Do you know all of them?"

"No," he said, sounding impatient with her.

There was one obscure fellow in the back and he was the only one Johnny really knew. He was sitting in a chair and was turned so that Emry could see only the side of his face. He was playing a guitar and he was slumped over it so that his long hair fell across his face. There were tattoos all up and down his arms and on every other exposed bit of skin, and as it turned out, he was the only one that Johnny knew. Emry wondered where he had found such a guy.

He shrugged indifferently when Emry said something about it.

But just then, Johnny's eyes looked past Emry and his expression changed in an instant. The change was so dramatic that Emry turned in her chair and looked over her shoulder. Every muscle in her body tensed. Abby was walking toward them.

It was Abby, but it wasn't Abby — not the Abby Emry had known, anyway. She approached with the same graceful step that had always complimented her long legs and her sleek, slender body. Her red hair swayed with just the right amount of movement, some of it falling across her cheeks, but her skin was pale and her lips unusually bright.

She was still beautiful, but she lacked something that she had had before. She had lost the gentleness of eye. There was a hardness there now that gave her a feral look like that of a threatened tigress.

Emry froze. She was actually frightened and in that moment, she could neither move nor speak. Abby continued to walk toward them and all Emry could do was sit and stare.

Abby stopped by Emry's chair and then she leaned toward her. It was like looking into the face of death itself.

"Well, Emry," she said. "I'm glad to see you." Her voice was different. It was an octave lower and rich, but at the same time oleaginous. She looked across the table at Johnny. "You brought her. Good boy." She sounded like a master praising an obedient dog.

Emry commanded her muscles to move and she spun around to face Johnny, her mouth opened in shock and surprise.

It was all beginning to make sense — the sullenness, the sunglasses, the long sleeved shirt on a balmy night — he was being turned.

"Oh, Johnny!" she exclaimed.

"It's okay," he said. He reached across the table and took her hand. "You'll see. Everything's okay."

"Come on. Let's go," Abby said.

"Okay," Johnny readily agreed and he stood up, but Emry only looked at them.

"Now?" Emry asked. "We just got here."

Johnny was excited and right away Emry could see he was impatient to go with Abby. Was she the one turning him? Emry imagined so. The look he gave her seemed to indicate a bond between them.

But then, Emry had to wonder why Abby was interested in Johnny. Yes, he was adorably cute, but there had to be more to it. Emry knew or she figured she knew. It was not about Johnny, it was about Emry, and when you came right down to it, that meant it was really about Victor.

The thought caused Emry to look around. Were the Balfours here? Was Victor here? Her heart began to beat heavily.

"Come on, Emry," Abby impatiently said. "We don't want to miss the party."

"Party?" Emry looked at Johnny. "You didn't say anything about a party."

He was not listening. Being near Abby had done something to him. It was almost as if he was intoxicated.

Abby pulled Emry to her feet and Emry frantically looked around. No one seemed to notice. The band played on and everyone's attention was turned in that direction. Emry wondered if she should scream, but somehow she knew that would only make her look like a fool. No one would know there were vampires among them and if she said such a thing, they would lock her away for insanity.

"Come on," Abby said again and this time she began walking, dragging Emry along with her.

Away from the coffee shop, it was dark. They had taken only twenty steps when the light faded away behind them and shadows surrounded them.

"Wait, Abby," Emry said, trying to pull back. There was no way to escape from that powerful hold, and even as she said it, she saw that it was useless to try. Van was there, just a few feet away, and with him were two other vampires.

He looked pleased. No, it was more than that. He was smugly satisfied.

"Well, hello, Emry," he said and remarkably, his greeting was so similar to Victors that it gave Emry a start. "Don't be afraid. You're among friends here."

"I would not exactly call you a friend," a voice from the darkness spoke and Stefan Balfour stepped out of the shadows to materialize beside them.

The vampires tensed and turned with a snarl — all except Van. He stood calmly at ease.

"Hello, Father," he said. "It's been a long time."

"Yes," Stefan agreed. "But do not call me father after what you have done."

Emry looked at Van and then she looked at Stefan. What were they talking about?

Van's eyes shifted to Emry and he seemed to read her

thoughts.

"Yes, Emry," he said. "I'm the scion of Stefan Balfour. Victor is my brother."

"Half-brother," Victor said as he, too, materialized from the darkness.

"Oh, yes, we mustn't forget that distinction," Van said. He showed no surprise as Artemus and Marius also appeared, completing a loose circle that surrounded the vampires.

"I wouldn't start anything if I were you," Van went on to say. "I have more friends with me. They're waiting in the crowd to make a distraction if I need one."

The Balfours looked toward the coffee shop. They knew what Van meant. He had done this sort of thing before and in a group like this it would be a bloodbath.

"Besides, you've got another problem that you aren't even aware of."

All eyes turned back to Van and he mockingly chuckled.

"Oh, come, come. She's a tempting little morsel, Victor, as you already know, but I'm not going to die for her, as you probably would, and may yet, I might add."

"Let her go," Victor said.

"Here, take her," Van said, raising his hands agreeably. "But aren't you asking yourself about my back-up plan?"

Emry was free and she ran to Victor. He defensively pushed her behind him and she clung to him while looking around his shoulder.

"It will reveal itself soon enough," Stefan said.

"Will it?" He looked around in mock concern and then,

anomalously added. "You seem to be missing someone. Oh, yes, Joseph. It's been so long, I'd almost forgotten him." His jeering expression suddenly turned serious. "Almost, but not completely."

Artemus was the first to react. He pulled out a Glock 21 Gen4 .45 automatic revolver and pointed it right at Van's heart. "You do anything to Joseph and the people you hide behind will no longer matter. I will kill a hundred if I have to to get to you."

Victor was only a second behind him. He pulled out a Ruger SP 101, 357 Magnum and held it between his two fists, aiming it with precision at Van's vulnerable heart.

Marius and Stefan were almost as fast, but so was Van. He pulled Johnny in front of him and Abby just instinctively put her back against his. The two unknown vampires took a defensive posture, one on each side of Van.

"Wait!" Stefan called out, seeing the charged atmosphere and realizing it was a lost cause. "Do not let him delay us. Go — go!"

They backed away taking Emry with them. Van and his entourage waited without a word until the Balfours were out of sight and then it was Abby who tensed with the anticipation of following them.

"Come on! Let's hurry before they get away," she said, but Van shook his head.

"No, let them go. Only a fool would follow them right now."

"But they'll mess up your plans," she insisted.

"They've already messed up my plans," he irritably said. "That's why I always have a backup plan." He thoughtfully looked into the darkness where the Balfours had disappeared only a minute before. "I'll get one of them, though — maybe two, and then I'll take Emry, anyway."

"What?" Johnny asked. He was in a bit of a stupor. Being near Abby had an odd effect on him. "Where's Emry? I've gotta take 'er home."

Van scowled. He had no patience when he was irritated. "Take care of him," he said to Abby. "And then meet me at the car."

"Come on," she said to Johnny, but her tone made him flinch. For a brief moment, a warning went off in his head, but just as quickly, it disappeared.

He looked at her and his pulse quickened. She was like a drug and he was the addict who could not resist. He did not even want to resist. Abby took his hand, and his mind filled with thoughts of pleasure. He was ready to go with her and he impatiently tugged at her hand.

She looked at Van and he jerked his head with an impatient gesture. She nodded and let Johnny pull her down the street.

And in the background, the band played on . . .

Chapter Twenty-four

Victor pulled Emry with him and when Van's group disappeared behind them, she suddenly felt a whirl of heart stopping sensation like having the bottom pulled out from under her or as if she had careened over a giant hill in a roller coaster. She had time only to catch her breath and then she was standing beside the Jaguar, Victor opening the door.

She swayed and he caught her and a second later she was seated beside him. He spun out of the parking space and raced down the street and they were almost out of Gainesville before Emry recovered enough to speak.

"What just happened?" she asked.

Victor's eyes shifted to her and then right back to the road.

"I had to get you out of there quickly," he said and then he reached across the car and gently took her hand. "Are you alright?"

She gripped his hand and nodded. "I think so," she said, but then she cast a glance over her shoulder and out the back of the car. "Johnny!" she exclaimed. "What about Johnny? We have to help him."

Victor carefully pulled his hand back and gripped the steering wheel. "We cannot help him," he said. "It is too late for that."

"He's one of them?"

"Not yet," Victor said, "but I have a feeling he has outlived his usefulness. Johnny is not going to make it."

Emry looked over her shoulder again. "We could try to help him," she anxiously said, but Victor shook his head.

"No, Emry," Victor said. "I cannot help Johnny even if there was time — and there isn't."

"How do you know?"

"Because I know Hugo."

"It doesn't make sense to kill your own."

"It makes sense to get rid of what you cannot take with you, and Johnny would only be a burden on them when they pull out tonight."

"They're leaving?" Emry asked. Did that mean Victor was leaving, too?

He looked straight ahead for a few seconds before answering. "Not right away. It is all coming to a head, Emry, and before this night is over, a lot is going to happen — most of it not very good, I'm afraid."

"What is happening, Victor?"

His foot pressed the accelerator and the Jaguar raced down State Road 20.

"Hugo is making his move," Victor said. "He has a strange sense of humor. He finds it funny to torment us."

There was a moment of silence and then Emry tentatively said, "I don't understand."

Victor turned his head and looked at Emry and the Jaguar held steady on the road without wavering an inch. "It has to do with bloodlines," he said. "I chose to be what I am, but Hugo was born to be what he is."

He looked at the road again and Emry carefully asked, "What is he?"

"He is a vampire — but not just a vampire. You see, he was born to my father after my father had been changed. He is a new creature, Emry — a frightening creature and it is all because of Balfour blood."

"So, he really is your brother."

"My half-brother," Victor reminded her.

Emry tried to get that straight in her head, but for some reason, she couldn't untangle it nor reason it out.

"You have different mothers," she said, trying to understand, "But who is his mother?"

"Her name was Geneva," Victor said.

"Was?" Emry asked. She wondered if Hugo had killed his mother just like Lorna had killed hers. The question was in her eyes and Victor seemed to read it there.

"He did not kill her, if that is what you are thinking," he said. "She died in her own time, just like everyone does."

"You mean, she wasn't one of you?"

He shook his head. "No," he said. "She was not."

"She was like me," Emry said. "Your father married a girl that was no different than me."

Victor's brow creased and his lips tightened. After a few seconds he nodded his head. "She was a lot like you."

"So, what happened? How did it happen?"

"It is a long story," Victor said, "but I guess it is time I explained."

"I think so," Emry said.

Victor looked at her again, but this time, it was a look full of questions. He hoped Artemus was right. If she was enough like Thomas Winters, she would understand, but if she wasn't, then this would be the end. Well, wasn't that the whole idea — to end it all forever? He shifted his gaze back to the road and tried very hard to convince himself that he had to do the right thing.

"You have asked me what I am," Victor said, "and I have skirted the edges of the truth in answering you. The problem is, I don't really know what I am."

"Maybe you *are* an angel," Emry said and his expression momentarily softened with amusement. It didn't take long for it to return to its former dark study.

"Before this night is over, you will know how wrong you are to say that."

Emry didn't agree with him, but strangely, she had a funny feeling.

"I was once a normal teenager, as blissfully ignorant as anyone else, I guess. We all were — blissfully ignorant, I mean," he said, referring to his family. "And then, Lorna brought Demetrius into our family."

He paused to wrinkle his brow as if giving that serious consideration.

"She was engaged to marry Marius, you know, but when Demetrius came along, it was like she abandoned all propriety and lost her sense of decorum.

"We did not know Demetrius was a vampire. At the time, it

was just her indiscretion that caused us concern. Looking back, it is so clear to me," he said with true sorrow.

"You can't blame yourself," Emry said, wanting to erase the hurt in his eyes.

"No, I guess not," he agreed. "It is just so frustrating to know now what I wish I had known then."

"Would it really have helped?" Emry asked. "Or would it have just gotten you all killed?"

He chuckled with wry humor. "It would probably have gotten us all killed," he agreed. "I have often wondered why Demetrius did not kill Marius, anyway. You see what a hothead Marius is. He has always been that way."

Emry smiled, thinking how she had changed her opinion of Marius. After this past week, she and Marius had become good friends.

"Anyway," Victor said, getting on with his story, "you know what happened. He turned her and then she killed mother." There was a slight tremor in his voice, but he hardly paused a second. "We set out after her and Demetrius — babes in the woods," he said. "We were babes in the woods with hate and vengeance on our minds. It is a bad combination. In three years, I had lost four of my seven brothers and Father had been wounded almost to death two different times, and yet, we had come no closer to getting Demetrius.

"That is when we found Brother Cavanaugh. He was an eccentric hermit of a monk. He lived alone in a cave where he practiced a religion that I am afraid was more liberal than his order approved. He had something we wanted, though — the power to kill Demetrius. He promised us if we would follow his teachings, we would have our revenge, and he was right."

He stopped talking and he looked at Emry. His dark eyes were like a black abyss at that moment.

"I cannot tell you what happened to me," he continued. "Maybe it was magic. I don't know. But there are powers in this world that with the right knowledge can be tapped into. Brother Cavanaugh had learned how. He said it was God Almighty, but I am afraid it was the Devil himself who taught him."

"The Devil wouldn't give secrets away to destroy his own," Emry pointed out and Victor smiled.

"Maybe not. I hope you are right. The truth is," he went on, "at that time, we did not care one way or the other. We were consumed with the desire to kill Demetrius and that was all we cared about.

"We spent two years there with Brother Cavanaugh and I am not going to tell you about what we went through during that time, but I will tell you this. It was not easy. I went to hell and back again but I would do it again given the same set of circumstances."

"Is that when you became a vampire?" Emry interrupted him.

"Yes," he honestly answered her. "And then I overcame the vampire within me and killed it."

"You can do that?"

He cast a glance her way. "With the proper training," he said. "And that is what Brother Cavanaugh gave us. My heart was beating just like before and I was free from the boundaries of the night, but I was not a man anymore."

He looked at the road. They were coming into Hawthorne and he slowed down when the speed limit dropped to thirty-five miles per hour. They went over the overpass and the road narrowed. Immediately, Victor sped up again.

"I had become what it would take to destroy Demetrius, and, after all, that was the whole idea, but none of us had anticipated exactly what we would be like after those two years — not even Brother Cavanaugh. We were unique. Maybe it was something peculiar to us alone and maybe it was the hate that was driving us. Whatever the reason, when we emerged from that cave, Demetrius fled, instinctively knowing that he could not defeat us, and it took us many years to finally catch up with him."

He paused as if remembering what else had happened when they had found Demetrius. He had killed his sister. He shook as if removing the thought and then he continued with his story.

"We had quite a reputation by then," he said. "And we always went wherever we were called, but we had lost the fire that had driven us before. We wanted to simply retire and settle down somewhere, and each of us tried.

"Artemus went back to his wife, and my father returned to a woman he had met in the southern part of Ireland."

Emry was quick to notice that he never mentioned what he had retired to.

"Her name was Geneva. Father had saved her from a vampire attack, coming upon them just as the vampire had begun to feed. He killed the vampire, but Geneva was in a bad way and he stayed with her, treating her wound and nursing her back to health. He left her after a month, but he never forgot about her. After we killed Demetrius, he went back, and she was waiting as if she knew he would come back one day. They married and a year later, Geneva was pregnant."

He stopped there and Emry watched the change that came over him. It was a deathly calm that gave him a feral look not unlike the one Emry had seen in Abby's eyes.

"No one expected that," he said. "It was not supposed to happen. We were told it could not happen, but there she was — just as pregnant as she could be."

"But how?" Emry asked, interrupting him again.

"I don't know. Maybe the vampire bite . . ."

His voice trailed off into nothing and he stared down the road in thought.

"We were stunned and some of us in disbelief," he said, suddenly talking again. "Marius insisted Geneva had been unfaithful and the child belonged to some man in the nearby village, but after Hugo was born, it did not take long to see that Marius was wrong. Hugo was definitely my father's son."

They came up behind a slow moving car and Victor went around it without incident in a no passing zone. His foot pressed against the accelerator and the Jaguar sped up. The road was narrow and winding and Emry nervously gripped the edge of the seat, but the car held to the road.

"There is something in us," Victor said. "Something that is passed down through the bloodline — something that is not normal even by the standards of what we are now."

He looked across the car at Emry.

"It goes from generation to generation," he said.

"How do you know?" Emry asked.

"Because Hugo has passed it on in his children and they to theirs."

Emry gasped. "Hugo has children? I never dreamed . . ." She flashed a frightened look at Victor. "What about Artemus? You said he went back to his wife."

"They did not have any more children and when all this happened, he and his wife mutually agreed that he should leave. He saw that his family was cared for, but he never lived with them again."

"So, she knew."

"Yes, she knew from the very beginning."

"I'm so sorry," Emry said as she thought about the handsome warrior of a brother that Artemus was. Perhaps hate was still driving him.

"Which brings me to what is going on tonight," Victor said. "It may have escaped your notice, but if I lost four brothers out of seven, then there are three of us left."

Emry mentally counted the Balfours. Stefan, Artemus, Marius, and Victor. She was counting Marius as a brother, but that was incorrect. He was Lorna's fiancé.

"You have another brother," she stated with great wonder.

"Yes — Father Joe is my brother," he said, using the familiar name.

Emry was so stunned, he could have knocked her over with

a feather.

"Did you hear what Hugo said tonight about Joseph? He was letting us know that Joseph is the target. That is why I am in a hurry."

He flew around another car just then and took an s-curve without slowing down.

"Then, it was never me?" Emry asked, relieved and aggravated all at the same time.

Victor cast a quick glance at her.

"It was you — and me, and Joseph. Hugo wants to destroy us, but first he has to play. He is like a cat with a mouse. Sometimes, that is to our advantage."

"You're going to St. Peters?"

"Yes, but first, I am taking you to my house where you will be safe."

"I've got to go home," Emry insisted. "My parents'll kill me."

"It will be better to deal with punishment from them than face what may happen if you go home tonight. You might be putting your whole family in danger."

Emry looked down the road, her heart in her throat. That was one of the things that had always worried her. She had always worried that her family would not be safe.

"Hugo would not send just any vampire to confront Joseph," Victor explained. "He will send his family. I cannot help Joseph if I have to protect you. I will probably lose both of you if that happens. Let me take you to my house so that my mind can be clear."

"I'm afraid," she anxiously said. "The house frightens me. I even slept with the lights on while I was there."

He glanced at her and then immediately back at the road. "Yes, I know," he said.

She stiffened and her eyes slowly made their way across the car where they rested on him. She had dreamed he had come to her. It was a beautiful dream, but one so full of passion that her face burned with the memory of it.

"How do you know?" she carefully asked.

"I occasionally checked on you."

"I thought you were out," Emry said.

"I was in and out."

She was blushing. She hoped he couldn't see, but she knew only too well how well he could see in the dark.

He reached across the car and touched her cheek. He found the stray wisp of hair that he always found and he moved it aside.

"It is all right," he gently said.

"It wasn't a dream, was it?" she said. It took her several tries to get it out, but finally the words made it past her lips.

"No," he honestly answered.

She swallowed. "How much have I forgotten?"

"Nothing. I would not do that," he said. "I would not make you forget something like that."

"Then, why did you make me think it was a dream?"

"I thought it would be easier on you when I left."

She jerked like she had been stung by a bee, but she felt like she'd been kicked in the stomach by a bull.

"I thought you were just going to make me forget."

"You will not forget everything — even if I want you to." He looked at her again. "And there are some things I want you to remember."

"You can pick and choose?"

"No, it has gone too far for that. It is all or nothing now."

"So the last two months of my life will just be erased. They didn't exist."

He shook his head. "No," he said. "That is not the way it works. I was a part of your life. Lots of people know that. I cannot erase everyone's memories, so I cannot remove myself completely from yours." He looked across the car at her. "You just will not remember me the same way."

She turned quickly toward him. "I don't want to forget you," she said. "I really want to remember you just like you are."

They came into the town of Interlachen and Victor slowed down. The red light caught them and he stopped long enough for a truck to go through the intersection and then he ran the red light. The road widened into a four lane and he sped up, running the next red light without even slowing down.

"If you only knew, one day you would thank me for making you forget," he said. He looked at her again. "I am not coming back, Emry. I cannot. And if I could make myself forget you, I would."

Something in the tone of his voice pricked her memory and she remembered something else from the night before. Victor had said he loved her. She remembered the words as clear as a bell and her answering affirmation that she loved him, too.

But did it count? Did he mean it or had it only been said in the heat of the moment?

She began to cry. He touched her face and ran his hand across her head and down her hair in comfort.

"Go ahead," he said. "It's okay to cry."

She cried all the way to Palatka, but when Victor turned the Jaguar down State Road 19, she had cried it all out. He was holding her hand by then but he turned her loose to get a tissue for her.

"Here," he said as he handed it to her.

"Thanks," she replied.

"Feel better?" he asked.

"No."

He didn't say anything and they rode in silence until he turned left on US 17. Bostwick was only a few minutes down the road.

"I have been thinking," he said, sounding perplexed. "I am afraid none of us has this figured right."

"What d' ya' mean?"

"Hugo set the stage and we jumped into the act just like he wanted us to."

"What else could you do?" Emry asked and just then, Victor's cell phone began to ring. He answered it and Emry could hear Stefan's voice on the other end.

"How quickly can you get here?" he asked.

"Five minutes," Victor answered. "No, make that a few more. I have to drop Emry off."

"Bring more weapons," Stefan said. "And ammunition."

"What is wrong?"

"Hugo's oldest son is here."

"Faust? I am on my way."

Victor laid his phone down and at the same time, his foot pressed the accelerator. The Jaguar shot down the road like a bullet.

He picked the phone up again, but this time, he held it out to Emry.

"Take this," he said. "If you need help, Artemus is number two on speed dial."

She took the phone from him and looked down at it. It was a smart phone and she wasn't sure she knew how to operate it. He gave her some quick instructions and then, he was turning onto Palmetto Bluff Road in Bostwick. Emry felt an anxiousness that sat it her stomach like a lead weight.

They passed Jim's house and then Ellen's. Emry looked at them, wondering how she was going to explain all this. She'd be lucky if they didn't have her committed.

The Jaguar stopped at the locked gate. Victor pressed in a code and it opened, letting them in. He drove swiftly down the long driveway, pulling right up to the back door and stopping.

"Hurry!" he said as he jumped out of the car. Emry understood the urgency and she moved as quickly as she could.

They ran into the house and Victor ran straight to the kitchen table. It was covered with an arsenal of weapons.

"I thought you needed wooden stakes and crosses," Emry said as she looked at the table.

"They work, too," he said with a smile, then more seriously, he added, "These are special. Artemus has designed the bullets and the weapons have been modified." He picked up a Glock and slid the top back to cock it. "If anything goes wrong, this one is ready to use. Aim for the heart."

He laid the pistol on the table and he grabbed up several others. He picked up boxes of ammunition and then he started for the door.

He stopped and he turned to Emry. His hands were full, but he leaned down and kissed her gently on her lips.

"Stay inside," he said. "No one can come in even if you invite them. Only I or one of my family can bring anyone in here so you are safe."

"Will you be safe?" she asked and he gave her a wry smile.

"I will be very careful," he said and then he kissed her again before rushing out the door. He whirled out of the driveway and in only seconds, he was out of sight.

Emry stood alone in the dimly lit kitchen. Only the single candle burned there. She took it up and walked down the corridor that led to the grand entrance of the house and once there, she walked to the staircase and set her foot on the first step.

She stopped there and then she looked around, first up the stairs and then over her shoulder. She had a peculiar feeling of being watched but she knew if Victor was right then no one could be in the house.

But were they outside watching her through the windows? She felt exposed and oddly, vulnerable, so she quickly ran up the stairs and to her room. She slammed the door shut and then she leaned against it, still holding the candle in her right hand. Very carefully she stepped into the room and set the candle on the table. She backed away from it and stood in the deep shadows.

Someone had pulled the curtains so Emry could not see outside, but something continued to bother her. She stared at the windows and wondered what was in the night. Could vampires come onto the property or like the house, were they barred from entrance?

Strangely, she was drawn to the windows. She stared at them for some time before slowly walking across the room to stand before the one on the right side of the bed. She stood there looking at the curtain, an odd feeling of anticipation and compulsion making her at last move the curtain aside.

A man's face was against the window pane. He was looking in at her with large, staring eyes and Emry screamed before almost fainting and falling to the floor.

Chapter Twenty-five

Emry scrambled to her feet and ran stumbling to the door, putting as much distance between her and the window as she could.

Something rattled downstairs and she paused at the door, holding onto the frame for support.

The vampires were here and they knew she was defenseless — or was she? There was a table full of weapons downstairs.

The candle flickered with light inside her room, but everywhere else was dark as pitch. Emry flipped a nearby light switch, but nothing happened. She wondered what that meant. Had the vampires disabled the generator, or was it simply not on? Victor had had too much on his mind to think about a generator. It was probably just not on.

She needed the candle, but she was afraid to go back into the room. She heard something overhead and she looked up. What were they doing? Were they climbing over the house looking for a way inside? Emry's legs began to tremble. She had never been so frightened.

She summoned all her courage and ran into the room, snatching up the candle off of the table just as something broke outside. It sounded like glass shattering and Emry fearfully wondered if a window had been broken.

She held the candle before her and ran down the stairs and

into the kitchen. Everything was just like Victor had left it, but Emry wasn't so sure it was. He said nothing could come in, but what if Hugo had figured out a way. Hadn't Victor said he was very much like them? And, he was a Balfour. Maybe that was all it took to get inside.

Emry looked around. Was she alone or was Hugo Balfour there with her?

She picked up the Glock and held it in her fist. She knew very little about guns, but she had seen enough police-type movies to know how to hold it.

The door rattled. The candle was giving away her position in the house, but she dared not blow it out. She considered shouting out a warning, but she quickly abandoned that idea. She told herself to just stay quiet and wait patiently for Victor to return. She sat down on a chair by the table and held the gun in her lap.

Two thoughts immediately popped into her head, and both of them sent a shudder down her spine.

What if Victor did not return or what if he returned and stepped into an ambush? She came to her feet so quickly, she almost knocked over the chair.

And then, she remembered the cell phone Victor had given her. Not ever having one herself, she had completely forgotten about it.

Emry was so relieved, she almost laughed aloud. She pulled the phone out of her pocket and following Victor's instructions, she called Artemus.

The phone rang one time and went to voice mail. Emry

looked at the phone in her hand with dismay. What did that mean? Was his phone turned off? Why would he do that at a time like this?

Something was wrong. Artemus was in trouble and if he was in trouble, then all of the Balfours were probably in trouble.

Emry saw something move past the window and she looked up. There it was again, a shadow that moved past the window like a cloud. She carefully laid the phone on the table and held the gun with both hands.

The face appeared at the window and Emry fired.

The vampire fell away and Emry didn't know if she had hit him or if he had simply jumped out of the way. She stood holding the gun before her, staring at the hole she had made in the window, and wondering what she should do next. She finally inched toward the window, stopping when she came to a place where she could see outside. The man was lying on the ground, but as she watched, he moved and then he turned over. He got his hands under himself and he tried to push himself up. He was having trouble, but he was doing it. Emry watched in mute fascination as he struggled to his feet, at last succeeding in standing up.

"Aim for the heart," she heard Victor say. She steadied her hand and pulled the trigger. The vampire went down, and he didn't get up.

A sound arose from the rooftop. It was a wail that made Emry's blood run cold. She looked up, more afraid now than she had been before. The howl died away and in the silence that followed, a train whistled long and lonely.

Emry stood very still, holding the pistol and looking out the window. Nothing happened. The train rumbled by on the nearby track and then everything was quiet. She relaxed and brought her hand down, her arms suddenly too tired to hold out straight anymore.

She had to do something, but she didn't know what to do. She wanted to leave, but she was afraid to walk outside, especially after hearing that bloodcurdling howl.

She wondered if she should call her daddy, but she immediately rejected that idea. Jim? Well, that might not be such a bad idea, but what would she say to him? If she told him what was really happening, he'd think she had lost her mind. Besides, he'd probably go straight to Stanley and then they'd both come over and get themselves killed.

The gun was suddenly too heavy to hold. She laid it on the table and then she sat down. She leaned forward and rested her head in her hands.

Her strength returned and with it, came an urgency to get out of the Balfour mansion. She looked at the window, wondering what was out there. It was vampires. She was sure of that.

Something banged against the side of the house bringing Emry to her feet. It crashed and then glass shattered. It scraped down the side of the wall and complained like boards being pried away. It sounded like someone was tearing a hole in the side of the house.

Again, she wondered if Victor could be wrong. Hugo was a Balfour and so were his children. Maybe any one of them could come inside.

She needed help. She picked up Victor's phone from the table, but she looked at it for a few seconds before doing anything. Not ever having a cell phone, the smart phone was a complicated piece of engineering to Emry. She looked at it in dismay, wishing she had a number for Stefan or Marius.

She didn't know their numbers, but she had friends and she knew their phone numbers by heart. Maybe one of her friends would go to the church and get Victor. She immediately thought of Brad.

Emry punched in his number and the phone began to ring.

She paced the floor while waiting for him to answer and praying all the while that he would answer. She heard a sound upstairs and she paused in concern. Had something gotten in? Emry almost held her breath as she waited, listening, trying to decide what it was she had heard.

Not another sound came from anywhere, except the phone ringing in her ear — once, twice, three times.

"Hullo," Brad said in his very distinctive southern brogue.

"Brad? It's Emry. Hey, where are you?"

"Ummm," he drawled. "I'm in Boogerville."

That was a tiny community on the Putnam/Clay County line. It was five minutes down the road.

"Where're you?" he curiously asked, "an' whose phone you got? I only answered outta curiosity."

"You'd never believe," she said, "but it's Victor's cell phone."

"Whhaaat! Victor Balfour?"

"I'll explain later," she said, "but right now, I'm in trouble and I need your help."

"Is he tryin' t' hurt you?" he asked. Emry could hear the concern in his voice.

"No. Victor won't hurt me. He's been trying to help me, but listen, I don't have much time. Can you go to the Catholic Church and get him?"

Silence.

"Hello . . . Brad?"

"Yeah," he said. "I'm here, but I don't think I heard you right. You want me t' go to the Catholic Church and git Victor Balfour. What for?"

"Tell him I'm in trouble. He'll know what t' do."

"What kinda trouble you in?" Brad asked. There was real concern in his voice now.

"The kind that only Victor can help me with. Please, Brad, can you do it?"

"It'll take about ten or fifteen minutes. Is that okay?"

"Yeah, just hurry."

She ended the call and dropped the phone into her pocket. The house was so quiet that it disturbed Emry in a way that the noise had not. She listened with her head tilted first one way and then the other, but there wasn't a sound anywhere. The house was as quiet as death.

Death? The word pricked a part of Emry's consciousness that made her pause and rethink what she had just done. She could not send Brad to the church. There were vampires there. What if the Balfours were all hurt — or dead, and she sent Brad there to his death, too?

Emry dug into her pocket for the phone, fumbling with it as she anxiously tried to get it out. Her hands were trembling and she almost dropped it, but she finally got in straight in her hands and again she punched in Brad's number.

"Hullo," he answered on the first ring.

"Don't go to the church!" she shouted. "Brad . . . Hey, Brad! Don't go to the church."

"Okay," he said. "You okay?"

"Yeah," she lied.

"You don't sound okay."

"I am, though — honest! Just don't go to the church."

"You ain't in trouble no more?"

"No. I'm sorry I got you involved."

"You sure one o' them Balfours ain't tryin' t' hurt you?"

"No," she said. She could hear the tone of her voice rising the longer she talked. "I gotta go."

"Emry?"

"Yeah?"

"Where are you? Are you at home?"

"No," she answered.

"I'll go get your dad if you want me to — or Jim."

"No! For heaven's sakes, no!"

"Then tell me what's goin' on. You got us all worried and upset."

"Us?"

"Me 'n' Beaker."

Oh, great! She was putting both Brad and Beaker in

danger. She should have known. They were always together.

She had to redirect his thoughts, give him a story he could believe, but one that would make him lay off.

"I'm gonna tell you something, Brad, but you gotta keep it a secret," Emry said. "I've been seeing Victor Balfour — you know, like, he's my boyfriend." She swallowed hard because she imagined Victor would be horrified if he knew she had said such a thing.

"Victor Balfour's yore boyfriend!"

"Cool!" Emry heard Beaker say in the background.

"We argued and he left. I was tryin' to get him back," she lied. "But he called. Everything's okay — okay?"

"Yeah, okay, I guess. You sure he ain't tryin' t' hurt you?"

"No, he wouldn't do that. He's really a nice guy."

A loud thump upstairs caused Emry to inhale with a loud gasp. "Hey, guys, I gotta go," she said. "Talk to ya' later." She hung up before Brad could respond and then she waited, looking at the ceiling in fearful anticipation.

She had to get out of the house. Something was in the house. She just knew it, and she had to get out.

Emry paced the floor. Victor said to stay in the house, but he didn't know something would get in the house. She paced faster. She had to get out.

The table drew her attention. The Glock Victor had prepared for her was lying there and Emry picked it up. She wondered how many bullets it carried. She had fired it twice. How many more shots did she have before it would be empty? She had no idea.

There were several other guns on the table. She picked up a small revolver and tested its weight in her hand. It had a good feel and it was small enough she was not intimidated by it. That gave her two guns. She was beginning to have more confidence.

Emry walked to a place in the kitchen where she could see out the window. The vampire she had shot was still lying there. She hoped that meant he was permanently out of commission.

She turned her head and as she did, her peripheral vision picked up a movement. Emry looked back again, but she didn't see anything. Carefully, she turned her head and sure enough, she caught a glimpse of a shadow that moved gently like a breeze. Without waiting, Emry lifted the gun and fired.

A girl came into complete focus. She grabbed at her shoulder and then stumbled, the look of hate making her face ugly with rage.

She appeared to be having trouble. The bullet had not killed her, but it seemed to have almost paralyzed her. Emry fired again, but she missed and this time, the vampire fell out of sight.

Four shots. How many more did she have in the Glock? Emry picked up a rifle that had a strap attached to it and she slung it over her shoulder.

Now's the time! She thought. While the vampire was partially immobile, now was the time to leave.

Holding the two pistols and carrying the rifle over her right shoulder, Emry threw the kitchen door open wide and ran out of it.

She was down the steps in a second and running as fast as

she could toward the back gate in another second. She made it over the gate without mishap, but then something appeared in front of her. She raised her arm to fire, but just as quickly, she brought the arm down again. Her house was in front of her. If she missed, she might hit someone in the house.

Emry lowered the gun. She wanted to go home. She would be safe there, but the vampire was between her and her house. She took off running down the fence line, hoping she could either get to her house or get in a position where she could shoot without hitting the house. She was following the path of her jogging and a sound caught her attention on the other side of the fence. Something on the Balfour's property was keeping pace with her. She thought she heard something behind her, too.

Emry was nearing the road when she saw Brad's truck.

What're you doin', Brad? she immediately thought. He and Beaker had obviously ignored what she had said. They were inching along, their heads craned toward Ellen's house and their attention completely on it.

At first, Emry was displeased and then she was afraid, but then, she saw their arrival as an opportunity to escape and maybe the only one she was going to get. It set fire to her steps and she sprinted to the road, running faster than she had ever run.

She was breathing hard by the time she came to a stop in the middle of the West Tocoi Road. Immediately, she turned raising her gun as she spun around. Emry planted her feet firmly on the ground, the Glock tight in her fist, ready to fire, but there was nothing there.

Brad and Beaker were only thirty yards down the road. They saw Emry with the gun in her hand and she standing in a defensive posture. They sped up to meet her just as she turned and ran toward them. A dark figure appeared in her peripheral vision and when she reached Brad's truck, she did not wait for him to open a door, she jumped into the bed of the truck and shouted for him to go.

"Don't stop, Brad! Go! Go!"

He spun off, leaving black lines down the pavement. Beaker opened the sliding glass window at the back of the cab and he reached out trying to steady Emry.

"Here," she said, passing the rifle through the window to him. "And this," she said, giving him the revolver. "Defend yourself."

"From what?" he demanded in a high-pitched voice.

Something jumped into the bed of the truck, appearing to come out of nowhere. It looked like a wolf, but as they watched, it changed before their eyes until it was a man.

"From that!" Emry shouted.

She fired the Glock, but it caused her to fall and she hit her head on the cab of the truck. She heard the revolver as Beaker pulled the trigger and the vampire disappeared as if he had vanished.

"Good, Lord!" Beaker exclaimed. "What was that?"

But Emry couldn't answer. She was down in the back of the pickup and she was having trouble getting up. Her foot was caught in a bucket and her head hurt like crazy where she had hit it.

By the time she got up, she knew the only way they were going to make it out alive was to get to the Balfours. Whether she liked it or not, they had to go to St. Peter's Church.

Emry pulled herself up to the window in the back of the cab and she put her hands on the opening. "You gotta turn around, Brad," she said. "We have t' go to St. Peters."

He was flying north down West Tocoi Road. That wasn't going to take them anywhere for a while and they all knew it. He hit the brake and did a quick three point turn. The Ford took off again, heading south this time, going as fast as it could toward Bostwick.

They had not yet made it to Palmetto Bluff Road when two more vampires jumped into the back of the truck. Emry lifted her hand to fire the Glock, but it was knocked away from her. Beaker tried to fire from the cab, but he was afraid he would hit Emry so he didn't.

"Move!" he shouted as he turned the gun first one way and then the other trying to get a clear shot.

"Don't point that thing at me!" Brad yelled as Beaker nervously swung the gun in Brad's direction.

He finally fired, but it was at nothing. Emry and the vampires were gone.

Brad slammed on the brakes and brought the Ford to a screeching halt. He threw open his door and grabbed the rifle as he jumped out and looked down the road.

"Where'd they go?" he shouted.

"To the church!" Beaker said and Brad jumped back into

the truck. He put it in drive and he and Beaker took off again, heading for the Catholic Church.

Chapter Twenty-six

Jim was standing at the front door, looking out of his house when Victor's blue Jaguar flew by. He was going much too fast, Jim was thinking, especially since he was making a turn just a few yards down the road.

He watched him with stoic but uneasy silence. The black Escalade had come in just minutes before, flying by just like the Jag was doing now and then it had flown out again. He wondered what all the hurry was about.

Jim rested his shoulder against the door frame and sipped on a cup of coffee. He never used to drink anything with caffeine in it this late in the evening, but Jim was a restless man and didn't sleep well anymore. A little caffeine wasn't going to make any difference one way or the other. Besides, he was alone tonight. Betty had gone to visit her sister in Middleburg and Casey was on a date. The coffee was a comfort to him when he was alone.

He was still standing there when he saw the Jaguar's headlights moving down the Balfour's winding driveway, coming out of the property.

He stiffened. "What on earth are you Balfours doin'?" he asked himself. He'd had enough. He was going to stop that Jaguar if he had to follow it all the way to Palatka. He was going to find out once and for all what they were doing.

The patrol car keys hung on a rack beside the door. Jim reached out and snatched them up, setting the cup down at the same time. He ran to the car and started the engine, quickly slamming it into reverse and backing it down the driveway. He backed right into the road and stopped just as the Jaguar turned onto West Tocoi Road. Jim turned on his flashing lights and he hit the siren with two short blasts. The Jaguar stopped and Jim got out of the patrol car. He had the words in his head that he planned to say, but when he looked at Victor, his courage as well as his words left him.

He's just a boy, Jim thought, but oddly, Victor did not seem like a mere boy. There was something inviolable about him, something visceral that caused Jim to step back in awe.

"What is it, Jim?" Victor asked when Jim didn't say anything.

"What's goin' on?" he managed to ask after several tries to get the words out.

"I do not have the time to explain," Victor said. "But you can help me, if you will."

Jim nodded. He was a man that knew how to control a situation, but he was completely submissive in this instance. Victor had control without even trying.

"There is going to be trouble and your gun is not going to help you." He reached across the seat and picked up a box of bullets. "Take these," he said, "and reload your gun with them."

Jim took them. "Why will these help when mine won't?"

"Because these are specially made for the trouble that is coming."

"An' what is that?"

"You will know it when it gets here. By the way, Emry is at my house."

Jim looked up with a start.

"She is going to stay there tonight — all night," Victor said. "I do not want her family to worry, but she cannot go home tonight."

"Why?"

"Because if she leaves my house, she will probably die."

"Where's Johnny?" Jim asked. "I thought she was with him."

"Johnny is dead."

"What!"

"The same person who killed him will kill Emry if you do not let me go so I can end this."

"I wanna go, too."

"It is too dangerous."

"I don't care."

Victor paused in thought. He had a feeling Jim had a part to play in all this. It was an illogical thought, but one he could not shake. Just as Marius had considered Johnny as deus ex machina, now Victor wondered if that role had fallen to Jim. He had another feeling, too, like there was someone else who should be here.

"Follow me to the Catholic Church," Victor said. "And when you get there, have the bullets I gave you in your gun and the gun in your hand."

"Okay," Jim said. He ran to the patrol car and Victor

steered the Jaguar around him while Jim reloaded his gun. They took out in tandem and were at the church road within seconds.

When they arrived at St. Peters, the black Escalade was in the parking lot, but no one was in it. In fact, there was no one in sight anywhere. Victor stepped out of the Jaguar, gathering up several weapons and ammunition before walking to where Jim was standing beside his patrol car, gun in hand.

The evidence of a fight was all around them. Victor's eyes swept the area, taking in the broken cemetery fence, the shattered glass on the ground, and the toppled down tree.

"Here. Take some of these and come with me," he said to Jim and they walked together to the rectory.

Joseph met them at the door and Victor sighed with relief.

"Is everyone all right?" he anxiously asked and Joseph nodded. He gave Jim a curious look, but a look that had no surprise or displeasure in it. It was a prescient look.

"You are just in time," Father Joe said. "Come this way."

They walked into the rectory, following Joseph to a room in the back. There was a table there and all the Balfours were seated at it. The only light was from candles that were placed here and there around the room. Everyone looked up and when Marius saw Jim, he came to his feet.

"Sit down," Stefan said to Marius. "This had to be."

Marius slowly sat down again, but his eyes left Jim only long enough to cast an accusation at Victor and then they slowly went back to Jim.

"What's goin' on?" Jim asked.

"It is right you should ask that," Stefan said. "Have a seat."

Jim sat down. He could feel the power in the room. It was so strong, it was tangible.

"Where is Hugo?" Victor asked. "And Faust?"

"They are here." Stefan said. "We had a scuffle when we arrived, but they withdrew."

Everyone was looking at Victor. He felt the attention like a charge against him.

"What is wrong?" he asked.

"We have learned some disturbing news," Stefan said. "Tell him, Joseph."

Joseph was standing alone, his elbow resting on the nearby counter. He pushed away from it and nodded.

"I have been doing some studying," he began. "You know, I have Brother Cavanaugh's records. I keep them in the church so they will be safe, but after the attack at the church, I brought some of them here to go over them. You see, the attack made me think of something I had once read. It is about a ritual that must be performed in a sanctified place — like a church, one that will strip a Peregrinias of his power and bring about his death."

"But a vampire cannot enter a church," Victor said.

"He can if he has the right relics and I believe Hugo has been collecting them for years. Do you remember the attack I had here in August? I believe it was a test. He was testing his ability to get into the church but he lacked something — something you have now given him, my brother."

Every muscle in Victor's body tightened. "What have I

given him?" he asked, but even as he said it, he thought of Emry.

"The girl you love," Joseph said.

Victor made a sound of anguish and he turned with a start.

"Hold on," Stefan said, seeing what he planned. "She is safe in the house but one of us will go and check on her. You stay here. Hugo needs the two of you together to make his plan work."

Victor hesitated in uncertainty.

"Artemus — you go," Stefan said, "and here, take my phone since yours is broken."

"Broken? Your phone is broken?" Victor anxiously asked.

"It was smashed in the fight," Artemus explained and Victor turned on the balls of his feet, his eyes staring.

"I have to go to Emry," Victor said.

"No," Stefan said, but Joseph held up a hand in warning.

"Something is wrong," he said. "I think she has left the house."

Everyone came to their feet in a mad rush.

"We will all go," Stefan said and they ran for the door.

Victor did not go to the car. He stepped into the yard and his body changed in a dazzling display of transmogrification. Jim stepped back in awe, his mouth open and his eyes wide and staring as Victor flew away. Artemus had to take him by the arm and drag him to the car, but once there, Jim came to his senses and steadied his gun in his hands, ready to fight.

They dashed out of the parking lot and flew down the road, not slowing down until they reached Palmetto Bluff Road.

Joseph did not go with them. He had manuscripts to protect and after the others spun out of the parking lot, he hurried back into the rectory.

He went straight to the study where he kept the manuscripts. He stepped into the room and abruptly stopped. Hugo was standing there waiting for him.

"You are all so predictable," he said with a dry laugh. "It's too late, though. Faust is already in the church with Emry."

Joseph sidestepped, making a circle away from Hugo.

"You cannot succeed," he said. "You need Victor to complete this."

"Or you," he said. "You love her. Oh, I know. It's not the same kind of love, but the Shepherd loves his sheep, nevertheless, and that's good enough."

Joseph froze. He had interpreted the manuscript to mean a secular love like the one between a man and a woman, but was he wrong?

"It will not work."

"It will," Hugo assured him.

"You don't have time. The others will be back in minutes. You should take Faust and go. Go now before they return."

"Your suggestions won't work on me," Hugo said. "But you are right about one thing. I don't have time to waste."

He jumped and landed on top of Joseph, taking him down to the floor. He put his hands around Joseph's neck, but Joseph rolled over and broke the hold. They wrestled, neither one able to get a successful grip on the other, but Joseph finally pushed Hugo hard enough that he fell back, giving Joseph time to get to his feet.

Hugo swiftly attacked, coming up from a crouching position and knocking Joseph into the nearby table. The table fell over and the candle hit the window, spilling into the curtain. It immediately caught fire.

Hugo cried out. Fire was one thing he could not survive, but then, neither could Joseph. Hugo turned to flee, but Joseph grabbed him. Hugo snarled and then a sound erupted from him that sounded like the hounds of hell. He tore at Joseph's face with hands that had turned into claws but he could not get away. Joseph held him fast.

Meanwhile, Victor arrived at the house and the first thing he saw was the dead vampire in the yard. He looked at the window and saw the broken glass. Emry had given them a fight. He ran into the house and called her name. She didn't answer. The house was empty and silent.

The others arrived just as he stepped outside again.

"She is not here," he said.

"Got one," Marius said, indicating the fallen vampire. Without another word, he pulled his sword and lopped off the head.

"Let us get back to the church," Stefan said. "He has taken her there."

"Has he? There is more than one church in this community. It would be like Hugo to misdirect us."

"You are right. We have to split up."

"I will go to the Baptist Church," Artemus said.

"I will go to the little church on the corner," Marius said.

They fled on foot and Stefan and Jim jumped into the Escalade. Victor took to the sky. He would check them all out.

Victor flew high and his eyes immediately caught sight of Brad's truck. It was going down the church road and it was moving faster than normal.

Hope arose in Victor. Maybe Emry was with Brad. He flew down and landed in the back of Brad's truck, changing as his feet touched the bed.

He felt the hot breath of the bullet as it whizzed past him even before he heard the report of the pistol.

"Don't shoot!" he yelled. "I am looking for Emry. Is she with you?"

Beaker's face appeared in the open window. "No. Something got her. Geez! What's goin' on?"

"What got her?" Victor demanded, ignoring his question.

"How should I know — somethin'. They either jumped outta the truck with 'er or disappeared. I'm not sure if I'm sane enough to tell ya'."

They were pulling into the church parking lot by that time and Victor jumped out. The rectory was on fire. He could see the smoke billowing out and the flames rising.

He ran to the burning building and Brad and Beaker followed him. "Joseph!" he called. "Joseph, where are you?"

The brightness of the fire blinded him. He held his arm up trying to shield his eyes, but he could not see into the flames.

"Look!" Brad said pointing a finger inside the rectory. There were two bodies on the floor. One of them had a wooden stake sticking up from his chest. The other one was out cold on the floor.

"What?" Victor asked. "What do you see?"

The black Escalade flew into the parking lot at that moment and Jim and Stefan jumped out. Jim ran to the burning building, but Stefan walked slowly, holding up his arm much the same way Victor was doing.

"There's two bodies on the floor in there," Brad immediately explained.

"Oh, God! Oh, God!" Victor cried. "It's Joseph! I am going in."

"No!" Stefan shouted. "It will kill you." He ran to Victor and pulled him back. "There is nothing you can do except get yourself killed."

"I have to try."

Stefan looked anxiously at Jim. "We cannot go into the fire. It is one of the things we cannot do."

"I'll go," Jim said. He removed the pistol from his side and laid it aside, but before he could move again, a scream arose from the direction of the church and they all turned.

"It's Abby," Brad said in surprise.

"No, not anymore," Victor said. "She is one of them."

Abby could not go into the church, but she stood in the yard between it and the cemetery. There was a faint light in the church and as everyone turned to look at Abby, they saw Faust inside, near the altar, holding Emry with her arms pulled back behind her.

Victor gasped. He was torn between his brother and the girl he loved, but it was Abby who became the deciding factor.

Two vampires joined her and they angrily shouted as if making a war cry and then they split up and ran in three different directions.

Stefan and Victor made a barrier in front of Jim, Brad and Beaker. Victor was unarmed, but Stefan raised his gun and fired, taking out one of the vampires.

It was an even match and he and Victor raced away, Stefan going in one direction and Victor chasing after Abby.

She ran to the corner of the rectory and Victor followed her. The flames had not yet reached where she stood, but the smoke was thick. When Victor arrived, she was already gone. He saw her run around the building and go in at the back door. Again, he followed her, but this time when he arrived, the brightness from the fire dimmed his sight. It was like a hot poker in his eyes and he backed away, afraid Abby would come upon him while he couldn't see. If Abby had run into the burning building, though, he knew she was no longer a threat. No vampire could survive in there.

He heard a gunshot and then another and Victor anxiously looked up. He turned and looked into the darkness, staring into the cool shadows until his sight returned and then he disappeared in a swirl of smoke, taking form again in the parking lot, but not as Victor. He was the dragon, ready for battle.

He anxiously looked around. Marius was there and so were Brad and Beaker. Joseph was lying on the ground. Someone had gotten him out of the burning building. Victor sighed with relief, but all of them were staring at the church so Victor looked, too.

Emry had been looking out the whole time and it was with great anxiety that she had witnessed the unfolding drama. Victor had come just like she knew he would, but something was happening that she did not understand. She watched as he ran — not to her, but around the burning rectory. He disappeared behind it and Faust cursed under his breath.

"Come on," he said as he moved for better advantage. He was talking as if to Victor, but only Emry could hear him. He pulled her aside, all but dragging her to the edge of the altar. It hurt her arms and she grimaced, but he did not care. He dragged her along, pulling her to a spot where he could get a better view.

It was Victor he was looking for but Victor was nowhere in sight.

"What're you doing?" he said, anxiously looking where Victor had been standing only a second before. "Come and get her," he said as if Victor could hear him. His eyes danced feverishly and he clenched his teeth. "Come o-o-on," he said as he moved around. "Come o-o-n."

Emry tripped and went down to her knees. Faust pulled her up and impatiently shook her.

"He'll kill you," she said with more assurance than she felt. "Go ahead and call him in and he'll kill you."

Faust laughed aloud. "No, he won't," he said. "He'll give me exactly what I need to destroy him."

Emry pulled back and the unexpectedness of it pulled her arm free of Faust's grip. She ran, but he caught her before she had taken more than two steps.

"Don't come in, Victor!" she began to scream. "It's a trap! Don't come in!"

Faust slapped her and she fell to her knees again. He laughed with great delight.

"That's a good girl," he said. "Give him a reason to come in. I'm running out of patience."

"And time," Emry said.

She was more correct than she knew. Faust had only minutes left and he needed both Victor and his father's relics in order to complete his ritual. The smile left his face in an instant and a dark cloud covered his countenance. He roughly pulled her to her feet but when he turned he paused with great surprise. Jim was standing inside the church door.

The building was small. There was no more than thirty feet between the front door and the altar where Faust stood. He stared in disbelief and momentary confusion. He had expected Victor. In fact, he was primed for Victor's entrance. Jim's sudden and unexpected appearance literally threw him off. It was strange, but Faust did not know what to do. He paused in thought and then he slowly relaxed.

Jim was no threat. Faust laughed at what he perceived as a stroke of luck. It would be like swatting a gnat and that was sure to hurry Victor along.

"Go back, Jim!" Emry called, but Faust encouraged him to approach.

"No, come in," he said with a taunt. "Come join us."

For the first time, Faust noticed the pistol in Jim's hand.

He chuckled, but at the same time, he turned so that Emry was between them.

"Do you know what I am?" Faust asked. "Your gun won't hurt me, but go ahead and fire it if it makes you feel better. Only, remember, Emry isn't so indestructible. You hit her and it's all over."

"I won't hit her."

"Then be quick with your plans. As soon as Victor and my father arrive, I'll be gone anyway."

"Your father?"

"Hugo," Faust said.

"Hugo is dead."

"You lie!" Faust yelled but his eyes darted with fear and expectation to the burning rectory. Hugo held all the relics except one. If he was dead, then Faust was unable to complete the ritual.

He was suddenly afraid. If Victor caught him without the relics, he was vulnerable. His eyes swept the parking lot, but Victor was gone.

Faust cried out. He did not doubt that Hugo was dead even though he had denied it. He looked around, expecting Victor to enter at any moment. Well, it was no mystery what would happen when he arrived. Faust would kill Emry and then run. He had no desire to fight Victor, although that was not why he would run. He was of the philosophy, live to fight another day, and it was the disappointment of his failure that brought him to his conclusions, that and his outrage at missing this chance for the ritual. It was a twofold disappointment.

The ritual would have freed him from the night and at the same time, it would have destroyed Victor. Victor would have simply withered and turned to ashes before their very eyes and whatever power he had possessed would have fallen to Faust. That possibility was gone for now and Faust had a poignant regret at its failure. He could remember the daylight and as strange as it sounded, the older he became, the more he longed to see the sun again.

He had not been born a vampire, although that was what he had become. It had been like a sickness, gradually coming over him his whole life. At puberty, there had been a significant change and it was with suddenness that he could no longer tolerate the sun nor eat food. He had lusted for blood. The desire had consumed him and he had satiated himself without remorse or conscience. After a while it had found its own place in his life and he had lost the hunger that had driven him in the beginning. Once a month now, he feasted just like any other vampire and it was enough although he was never completely satisfied. The blood lust was always on him.

He had wanted this ritual — wanted it badly, but he had not wanted it in order to free himself from being a vampire. There was too much power to be lost in that instance and Faust would not want to be a mortal man for anything in the world. That was one reason he hated the Balfours with such a passion. He wanted the power they had and the freedom of their movement. The Balfours were restricted, but not like he was. And the power they had — how he craved it!

Jim took a step toward them and Emry again warned him.

"Go back!" she shouted. "You can't kill him. He's a vampire!"

Jim stopped and Faust laughed. Fear excited him and he could feel the fear so strongly that it aroused an excitement in him he could hardly contain. Emry pulled away from him and he let her take a step before reaching out and grasping her hand. He did not pull her back. His attention was on Jim but even as he watched Jim raised the gun and pointed it directly at him.

Jim fired, but at that moment, Emry pulled hard against Faust's grip, trying to pull herself away from him. Faust moved and Jim's bullet, aimed for the heart, missed completely, but the second one caught him in the shoulder. He fell as the special bullet magically drained the strength out of him. His shock was no greater than Emrys. Neither of them knew that Victor had had Jim change the bullets in his gun and neither of them had expected the results it gave. Faust was on the floor, but even as Emry looked, he pushed himself up and began to crawl.

Emry did not hesitate. She ran to Jim and he took her hand. Together they ran out of the church and down the steps.

They both abruptly stopped in amazement. Victor had just appeared and this time there was no question about it. He had materialized in a cloud of smoke but he did not look like Victor. He was not a man, at all, but some strange and beautiful creature with dark wings that spread out from his back and down his arms. His face was like a mask but his eyes were piercing like daggers of flame. He had raised his wings as if to fly, but he lowered them and his whole appearance changed until the dragon he had become disappeared and the man stood before them.

Emry could not move. She stood rooted to the ground, staring in disbelief at what she knew was the vision she had seen before. Victor was the fairytale swan she thought she had dreamed about, but it was no dream. It had really happened and with great revelation, Emry at last understood the impossibility of their relationship. The hope leaving her was like something dying inside her. She covered her face with open hands and fell to her knees sobbing, and in the distance, sirens pierced the night.

Chapter Twenty-seven

"Get up! Get up," someone was saying to Emry but she couldn't find the strength to push herself up.

There was a roar of commotion around her and the burning building in the background added an element of unbridled power to the already chaotic scene.

She looked up. Victor was not there and it was Jim, Brad and Beaker who were urging her up. Her eyes swept the parking lot, but she did not see him.

The sirens were louder. The fire department would soon be there and Emry imagined the Balfours would want to be out of there before anyone arrived. Where she knelt, she was in the way and they were right to encourage her to move.

She came to her feet and together she walked with Jim, Brad and Beaker to the place where Father Joe sat resting against a corner post of the cemetery fence. Stefan was there, but still there was no sign of Victor.

Artemus appeared quite suddenly, stepping into the light from the fire as if by magic. Marius came to stand beside him.

"Where is Faust?" he asked.

"I shot him," Jim said and everyone turned and looked toward the church.

"Where is Victor?" Artemus then asked.

No one knew, but as they looked around in wonder, he

walked toward them from the side of the church.

"If we hurry," he said, "we can catch Faust. He is hurt."

"You stay here," Stefan ordered. "Artemus and Marius will get him. You have work to do here."

Victor's eyes darted to Emry and then slowly they made a pass over Jim, Brad, and Beaker.

"Yes," he simply said as Artemus and Marius took off on foot for the church. They ran to the corner of the building and disappeared as they made the turn.

Lights were flashing and sirens were screaming as Jim herded the small group to a spot closer to the church.

"You've got to get out of here," he said and Stefan nodded.

"Yes," he agreed. "Victor, take the children with you and I will stay with Joseph."

"Where're you goin'?" Jim asked Victor. Jim was slightly uncomfortable with him, not understanding what he had seen a moment before and wondering if it was safe to be with him.

"To our place — just for a little while."

Stefan saw Jim's anxiousness and he put a hand on his shoulder.

"Do not be concerned. He will not hurt them."

Jim wasn't so sure. It had been a frightening thing to watch Victor's transformation although Jim marveled at the beauty of him.

"What are you — angels?" he asked.

Victor and Stefan exchanged glances, but neither of them were quick to answer.

"No," Stefan finally said. "We are simply strangers who

come when we are needed and then go when our work is done."

Emry looked at Victor. He was looking at her but she could not read his expression. Everyone was perplexed, but it was a still and grave look that he gave to her. Emry dropped her eyes, unable to look at him.

Jim slowly relaxed and as he did, he felt better.

"Go," Stefan said to Victor, seeing that Jim wavered.

Brad drove his truck and Emry and Beaker rode with him. Victor led the way in the Jaguar. It was a quiet and subdued trio that stopped before the locked gate on the Balfour's property. They waited as Victor punched in the code and the gate opened for them. They drove in and parked near the back door. By the time they got out of the truck, Victor was waiting for them by the back steps.

He was looking at all of them, but his focus was mainly on Emry. He knew what she was thinking and he was trying very hard to convince himself that it was a good thing.

It was a good thing, he told himself. It would accomplish what he could not do on his own. He had lost that power once he admitted he was in love with her. At that moment, he had lost control and once that was done, he had gotten completely out of line. Now he was back on track. He told himself to leave it as it was and just do his job. After all, that was what he had been created for. There was no going back.

Brad and Beaker were in awe of the old mansion. They stared with wide eyes and curious glances, but when Victor spoke to them, they cautiously turned to him. He spoke again and the fear left them.

He is an angel, Emry thought. She could almost imagine him saying, "Fear not" just like the angels in the Bible always did, but then she remembered the provocative touch of his hand and his passionate kiss and the idea of him being an angel vanished in an instant. He was something both great and terrible but he was no angel. Emry suddenly felt very lost and lonely.

They went inside and Victor walked with them, talking all the time in a voice that no one could resist listening to. Emry knew what he was doing. With every word out of his mouth, Brad and Beaker were succumbing to his redesigned reality. When he was finished, their recollection of what had happened tonight would be drastically altered and they wouldn't even know anything had changed. For some unknown reason, she was not affected. She had clarity and her thoughts were her own. He wasn't touching her. Maybe that was it. She had always suspected that he needed contact to make his magic work. After a while, she left them and went to the kitchen area where she waited alone until they returned.

Victor gave her a sharp, but curious look as he walked into the room. He approached her and stopped closely beside her. He had been acting as if he was afraid to come near her, and maybe he had been. He didn't know what her reaction would be, but he could no longer put it off.

"Go with them," he said, referring to Brad and Beaker. "They will take you home."

She turned quickly. "What do I say to my parents?" she asked. "I'm past curfew and they're going to hear what happened. I've got to tell them something, but I can't tell them the truth. They'll have me committed."

Victor smiled even though there was no humor in it. "Johnny and you argued," he said, giving her the story as Brad and Beaker would remember it. "He left you in Palatka. You called Brad and he and Beaker went and got you, but thinking Johnny might hurt himself, the three of you went first to Jim.

"Jim, however, was at the burning rectory when you arrived in town," he went on with his story. "So, the three of you went there."

He was silent a moment and then he softly said, "I think Johnny is dead, Emry."

She knew it even though she tried not to think of it.

"I know," she said after a thoughtful moment.

"I am not being callous when I say his death will help make your story believable."

"I know," she said again.

He didn't say anything for a few seconds and then he carefully added, "I am leaving, Emry. But I don't suppose you will be sorry to see me go."

Her eyes flashed as she looked up at him.

"After tonight, I mean. You saw what I am — or what I can become," he added. "I never wanted you to see that."

She looked away. "I'd already seen it," she said, thinking of the night she had awakened with her head on the window sill. Victor had landed in her yard as a beautiful swan — or that was what she thought she had dreamed. Now she knew it was no dream, only Victor was a dragon and not a swan. Either way, it was a sobering fact. "I just didn't know what I was seeing."

"Well," he said, looking around while trying to find the words he wanted to say. "It is time to go. Let us get this over with."

She turned again until she was looking squarely at him. "Not now," she anxiously said. "Let me see you one more time before you go."

He smiled derisively and then he leaned back against the window frame as he considered her request.

"No," he finally said.

"Please!"

"No, Emry," he repeated. His voice was soft, almost apologetic, but adamant, just the same. "We have to be realistic. You saw what I am."

Her eyes searched his face before replying. "I'd be lying if I didn't tell you it frightened me, but then, well, it's still you and . . ." She paused. "You were beautiful!" she softly whispered.

He didn't know what to say. He had never thought about the way he looked to other people. To himself, he imaged he was a hideous thing, but it was marvelous to soar in the sky as a dragon.

He smiled, but he looked away from her in thought, a pensive expression filling his eyes. "I should be firm," he said as he looked back at her. "But I find I cannot be. One more time," he agreed. He lied to himself, saying that it would be easier if they were alone. The truth was, he wanted to see her again — wanted it to be just the two of them alone one more time. "Meet me later. I will wait for you under the big oak." He pushed himself away from the window frame. "Go quickly now. It is important that you get home soon."

They returned to the church where Victor gave Brad and Beaker one last instruction. They went home from there, not even realizing they had left and gone to the old Balfour mansion. They took Emry home and Victor watched from a distance to make sure they all arrived safely at their destinations and then silently he made his way back to the old mansion, changing from the flying form he had taken back to the man he wanted to be when Emry came to see him. He walked to the gate and he waited there, watching as one by one the lights went out in the Winters' house.

It was a long time later when Emry came stealing across the lawn, her direction straight as an arrow to the old oak tree.

Victor was waiting as she stepped into the darkness under the tree. He stepped forward and took her hand and together they walked to the back gate.

Once there, he wrapped her in his arms and they simply stood there holding each other but saying not a word. It was some time before Victor changed position and moved his arms. He touched her hair and she looked up at him.

"How did things go at home?" he asked.

"Just fine. Jim came in and confirmed everything I had said. I guess you got to him, too."

Victor smiled. "I guess I did," he agreed. "Your parents accepted your story?"

"They did."

"Then you are all that is left," he said, his voice wistful.

"I won't tell anyone, Victor — I promise."

"That is not what I am afraid of," he said.

"What are you afraid of?"

He smiled, but then ambiguously, he shook his head. "Nothing you can do anything about," he said. "Let us not talk about it. Let us just enjoy these last few minutes together."

He pulled her closer to him and held her tightly against him. She trusted him and she embraced him with sweet tenderness, never once suspecting what he was planning to do.

"I love you," she whispered.

The wind stirred softly and Emry felt a chill even though she was safely wrapped in Victor's arms. She buried her face against his shoulder and rested against him.

"I love you, too," he whispered, his voice as light as the wind. "But—"

He paused, hesitating while he fought with his will. He closed his eyes and gripped her even tighter.

"Emry?"

"Hmmm?"

"Forget . . ."

Made in the USA
Columbia, SC
31 March 2018